EXPOSED

Other books by Cris Mazza:

How to Leave a Country

Animal Acts

Revelation Countdown

Is It Sexual Harassment Yet?

EXPOSED

CRIS MAZZA

COFFEE HOUSE PRESS • MINNEAPOLIS • 1994

Cover art by John D. Koch

Back cover photograph by Cris Mazza

Book design by Nora Koch

The author wishes to thank the editors of the following publications where portions of this novel first appeared: "Second Person," and "The Kind of Sadness Which Makes You Sad," in *Is It Sexual Harassment Yet?* by Cris Mazza, Fiction Collective Two, 1991. "Second Person," in *Alaska Quarterly*, Vol. 5, No. 3 & 4, 1987.

The publishers would like to thank the following funders for assistance that helped make this book possible: The National Endowment for the Arts, a federal agency; Dayton Hudson Foundation on behalf of Dayton's and Target Stores; The Lannan Foundation; The Andrew W. Mellon Foundation; Star Tribune/Cowles Media Company; and The McKnight Foundation. This activity is made possible in part by a grant provided by the Minnesota State Arts Board, through an appropriation by the Minnesota State Legislature. Major new marketing initiatives have been made possible by the Lila Wallace-Reader's Digest Literary Publishers Marketing Development Program, funded through a grant to the Council of Literary Magazines and Presses.

Coffee House Press books are available to the trade through our primary distributor, Consortium Book Sales & Distribution, 1045 Westgate Drive, Saint Paul, Mn 55114. For personal orders, catalogs or other information, write to:
Coffee House Press
27 North Fourth Street, Suite 400 Minneapolis, MN 55401

Library of Congress CIP Data
Mazza, Cris
Exposed/Cris Mazza.
p. cm.
ISBN 1-56689-019-5
1. Women photographers—United States—Fiction. I. Title.
PS3563.A988E96 1994
813´.54—dc20 93-23689
CIP

10 9 8 7 6 5 4 3 2 1

Printed in Canada

TABLE OF CONTENTS

To. H.W.

I chased *this one a long time.*

I

The Pit Where the Orchestra Sits Below the Stage

• • •

Last night I noticed I've been marking my place in books with a faded brown photograph of bombed-out shells of buildings in World War II. It's an aerial shot. I found it, along with a liberty pass, in my father's French dictionary. It doesn't get to me, the honeycomb of walls with nothing inside, maybe because I wasn't the one there to see the scene and take the shot. Maybe also because the photographer wasn't stirred either. My father took the picture, but I don't think he understood what I mean. He had other photos from Germany—of himself, standing in the rubble, a soft layer of snow covering the jagged edges of the remaining walls. I'm not sure if a friend took those shots for him or if he put the shutter on timed-release and let the camera work alone. But disaster is just like anything else—Mount Rushmore or a birthday party—you're not supposed to put it on film just to prove you were there. It's memory, like if your brain was the camera and darkroom. It's part of you at that moment, and when someone else sees it, that part of you should become part of them. That's why it's stupid to want to jump into your own pictures before the camera clicks. The photographer can't be *in* the shot—the photographer *is* the shot.

I've never even considered doing a self portrait. Not superstitious or afraid the negative would be blank, like a witch in a mirror. I'm just already aware of how worthless it is. Someone inevitably tries to use a photograph to cure amnesia victims on television, but it never works. They always have to be hit on the head a second time. A guy where I used to work liked to take his own picture. "You never know," he said to me in the darkroom, "you might see someone different who you haven't yet noticed or even met when you're looking in the mirror shaving or putting on makeup." I barely listened to him. But maybe that different me is the one who takes over after I'm finished reading in bed—after I close the book and my eyes—and does my dreaming for me. Like two clerks who work in the same office, different shifts, incomparable functions, seldom see each other, want to kill each other.

The pit where the orchestra sits below the stage is like a cellar to hide in with an overly dramatic war overhead. I'm very comfortable, of course. When I auditioned to play cello here, they asked me why I would quit my decent job to play in a theater pit orchestra three nights a week plus daytime rehearsals. I said, "Is having a good enough reason one of the qualifications?" But now that I'm down here, I know I *am* qualified—not because my father made me practice two hours a day for 20 years, but because it's dark. Audiences sit quietly in the dark to watch movies or listen to music. Likewise most recluses find comfort in the dark. That's where I've spent most of my time—in film developing closets which are opaque, where the air tastes like black chalk. My body may feel swollen and fill every corner, or I might be a speck on the floor. Mostly I don't feel myself at all. I'm all hands, winding film on spools . . . the closeness of the chemicals makes my head empty. Also in the printing darkroom, where dim lights in the ceiling are covered with yellow filters, it feels like swimming underwater at night. I dive into each scene on the enlarger then paddle to the chemical trays. It's gold-black and always a comfortable warm. It's the darkness at night that's sometimes too hot. Nearing the end of January and I still have to keep my window open when I sleep. When I don't sleep, I lie in bed with no electric lights in the room—the area illuminated only by the moon outside, or the stars, or someone else's porch light, or some light left over from daytime because the world is not an ideal light-tight darkroom. Through my eyelids *any* light is too bright, too hot, I feel as though I'm melting into a puddle on rubber sheets. The dreams are coming, humid, lurid, pulsating. Not mine. I try to distract myself by concentrating on books I've read, movies and television shows I've seen and how I would film them differently, photo stories I've planned but never completed . . . self-defense techniques. . . .

I try to tune my cello, but I'm always off, halfway here, halfway there. The center of pitch can't seem to get through to me. It's too perfect, too thin, like a needle pushed so slowly into a bubble that it can't make the bubble pop.

But the pitch is broken anyway, and painted actors flood into the pit, coming in among the pale-skinned musicians. It would make a good photograph, if I had my camera: the colorful actress who's speaking—her stained red lips and flushed cheekbones, her chalky-blue eyelids—and the equally surreal lank-hair musician who's closest, with his pasty skin and black-rimmed eyes.

"There's a body in the parking lot!"

"They say it was a gang fight."

"It's a kid—I mean, someone ran over a kid, so they hung the guy who did it."

"No, they dragged a guy around the parking lot, then they hung him."

"I saw him, someone chopped his face up with an ax."

"No, they put a rope on his neck, dragged him around, then ran over his head."

Still plucking this tuning note, I look at each of the vivid faces, beaming in spite of the dim music-stand lights. From looking at them now, you'd never know there was a body waiting in the parking lot when the players arrived at the theater.

Everyone would probably ask you to take a picture for the newspaper from the back, from behind the gore, showing shoulders and a head. The photographer might as well get an actor to lie in the street, use a gauzy effect or vaseline on the lens while he's at it. The slightest shocking detail, they write letters to the editor asking why it's necessary to revolt them when they open their paper over their morning juice and coffee. But why *wouldn't* they want the photographer to give them the same fist-in-the-gut feeling that hit him when he got to the scene—a body crumpled in the parking lot, nameless and, presumably now, faceless?

Any musicians who aren't trapped in their seats by wires—slung everywhere around the pit to provide the scanty light—get up and run. Clarinets fall off chairs, a trombone topples like a tree onto a music stand that flips a trumpet over and rattles the snare. A wire pulls tight and upends four chairs. I'm still trying to tune my G string. I have to share my chair with this cello, I can't get up and dash with them to the parking lot.

"Well, this is interesting," says Ron Galvin, holding a baton over one woodwind player, one percussionist trapped behind the tympani, the harpist afraid to leave her instrument, and me, in the seat closest to him. He turns pages of his music score, flicking past his stand-light like movie frames. He is, after all, the one who gathers and keeps actors and musicians together. He'll either have to excite flat chords to match their melodramatic vocal intercourse, or arouse the action on stage to keep pace with the music. When they first turned the house lights off and no flood or spotlight found its way into the pit, and none of the musicians had turned on their own bulbs yet, Galvin's light jumped up at him, a cue to start the overture. He was the only one visible. Something about his equipment makes the light shower over the whole podium while mine has difficulty lighting the music down to the last line. So he shouldn't be able to see me as well nor as easily as I see him. So why do I suddenly feel too exposed?

The director walks across the stage calling for the players. "Where *is* everybody?"

Still trying to tune—did I ever stop plucking this G string?—I bend an ear close to my cello. But the orchestra begins to climb noisily back into the pit, some from the cellar door, some from over the top, soldiers back into the foxhole. Someone curses because his trombone was left so rudely on the floor, but a cymbal falls off the drum set the same moment the petite concertmistress apparently finds the proper name to call the trombonist. Galvin laughs.

"You couldn't see anything," the pianist reports. "The police wouldn't let anyone near. He had long hair and a leather coat."

Galvin turns to me and it seems to take several moments, once again a film flicking frame-by-frame. I almost see a projector bulb flash in the clear strip in between. A movie can't see the audience, but he looks at me with moon-eyes, making me flinch because I think he sees through my head to the wall behind.

"Why didn't you run out there, Connie?" he asks me. How does he know my name?

"Maybe I would've if I'd had my camera. . . ."

He squints at me, making his eyes crease as though they're laughing. And his voice is amused: "What?"

"I probably wouldn't have taken a picture, but at least with a camera I wouldn't be part of a stupidly gawking crowd."

"Is that a hobby—photography?"

"Not really. I mean, it's no hobby."

"A profession?"

"Yeah, I guess so."

I see myself in his dilated eyes. The darkness opens them up, exposing all those tender nerves. A gentle flashlight could really hurt him.

The violinists have their instruments under their chins and the horn players have theirs in their mouths. I never did get my strings in tune. Galvin is silently tapping his baton in the air to show us the tempo of the next song, but still looking at me, he says, "Do you make a living at it?"

"At what?"

"Photography—do you just *want* to be a professional or do you have experience?"

The song starts and I'm already lost. He's still looking at me. "Five years at the newspaper." I have to say it a little too loud because the trumpets made their entrance. Galvin nods and turns back to his music, begins conducting with both arms, making eye-contact with the singing actress on stage. I still don't know where we are. I don't think I'm on the right page.

"Five years, huh?" Galvin says. "You must've gotten an early start. What are you, twenty-one? Twenty-two?"

"Almost thirty."

He smiles. "You must've been keeping yourself preserved in an air-tight container. Maybe you went to the University of the Fountain of Youth?" He doesn't say anything about how I didn't play in the last song until the final chord. It's a lot more difficult to play a part in an orchestra than it is to play concertos in an empty practice room.

"I didn't go to college."

"Well, we'll need a photographer to do stills and publicity shots. You could do it."

"How can I take pictures and play the music both?"

"It only takes one dry run-through to take pictures."

None of the excuses that come to mind would be a *total* lie. I could say I'm not going commercial, or that I don't have a camera to use at the moment. Or tell him I'm really just a darkroom technician. But before I decide which to say, he asks, "Did you *quit* your newspaper job for this, or just take a vacation to see if you could hit the big time in musical theater . . . starting on the very bottom rung, of course!" Still smiling.

"Neither. I left over a year ago." And ran all the way home. To my own darkroom and studio. My TV room. My music room. My quiet bed, untortured, at that time, by any damp dream that hadn't come from cool real memory.

"It was meatball photography, huh? No time for art?"

"No . . . I had lots of time for extra work. I could shoot anything I wanted. I could've sold to magazines if I'd wanted to. I had offers."

"You make it sound easy." He smiles.

I shrug. My camera could call me a coward too—it sat there looking at me with its one blue eye. So I locked it in a dark vault at the bank.

"And what've you been doing since?" he asks.

"I was a darkroom technician for a photo-developing lab."

"That doesn't make sense."

"It doesn't?" I look at him for a moment. He must be waiting for some explanation. I'm not obligated to tell him anything. We're just sitting down here in the dark together. . . . But going to the lab taught me how people all think they're photographers without knowing what it means. Taught me how they spend their vacations and holidays worrying about getting snapshots of their vacations and holidays. Showed me how people believe those ads on TV that say some kind of instant camera can bring people together faster, even be the life of a party. They're tossing this thing around, the flash popping, everyone laughing with arms around each other's shoulders. Such crap. A real photographer looks through a camera long enough, she knows that when the eye blinks it sucks part of someone else inside it, as well as part of herself the moment she shoots.

I wait longer, and finally he says, "I mean, you left something that allowed *some* expression for what's almost factory work."

"It *is* factory work. Worse." He won't stop looking at me. "Did you see that picture in the paper of the baseball player pushing people away as they asked for autographs? He has his hand right in a kid's face, knocking him over."

"No."

"Well . . . I took it. The sports page didn't want it, and I didn't care if it was ever published, it was *mine*, I didn't take it for anyone else. But the assistant sports editor got the Life-and-Living editor to put it on the society page."

"So they *fired* you?"

"No, I quit."

"Why?"

"I'm not sure."

"Were they threatening to fire you?"

"No—the paper was backing me up."

"Against who?"

I don't know why I've gone this far, telling him. Everyone told me it wasn't that big a deal, every time someone came into the darkroom, they'd say, You're not really quitting, are you? Dumb stuff like this *always* happens. "I'm not sure who was against who," I say, "I didn't need a model-release. It was probably the caption that caused the trouble, but no one knew who had written it. It was too confusing—too many lawyers and threats and phone calls. Even the commissioner of baseball called me, everyone asking questions and shouting, trying to get me to say that it really wasn't a picture of what it looked like."

We sit without saying anything for a minute. The dialogue on stage almost inaudible. I pick a loose hair off my bow.

"Wouldn't it have blown over?" he asks.

"I don't know. It's over now."

"Does this mean you wouldn't want to take pictures here?"

Is that my spine prickling? "I don't know."

"Let's talk about it later, okay?" he says. "You free during the break?"

"Yeah, sure. I mean . . . okay."

Vowed I would give up photography forever, but was like an alcoholic, hiding the camera under the bed, in the linen closet, in the freezer. Just who was I hiding it from? And why? Just because one of my pictures finally stirred a response? Not the response I wanted.

It never stayed hidden any place very long. I'd go get it, hold it, put it down, hold it again. Finally took it to the vault at the bank. Then the job at the lab stopped my urges to retrieve the camera from its cell. I know a lens and film will always allow me a sort of magic: freezing an image at the right instant, making the memory of that instant—the thoughts and sensations—something real to hold and keep. That's why it's so strange that I can actually lose control over what it's a photo *of* as soon as other people see it.

At places in the show where there's no musical accompaniment, we like to watch. The entire ensemble comes to the front of the pit, lines up on Galvin's left and right; we press our backs to the ten-foot cement wall, raise ourselves on our toes or stand on chairs. Three or four lines before the cue for a song, a terrified actor glances into the pit and sees the whole orchestra straining up against the wall.

The director cuts it anyway, so we don't need to clamor for our chairs. They're working on the dialogue before a kiss—they want to rush through the words. My guess is they'll change the lighting on contact, so if I photographed that kiss, I'd have to prepare beforehand—know what they're doing and what's coming.

The girl up there is chanting, "We don't *know* what we're doing," which makes her sound like she's hiccoughing into the kiss. As soon as the first smartass musician opens his mouth —"Someone tell them they just need to chill-out"—Galvin sends us back to our seats and stays alone against the wall. Can almost feel my camera against my eye as I watch the lighting changes bounce off his face. Deceivingly bland, hardly lucid, his wide eyes, flat cheekbones, square chin give no sign of thought. But as the lights soften the stage mood, his expression becomes sharp, tightening the corners of his mouth, flexing a muscle on his jaw, pulling his eyebrows together as he shakes his head.

"Chill-out," he says, "where'd that expression come from?" Afterward he looks down at me. I'm the only one paying attention, and I sit next to his right knee, so I guess he's talking to me.

"Someone once said that to me. This guy on a bus kept trying to talk to me, but I had nothing to say to him. I was winding some film backwards inside my camera, trying to stop it with the tab still exposed. He said, C'mon, baby, chill-out. So I said, Chilled is what fruit is, or jello. I'm not a pear, and you're no banana." Actually I only wished I'd said it.

Galvin's smile is so slow, it doesn't catch much stage-light at first. Then the lights change to blue and his eyes gleam. "So you're not a good target for the casual pick-up," he says.

"I don't know if that's what he was doing."

They start the kiss-scene over on stage. Galvin puts his baton down and sits on the podium, his legs stretched out in front of him, crossed at the ankle. This way our eyes are level. He looks at me with his mouth pulled over to one side. "The best pick-up story I ever heard was from a friend of mine. He graduated from college young, got his master's young, and was a young professor. There was a girl in one class he liked to look at. One day as she was leaving class, he grabbed her and told her—physically—how he felt about her. They were married in three months."

"You're kidding!"

The murmuring noise down here pulsates, but not evenly, not a throb. Not like a lawn mower going back and forth outside a window. There are sharp peaks, stunned silences. As each conversation stops at once, and everyone looks around for something new, it seems as if everyone has stopped to listen to us, and everybody stopped to stare at me the way Galvin is staring. My chair is a little hard, I need to stretch, I'd like a drink of water, but if I get up and leave it might make them stare even harder.

Someone nearby is eating an onion sandwich. Someone is turning pages of a magazine which get caught on his stomach as they pass. Someone is plinking a note over and over on the piano. Someone is scraping a knife against a reed. There's actually no one but Galvin watching me through the darkness.

"Anyway," Galvin says, "she kicked him out three years later. He grabbed another girl in another class, and his wife didn't like it. He said he should have that right, to follow honest impulses."

"What about *her* honest impulses?" Were three lessons in self-defense, so many years ago, enough to have made me able to respond with immediacy, jab eyes, break fingers, deflate testicles, spray mace, and run like hell?

"He said she could do the same. She just didn't *want* to. She was brought up *not* to want to. Her father—"

"If she was brought up not to *want* to, wouldn't she be scared when he first grabbed her?"

"She probably was, but she liked it. She couldn't help liking it. If a girl hasn't experienced that feeling by that age, something's wrong."

He's saying something can be wrong when nothing has happened. I look down at my cello—I never played any parts wrong before I picked up the bow. But isn't it wrong to completely miss whole passages? I never did anything wrong *before* I pressed a shutter-release. But it *is* wrong to miss a good shot because you're fumbling with film or exposure settings . . . or worrying about who's going to see the print and what they'll say. *Is* there something wrong with me? You're a strange girl, they said when I quit.

"Hey!"

We all look up at an actress peeking into the pit. She's kneeling on the stage floor. Her hair swings around her face like black silk fringe.

"They identified him," she says to the pianist.

"Who?"

"The guy in the parking lot. He's an escaped convict."

"He is not. I already heard he was an ex-con."

"Same difference." She tosses her head and her shoulders as she stands up, and tosses her ass as she walks along the edge of the pit toward the right wing.

"Bitch," someone says.

"Still, it's not a good motive for murder," the pianist informs someone else.

"*Is* there a good motive for murder?" I say just loud enough for Galvin to hear. He's close enough to touch with my cello bow. So I must be talking to him.

"Someone must think so. Someone made up varying degrees of murder."

"I bet that guy would rather be dead and buried," I say, "than try to understand *why* someone would want to kill him."

Facing me, Galvin's huge black pupils reflect the tiny sparks of five or six music-stand lights. "I had a dream once that I was being buried alive," he says. "I remember as they piled the dirt on, I felt warmer and warmer. The weight of it was so tight and it was so comfortable, I wanted to stay that way forever. Then I realized that in order to enjoy that warm weight, I would have to die. I *would* stay that way forever. I had to decide to either die, or fight to get out of there."

Certainly better than *my* dreams. Which I won't share.

It's time for another song and Galvin groans a little as he stands up, stretches, presses his songbook flat on his music stand. "We should have lunch sometime," he says, "so we won't continually be so rudely interrupted."

When sitting below the stage, the cement wall on my left towers ten feet over my head. On my other side, on the stage, I can see heads bobbling in legless dances. Something goes on up there—they live tightly plotted lives, but are just heads until they thump forward and teeter on the brink of the pit. Then I see trunks and arms, and sometimes, if I flatten against the wall, legs and knees. They deal with their complicated lives by saying what's prepared for them up there. But they spit when they talk and we have to duck.

They're ready for the second act. The theater lights burn out in sequence, and the music-stand lights once again are all we have, a little private room for each musician. My stomach always burns for the first few minutes before we start playing, while the darkness is settling and we huddle down here in silence.

I'm not moving, not talking, probably breathing and could prove it with a mirror. There's a pitter-patter clatter behind me, behind the drums where they store the thunder. But there's no storm in the script. Fluorescent sunlight blazes on the stage after the entr'acte. Up there—the ones who have to be concerned with plot and development and sub-plot and rising action. I love the silence we therefore maintain . . . usually, except a few scuffles. But I can look around and see each weak light bulb glow on someone's brow, flicker in pale eyes or on sweat-shiny skin, and not know who moved. This time Galvin flashes a white palm in my face: shut up. No matter how it's said—lower your voice, calm down, please be quiet—it's all still *shut up*. One of those lawyers kept screaming it over the phone and I wasn't even trying to say anything.

Galvin's *shut up* settles like a blanket over the pit, but before I crack into a sweat, he calls to me: "Connie."

I turn and he's right there, two eyes inches away—blue like the daytime sky or a swimming pool, like the inside of a mussel shell bleached in the sand; blue like the middle of a flame, like a thin trickle of smoke, like a new bruise, like old mountains. Blue like when the first star comes out or when the last one goes in. There are so many different blues to see when it's close enough. I haven't moved away yet. And he *has* read my mind. Am I a lunatic hermit who mutters out loud?

"You know, some people don't like to be told to be quiet," Galvin half whispers. His voice never loses substance. "Even when they're polite, courteous people. Even a nice little thing like you—I saw your fuse spark! Maybe I should make you really mad and see what happens. What would it take?"

Why don't I move or back up? Remind him to ignore me—photographer's chant—*don't be so aware of the camera, pretend I'm not here!* "You'll see," he says, "crammed down here together for so many hours, pit musicians get to know each other pretty fast. We have a unique rapport." I still never moved back. That's why I feel his hands on my throat. Isn't this the time for self defense? Why aren't I moving? I wait for his thumbs to push into the soft space between the bones, closing me off like a balloon about to be jet-propelled into crazy circles, or popped.

"Let's have a pit-orchestra silent wrestling match. First one to make a sound is out!" His mouth makes hard ridges when he tries not to smile, white and firm, not like my thin dark neck waiting to be punctured without a fight. But he steps back up onto the podium, takes his long arms with him, and finally looks away. There's a sweet humming somewhere, like in my stomach. I squeeze my eyes shut.

Somebody calls "time," and immediately all the musicians are standing, stretching, putting instruments away. The action on stage has stopped also, replaced with loud laughter, thumping feet, and practice dance steps. But the lights stay off down here; the lighting crew is already taking their break. I loosen the bolt on the bottom of my cello and slide the endpin in, then lay the cello on its side and close my songbook. Someone is calling me. Not a loud call. Just my name, "Connie," in a regular speaking voice, but not close to me. I look around—Galvin is over at the door leading out of the pit, into the basement areas of the theater. He's motioning to someone. I don't move, look around to see who he's talking to, but he points at me and motions again for me to follow.

In the hallway to the basement rooms, with musicians and cast members pushing to get out, he pulls me aside. "Hey, why not have lunch with me today? I keep my food in the refrigerator in the prop room. Why don't you go wait for me there. I've got a thermos of coffee too. You want me to bring you anything? I have to go talk to Harlan for a minute."

"What?"

"Coming through!" A prop man squeezes past with three more music stands for the pit.

"Lunch—you want anything?"

"Oh . . . no."

"You know where the prop room is? Upstairs next to the chorus dressing room and makeup."

"Oh."

"Okay, see you in a few minutes." He pushes back into the pit, against the flow of traffic. I can still see him as he gets back on the podium and talks to someone on stage, flipping pages of his songbook.

The prop room door feels locked but someone passing by says "push hard, it's open." The door makes a horrible screech on the cement floor. There's a window with daylight coming in—a square of sun with distinct edges and corners, filled with flying dust. Potted trees are lined up under the window—all of them plastic and faded. The palm tree is almost yellow. A shopping cart is filled with plastic cups and plates, a few stuffed animals mixed in. There are some light pieces of furniture, thick with layers of paint, spindly tables, dressers, bedframes stacked against the wall. A mounted deer head is on the floor, beside it a hat with antlers and yellow braids attached to the inside. A corpse of a knight lies twisted on the floor too, one leg bent under, his head askew. The refrigerator is next to a stove, and beside that is a pile of framed paintings leaning against the wall, the top one a bull-fighter painted on velvet, so ugly I have to put it at the back of the stack. The next painting is awful too, but not in the same way. It's a seascape—out of proportion and blotchy, colors over-lapping, round brown blobs that are supposed to be rocks, blue spatters for water. Horrible. Makes me sick. Reminds me of my father's paintings. I actually only remember a few of them in de-tail. Like the one that looked like a tree stump growing in front of a big hole in a wall, stretching its two branches up toward the sun—it's hard for an artist to disguise the sun, no matter how bad the artist. And there appeared to be red liquid running down the tree stump's body. I don't know how I remember it so well—I think I was around twelve when he painted it. When I asked my father what the painting was, he stared at me—I thought he wouldn't answer, not so unusual—then he said it was a hermit who had lived his whole live inside a cave, and finally one day comes out and sees the sun. But as soon as he told me—probably while he was telling me—I decided the way *I* would've painted the picture. First of all it would been realistic like a photograph, or maybe it would have *been* a photograph, a whole photo story. The hermit lived in the dark cave and finds a mirror—a wet rock or a puddle or a piece of glass lying around—so he sees his own pale, waxy skin. Who would want to know him? Horrified—both hands full of limp hair, spurting through his fingers—he rushes to the desert and lies in the sand. But instead of getting the suntan he wanted, the sun fries the hermit in his own juice. Blisters rise and burst and ooze, leaving him glistening, and his eyes melt and run from their sockets when he sits up and sees what happened to his perfect body. I know my version of my father's hermit is pretty stupid—I mean, I had an excuse, I was in junior high—but his was *awful,* and yet the bleeding tree stump wasn't even the worst of my father's paintings. The worst was his painting of my mother. I saw it the first—the only—time after I was old enough to have the guts to ask about my mother. All I knew was the horrible name she'd given me, Constantina, which he, thank god, never called me. Once I asked him, though, if he could call me Constance instead of Connie. He said, "You can have your name changed legally if you want," but never stopped calling me Connie, the few times he ever called me anything, which isn't necessary with only two in the house ever at a time. Anyway, when I did ask about my mother—a rare exchange of more than three words between us—he said, "I was waiting until you wanted to know," and he brought out a frame wrapped in brown paper. I ripped off the paper eagerly, but the portrait was just an indistinguishable form. I threw it down and cried. "Where *is* she, what's *this?* It's not my mother!"

"This is how I want to remember her."

"Why? Without a *face*—just a pink circle? With one arm as big as her whole body? Without feet? No fingers? No neck? This is a *thing*. You can't remember her this way—she didn't look like this!"

"It's not supposed to be a mirror image." He was getting mad, but in an unusual way—he was still talking, going on and on. "When are you going to learn that perception is more than an exact photograph."

"Why? What's wrong with a photograph? That's what I wanted!"

"It's my *perception* of her, don't you understand? Can't you understand a little more about her this way?"

"No. I don't remember anyone like this, and neither do you!"

Of course I was supposed to be learning painting myself. But none of the paintings I started was ever finished. He always said he would rather be a successful painter than rich. Instead he got rich, because, he said, he wanted *me* to be able to paint without having to worry about going out every day with a bunch of other people making money off each other. He painted only in his spare time. In *my* spare time I experimented with the old Nikon that he kept on a tripod to take slides of his paintings to send to galleries. I could never paint things the way I remembered them. It was as if the paints had a mind of their own. But if I watch something through a camera—or even pretend I have a camera—it's like I'm the only one watching, it's *mine* to watch alone, and whatever or whoever it is—even if it doesn't know I'm around, isn't aware of the photographer watching, as though the photographer isn't there at all—it still, in a way, knows it's mine. If I'd taken a picture of my father painting one of his ugly pictures, that would've been a different story—I could've looked at the painting in the photo without getting sick. But I never did—I wasn't allowed to fool with the Nikon except when he didn't know, just like the TV. I also wasn't really allowed—not very often—to hang around much when he worked, so I don't actually know what he was like when he painted . . . maybe humming to himself, or listening to a football game on the radio, but no more affable than the man in a gray suit and briefcase going through the kitchen at 7:30 in the morning, grunting good-bye as he passed me, still in my pajamas, making a peanut butter sandwich to take to school. When I still went to school. He let me quit when I was 16. Studied on my own in the library he'd made from an empty bedroom. Had an equivalency diploma before I was 18, avoided all the jousting complication of high school halls. He said, "Good, now that's out of the way," and had me in his studio painting from 8 to noon, then in the music room—another converted bedroom—with the cello for several hours in the afternoon. I think I took lessons when my mother was around, but practiced on my own after that, all those years, at least two hours a day. The only other lessons I ever had were in self defense when I was 18, in-home private sessions, but I quit after three meetings. I got more out of watching the films the teacher brought. I even watched the slow-motion parts in super-slow, but the bulb in the projector started burning the frames. There were scenes on TV I wanted to watch over, in slow-motion, but that was before VCRs. After dinner, which I ate in the kitchen, I sneaked as much TV as I could until he came home. He suggested a book in the library instead. I switched some things around after he died—books in my bedroom, TV in the library. If things get much worse at night, if I can't stop dreaming those dreams, I may move the TV next to my bed too.

After my father died, needless to say, I abandoned painting completely for photography—threw away all his paints and brushes and canvasses, packed away his paintings and began replacing them with photographs on the walls. I was 21 or 22 and hadn't been away from home for . . . maybe six years. Well, I went, as they say, out into the world after that. Thought I was ready, but at the newspaper they called me Howie, for Howard Hughes, but not, as I first thought, because of the money my father left me—it was because I spent so much time alone in the darkrooms. Nothing had changed except I wasn't at home. I went out, did my assignments, but didn't hang around the editorial conference tables where the donuts were. They probably didn't even know my actual name, and I probably never told them. But maybe I'm not so bad now, growing out of it, taking it slowly. At least in the orchestra pit I'm not *alone* in the dark. And all that cello practicing was of some use after all.

"Hi. Maybe I have a few minutes left in my lunch break." Galvin comes into the prop room. "Sorry, I didn't mean to startle you. God, you jumped a mile. Why is it no union rep says, Hey, asshole, you can't work on tempo problems during the conductor's break!" He grins, opens the refrigerator and takes out a box of fried chicken. "Hungry?"

"No."

"What's the matter? First day in the pit kind of intimidating?"

"No. Not really."

"I'll take you *out* to lunch tomorrow if you want, but I had already brought my lunch today."

"That's okay." I sit on a wooden box. He's pulled a chair up to the rickety table.

"I feel like I have to hide during my breaks," he says. "Otherwise Windrem would be on my ass during every free minute. He actually tried to get me to dig up some publicity for the show by making phone calls to critics in *London.* The guy's always got publicity coming out his butt. The music director working part-time as publicist? I wouldn't be surprised if he put that body in the parking lot himself, offed some dude and dragged him here, to get some press. He was out there trying to give a statement when the cops were here."

"Who are you talking about?"

"Windrem, you know, the producer. He put this thing together. Small-man complex. Oh, I guess it was a good enough idea. Puts this old theater to better use than the occasional local rock concert." He smiles again. "But it's such a two-bit power trip. Opportunity Players—did you know that's the name of this whole outfit? Got money from somewhere to lease this theater for a series of shows. This isn't even the only rinky-dink production he's got planned!" He chews on a chicken leg.

"Who's getting the opportunity?"

"You." He chews more, then swallows. "People like you. It's designed to give local inexperienced people their first chance in a professional production. Most of these people were strictly amateur before this—can't you tell? But he has the power to decide who gets their first big break and who doesn't. He gets some kinda cheap thrill out of that. Hey, I don't want to talk about him. I want to know more about you."

"Okay."

"He wants Harlan and me to ride in his fat-man's car when we go on tour," he says. "Probably wants us to look like his chauffeurs."

"Who's Harlan?"

"The director—where've *you* been hiding? You're such a quiet little thing down there behind that cello."

"What tour are you talking about? You mean . . . traveling together, staying together. . . ."

"That's what a tour's all about, close quarters with a lot of other people you may not really like very much. And a bus tour at that—god, this thing's rinky-dink. Naturally we're not taking the orchestra. The only reason there's live music for the performances here is one backer's a nut for the real thing. No canned music—except on tour. I'll be conducting a sound system, probably a boombox!" He empties his thermos of coffee into a cup. "But we could bring you along since you could document the whole thing with pictures—for *real* publicity, and for the investors. You can help *me* drive, since I have no intention of either riding the bus or going with Windrem and his puppy." He hands me a container of cole slaw, closes up the chicken box and puts it back in the refrigerator. I guess it's time to go back to the pit, so I stand, leaving the cole slaw on the prop box. But Galvin doesn't go to the door—he comes to where I am. "I'd like to see some of your work."

"Haven't you heard me playing? I know I've been terrible, but I'm usually better than that."

"No—your photography."

"Oh that."

"Could you bring some tomorrow?"

"I don't know."

"Is something wrong? I don't want to seem high pressure. I guess I just talk fast because breaks are the only time to get to know someone. Maybe we should have dinner. What do you think?" He leans against the wall with one hand, his arm locked, right next to my head, trapping me and I can't breathe, my throat catches. Then he moves, bending over to pick up the hat with antlers and braids. "Hey, lookit this, let's try it on you, change your image, become Viking Woman!" With both hands, he's lowering the hat onto my head. My eyes are closed. Something tickles, it's his breath on my face. Then I feel his fingers brushing my frizzy hair out of my eyes from where the hat has smashed it down, his other hand on my shoulder. I don't have a camera. . . . Even if my eyes were open, I wouldn't be able to see what's going on here, wouldn't have a freeze frame or slow motion or enlargement. I should back up, shake my head to get rid of the hat and his hands and the tickle of his breath, but . . . why don't I want him so close to me? My low voice comes from somewhere without warning, "I know self-defense."

Neither of us moves for a second. Then the hat is taken from my head. I hear it fall to the floor. His arm braced on the wall again. "Anyone else might be joking," he says, "but I think you've got real problems. Real problems, girl. Time to stop crouching in corners, don't you think? You watch everything. I've seen how you take it all in. But I wonder, what do you think about, sitting there in the pit looking around? What do you want? What are your goals? What do you dream—"

Suddenly, my fists protecting my face, I'm ducking under his elbow, almost tripping, but stay on my feet and run out the door which had never shut behind him when he came in.

II

The Off-Stage Wings Where the Actors Hide and Watch

• • •

The musicians bring the smell of coffee and egg sandwiches and bacon with them when they gather in the pit in the morning. Yawning, stretching, as though a 10 A.M. call is too early. Except Galvin. I'm not looking at him, but he's there on the podium, right in front of me, close enough to touch, if I wanted to apologize . . . for anything . . . at least for missing the afternoon rehearsal yesterday. What kind of strange girl am I? Running home in the middle of the day . . . sitting in my darkroom with the chemical trays dry, the water not running, the enlarger cold.

From the stage, Harlan, the director, standing squarely, hands on hips, looks down, past his feet, into the pit. Beside him, I think, is Hal Windrem, who points and whispers, points and whispers.

"Windrem was asking about you." Galvin's voice sounds no different. Should it? "He has this plan. I said it was garbage, but I don't have a vote. I shouldn't say any more. Maybe you'll have fun. Maybe a few moments of attention will be good for you. You'll have your allotted fifteen minutes of fame."

Windrem says something, inaudible because backstage they're dropping scenery.

"What?" Galvin calls up.

"I'm coming down," says Harlan.

It's nearly silent once again down here as everyone waits. I tap my bow on the toe of my shoe. Galvin clears his throat. "To Windrem, publicity is more important than putting on a good show. He'd scrap the show and just crank out the publicity if he could. But if you can forget that, this might be good for you, as I said."

My head jerks up—I'm suddenly staring at him. Just for a second, then I have to look away again. Maybe I saw a bruise on his cheek.

"Just let me know if you really don't want to do it," he says, "and I won't let him make you. It's not that big a deal, but he can't make you. Unfortunate that your resume was so perfect, he won't let go easily."

I hear footsteps thumping down the stairs from backstage to the basement. Then Harlan hesitates for a moment by the door to the pit before he begins to plow his way through the orchestra. Musicians take their clarinets and flutes off their floor stands to protect them between their knees; string players hug their violins and violas to their chests. Most times I climb in and out of here without crashing, although I feel like I have a leg-and-a-half. But here's Harlan falling, tripping, stumbling through the pit like a gazelle dying in an ecology movie.

Finally he ducks under Galvin's music stand and sits on the podium facing me. Galvin puts his baton down and also sits. I hate having this huge cello between my legs as they face me up-close. Shoulder-to-shoulder, two portraits side-by-side, no two could be more different, except the color of their eyes. I don't need to look very long to see that Galvin's unflinching blond face—wide at the cheeks, heavy-jawed, straight lips, far-apart dry blue eyes, no lines around his mouth or eyes—is changed by the bruise. I think it's a bruise. It makes him look sad. Harlan is a darker man, but lit-up now by Galvin's stand-light. His hollow cheeks are perpetual dimples, his mouth small in order to fit between his lean jaws. The corners of his mouth seem always tight, small firm muscles there, with not as much blood-color as the rest of his face—they catch the highlights, as do the subtle peaks of his fragile cheekbones and his omniscient, luminescent blue eyes.

"We have a part for another extra. Wanna leave the pit and go up on the stage?"

"Well, I— Why? Can't you hire someone?"

Galvin says, "Has Hal gotten anyone for the stills yet? She's a photographer."

"That's Windrem's job. I just need another extra. A cocktail waitress. How about it?"

"Well, I—"

"We'll explain upstairs. Interested?" Harlan's smile is pointed, could poke me in the stomach if this clunky wooden instrument wasn't in the way. There's also a pointed lock of nut-brown hair falling over his forehead. But despite his swarthy skin and thrust-forward features, his eyes are un-brittle blue.

"You'll probably fit the costume we have," he says.

"What is it?"

"You know, a little . . . thing. Lace and satin. It rustles."

"Oh." I remove my cello from between my knees, lay it on its side and promptly stab Harlan in the shin with the endpin.

"Just say no if you don't want to. You don't need to attack me with your cello."

"I want to." Still don't look at Galvin. Does he know why I answered so quickly? Maybe he's right about me. I don't want to be a strange girl anymore. Time to start being part of things. What better way than a part in a play. Do I look as sad as he does? I make myself smile, but not *at* either of them.

Harlan slaps his knees, standing up. Fat men do that—but all of Harlan's lines taper toward his narrow hips, which he now manages to twist out of the way of every chair, music stand and unprotected instrument, while I clump along behind.

I hear Galvin say, "Don't go too far, but take ten." He must've scaled the wall because he meets Harlan and me coming up the stairs from the basement.

"Wait a minute," Galvin says, and before I can react he has my arm, pulling me aside. Harlan doesn't even flinch—continues going through an exit door next to the first row of seats.

"No—I have to go with him."

"Just wait a second and listen," Galvin says, then he takes a second to inhale. The bruise is really no more than a shadow.

"Look, Connie, I did say that this would probably be okay for you, and it isn't really that big a deal so I don't know what my second thoughts are . . . or why I should care. They looked through the résumés on hand as a stab in the dark before trying to find someone like a secretary's sister or friend-of-a-friend-of-a-cousin, and bingo, there you were, mixed in with the crew's résumés because yours had no musical experience on it, someone didn't know where to file it and just guessed." I'm staring at Galvin's hand holding my arm. He releases me. "There you were, as though dropped from heaven—like that dead guy—fitting a plan for a little more press, someone who'd never had anything to do with entertainment, to fit the story he's already made up."

"What are you talking about?"

"Aren't you listening?" He grabs my arm again, but then lets go immediately. "Okay, I just want to mention something to you— A lot of people, especially young women, it seems, have felt they want to follow Harlan anywhere . . . I don't know . . . he hasn't directed anything for several years . . ." I'm staring at the exit door where Harlan disappeared. "He sort of dropped out of sight after becoming the hottest young directing talent on the East Coast. I wonder why— Maybe I ought to find out." He pauses. I head for the exit door. "All I know is Windrem and Harlan worked together in the past and something happened," he says. I'm slipping through the door, but his voice, and apparently his body too, are following me. "Maybe I ought to try to find out what it was."

The door opens into a hallway—to the right another door leading back to the dressing rooms, to the left a flight of stairs. Galvin heads that way and I have no choice other than to follow him up to an office that Windrem fills with cigarette smoke, where a sullen mousey-haired secretary flings a contract at me, and Galvin says, "Connie's an experienced photographer, Hal, have you gotten anyone for the publicity stills yet?"

"Let *me* worry about when to hire who for what." Windrem looks at him, blows smoke out between us and keeps looking until the smoke clears. "God, she'll even fit the costume. She's even got legs, I think, somewhere under the jeans. How about this for a release, 'Even an unnoticed . . .' what, what do we call her, *cellist? musician?* . . . anyway, 'even an unnoticed . . . *blank* . . . who always coveted a chance on the stage is getting her big moment with the Opportunity Players.' I mean, the way to get more press is use the vehicle, you know, the *mission* of the group. This might not just get press, might find another investor or two. Better yet, a sponsor. They give money to homeless missions, why not to us, it's almost the same thing, keep these starving actors off the streets for a few weeks." He takes another drag, fills the space between us with smoke again. "But you know what," his voice gets more nasal, "as a photographer, it might be funny," he grins, not at me, "like she was part of the play, except she shows up in the aisle setting up a telephoto, setting off a flash and flashing a little cheesecake, bouncing her ass up and down the aisle during scene changes."

"Where in the script is there anything even remotely like this?" Galvin says.

"Who needs it in the script. Have some imagination, man, jeez, think about it, it's like an innovation, a statement, extending the play beyond the boundaries of the stage, extending not only off the stage into the audience, but extending the play into the crew—the technical side *is* part of the show, it's part of the art. That'll get us noticed, maybe even a pre-opening review in the artsy-fartsy community. Keep us from just being a musical full of crotch shots, have this sleazy part in the play flouncing around with a camera covering her vital parts, taking pictures of the rest of the play. Looking at ourselves, we come off as legitimate art. Isn't that how they think in that quarter?"

With a hand covering his smileless mouth, Galvin looks at a wall calendar. Harlan is behind me. Windrem's eyes still on me, from knees to neck, I itch all over like I've got fleas or lice. Don't know where to put my eyes, they've got me covered from every direction. "I'd like to see what she'll look like in the costume, but, this is going to make it, I really think we've got the right combination here, and—" He claps his hands. "Actually, it's *perfect,* even better! Listen, how about: we even give our *photographer* the chance of a lifetime!"

"She's a *professional,* Hal," Galvin says quietly.

"Well, the whole thing's an administrative decision for *me* to make, isn't it."

Without looking at me again, Galvin gets a cup of coffee from the stained yellow-glass coffee pot and leaves. I bury my eyes in the small print of my unsigned contract. I can't read anything, it's so tiny, but typed on a line, *C. Zamora,* and on another line, *Non-speaking.* They don't want me to talk. Oh, I guess that's my part in the play, a mute stripper cocktail waitress. Over my shoulder, very close behind me, Harlan hangs his head, reading . . . my contract? the back of my neck? Surely not my mind.

"Let me think," says Windrem. So we let him. Me in the center of the floor and Harlan with his head hanging over my shoulder.

I drop my contract to one side; he still doesn't move. I peek sideways, tilt my head a little—still only see his straw-straight brown hair falling forward, long brown lashes down flat on tan cheeks—until I turn all the way to face him, and his blue eyes open.

"Okay, I've decided, we'll go with it, it's even better than the original plan. I'll get releases out this afternoon."

"Fine," Harlan says, with one hand nudges me toward the door. "We've got a rehearsal."

I'm ahead on the stairs, three or four down, while Harlan and Windrem have a few more words up there, concluded with "back off" or "back down" or "lay off" (lay down?), and Harlan shuts the door. So I turn and wait, one foot braced below me, and don't even panic or flinch as he turns toward the dark stairway and falls at me. My hand against his ribs, his two hands both clutching my arm, I prop him up. He stays on his feet.

•

In the wings the next morning, Harlan sits under a caged light bulb and calls to me. I notice, not tripping over anything, how, in the dark, it's much easier to walk toward a light than away from one.

"I didn't sleep well last night, Connie," he says.

"Why?"

"I kept thinking about what happened in the office yesterday. I *am* sorry about it." Speaking softly, he isn't whispering, pushes the words against me as though tapping me with a finger. I wait for more, for something else, at least a smile . . . which he doesn't keep me waiting for. . . . Even that body in the parking lot might be glad to be lying there without hope if he had Harlan's blue eyes over him to say he was sorry. I follow him onto the stage.

From up here, that pit is really a hole. I can imagine when they flash the floodlights up, dazzled blinking actors may not see the edge of the stage, the drop-off into the pit. So Galvin will wear a white coat. Standing up, his head is still below the top of the wall on the audience side, but from the stage they'll see all of him, drenched in his own spotlight, in white. Of course they'll have to watch him for musical cues, for tempo, for facial grimaces. Will they notice the bruise?

I left my cello down there. I usually always leave it during breaks and even over-night. I don't like to cart it around like an extra body. I was always glad I didn't have to take it out of the house because of the case—someone (my mother?) wrote CONSTANTINA ZAMORA on it with red paint. But I can't leave it if I won't be down there anymore.

Voices are rising out of the pit. The call for musicians is hours later than stage players today, so there shouldn't be anyone there, except Galvin, maybe a pianist.

"We can't add anyone down here," Galvin says. "We're full."

"You lost one yesterday." Windrem's voice.

"I don't like to add cold musicians to a rehearsed group."

"Hey, we're going to give some musician a big chance too. Both stories could hit at the same time."

"The scene doesn't call for a harmonica."

"I want to try something different."

"Isn't this high-schoolish production company different enough?"

"Stop trying to make my decisions for me, Galvin, I'm the producer."

"No producer worth his shit will fool with the look or sound of the finished product when he doesn't know what he's doing."

"Don't tell me what my job is."

I know why it sounds familiar. The neighborhood crowd playing Civil War in the street—there was always a long process before the war could start while they discussed and fought over who would be boss that day and decide things like which prostrate position would signify death and which meant the soldier was only wounded. At first I watched from the kitchen window, then moved out to the front porch, finally sat on the curb or lay on the front lawn and watched the Civil War over and over, every day, without once getting shot.

I've circled the pit like a movie camera panning from a crane. Galvin, his light off, is standing on the podium above Windrem, who is on the floor near where I once sat. From the top Windrem is bald. He must've added a permanent to the thinnest wisps of hair, so—usually back-lighted—his hair on top looks like a thin white frizz, which doesn't match the stuff that goes from ear to ear around the back. But all the hair I'd thought he had must've just been *light*, because now I can see it's unmistakably skin. As I pan, I come around to his face and small, dull features, flat gloss on his skin, bestial brown eyes, blackened eyelids above and below, a child's round nose.

Galvin doesn't part his lips again. His silence seems immobile while Windrem's voice stops being words and becomes a nasal white-noise. I squat—thighs to my chest, arms wrapped around, rest my chin on my knees. The only way Galvin could get down off the podium would be through Windrem, so he turns to his music, the thick black songbook under his light. But as Galvin's arm reaches for the songs, Windrem's hand snaps out, grabs Galvin's wrist. "I'm talking to you!"

All Galvin does is try to pull his arm away from Windrem. But he pulls Windrem along. Galvin steps backward on the podium while Windrem leans forward, teeters forward, sways silently—just for a second. But Windrem has no room to *step* forward. All he can do is fall sideways.

"Watch out!" Harlan's voice, on stage, straight across the pit from me.

I stand as Windrem topples in clumsy slow-motion, catching

a music stand, knocking his hip on a wooden chair until his knees finally smash through the innocent pine shell of my cello.

The crunch of the instrument brings the cast onto the stage with the same urgency as when they went to see the murdered man, but they don't know where to look. Harlan swiftly moves away from the edge of the pit, calling them around him. Galvin steps over my cello's broken body,off the podium, and disappears toward the rear of the pit. Windrem is sitting in my chair, but I back away from the edge before he can raise his head to see me.

Sitting on a prop box, Harlan sweeps his arm in an arc, his hand flashing over the assembled heads of the cast. I stand on the outskirts. He claps and holds his two palms apart over their foreheads; they move inward and quiet themselves.

"I've been thinking lately—as I drive home and listen to tapes of some of you singing—about what if a production was made of individuals, rather than being a *company*. . . ." His pause is on an upbeat, catching them waiting. No ad-lib one-liners under their breaths or into their hands. So he moves on. "We have some different kinds of people here. Like the Big Idea person—he looks at the moon and says, someday I'll get there. The Analytic Thinker starts to determine the rocket size, thrust, fuel consistency and chemical makeup, inches and angles and seconds and energy. . . . You ever heard this, about the four kinds of people? . . . . Well, there are four basic types of people. The Big Idea and the Analytic Thinker are two. Plus there's the Salt-of-the-Earth who only wants to do everything right, no matter what, and always expects he *will* do right, and if he doesn't, he cries. And then there's the Reactor who reacts to everything—*bang*—right then. You can tell the difference if you hit them." He hops from the prop box, smacking one fist into an open palm. "The Reactor's gonna hit you back. The Salt-of-the-Earth cries. The Analytic Thinker figures weight and arc of the swing and distance and resistance and—okay, the bruise will last about a week. The Big Idea wonders, where is the origin of this hostility? And we've got all these people out here, all types mixed together." With one hand he stirs a whirlwind, smaller and smaller toward a point near his feet. "The Reactor will always snap and fire back; The Salt-of-the-Earth's gonna try and cry; the Analytic Thinker counts his heartbeats and regulates his breathing to less than sixty breaths per minute and figures out how many miles he can see; and the Big Idea wonders *why*—" His smile is trying not to smile, making it more pointed than ever. He brushes the straight hair away from the eye it points toward. Stretching his arms, embracing the stage area: "And we put all these people in one theater together and tell one-half to enter from the left wing to center-stage, and the other half the same from the right. The Salt-of-the-Earth says, Okay, I'm ready. The Big Idea sees the pattern that a portion of any given population is always going ass-backwards, and the symbolism—people from different poles running together and butting heads. The Analytic Thinker nods and sees we've got 50% moving from point A to B, and 50% running from C to B, so we'll have two people arriving at point B at the same time, which we know can't be done." Harlan lines his hands up edge-to-edge in the center of his face, one eye looking on either side; gives us a profile of this. "So he figures speed and time of arrival, and counts the steps, and knows if he'll land on his right or left foot, so he changes his angle a millimeter to one side and thus avoids collision." A palms-up shrug: "The Reactor says, Why the hell should I do this?"

Harlan takes a moment to look around, catching eyes. Misses me, off to one side. "The point, I think, being that nothing much is getting accomplished—which is why a company *can't be* a group of the four kinds of people." He sits back down on the prop box. "Okay, different subject: We're having technical rehearsal tomorrow. After that no one, but no one, touches a prop except props technicians, no one fools with a set except set crew, no one touches any lights or the circuit board except—guess who—lights technicians. Clear? Good. Now if you're not warmed-up, do so. We're gonna run the second act with piano in fifteen minutes."

Of course some smartass says, "Why the hell should I do this?" But they dissipate quickly into the wings and large off-stage areas, loving to warm-up, loving to show off for each other.

I stay on the stage—look once into the pit. Windrem has abandoned the splintered cello. From the prop box—not under a direct light, his face dark in a shadow from the long side curtains—Harlan beckons me with one finger.

"I probably should've said this earlier," he says. "If you don't understand, say so and I'll explain."

"Okay."

"Whenever there's a controversy, I do choose a side. It may not be apparent to you, but that shouldn't matter. All I ask of my cast is to do their best in their individual parts and have a good sense of the total *show.* Just the show. That's all that's important to you."

We stare at each other. As though he's not finished.

"Why are you telling me this?"

"I just wanted to see if you understood." He doesn't leave. He puts his two hands on my shoulders. "There's a lot of personal conflict here, that's all, no big deal—every show has its share. I just want you to be prepared."

"Oh."

Someone switches a light onto us, a white spot from the balcony. The technicians fooling around. Harlan drops his hands, folds them between his knees.

"Now listen, this is what I mean—don't get in the middle of anything. You can't protect anyone."

Even in the white glare here, even with pupils like pinpricks as he faces the spotlight, his glossy eyes are still soft.

"Okay?" He taps my backside as he walks past me into the wings.

The leads get a call to run a scene, so I melt back into the off-stage wings where the actors hide and watch. I haven't had a single staging instruction; I don't even know what scenes they want me in. But I do know one place I can almost walk without tripping.

The orchestra still isn't here. Galvin, at the piano, has his back to the pit entrance. This was a nice place once. There aren't many instruments to be careful of now. Only the large ones stay all night. I walk on a row of chairs, stepping quietly on each smoothed board. How many years of hours have these seats been warmed by soft-flanked musicians?

We sat down here in the dark with something happening right over our heads—and we never completely knew what was going on. I could always tell that they intended to shoot threads of emotion out over the pit, one by one, into the audience, spinning a complete web, trapping them hopelessly . . . while the actors themselves, like spiders, have to learn to walk on the parts that aren't sticky. But from the pit—I see now—it's too much like listening to someone—your own lover, probably—falling in love during a one-way conversation on the phone. Nothing to see. You might lie in bed together, and he/she takes the phone from *your* side, the cord right over your head; they have to speak in riddles, keep you from knowing, keep you guessing. Something going on none too subtly right over your unsuspecting head.

As I hold my cello up by its broken neck, still strung together, now forever out-of-tune, Galvin abruptly stops pounding at the piano. I feel him watch me slip the cello into the canvas case, which holds the pieces together like a limp splint. Then when I look up, he says, "He forgot one type," his eyes flashing over the piano.

"Huh?"

"The kinds of people, he forgot one: the one who sees something that he's not getting enough credit for, so he has to get his hands into it." The piano blocks him from the bridge of his nose down. Without a mouth, his eyes speak for themselves, become brittle, bite off the words. But it's too dark down here to see any bruise.

He says, "You see that he pays for that thing."

Holding it in both arms, I start to walk back along the chairs. As I hop off the last one, near the piano, Galvin stands, leans his elbows on the top, hands folded. "You watch it. I mean, watch *out*, okay?"

The mark on his cheek is almost gone. Maybe it was only a smudge of dust from the prop room—I might have been able to brush it away myself. I'm not sure.

"I told you, I'm going to find out what's going on." His eyes glare in the dark . . . my stomach jumps. . . . I had assumed a small-time theatrical company wouldn't make headlines, would be fairly harmless, that's why I'm here. Why should anyone need to be protected from a touring show?

Stage players seem to be here longer and work less than musicians. The orchestra doesn't have to arrive until afternoon some days. But I've been here since eight this morning and I still haven't done anything. They're running the whole second act, which should take at least an hour, maybe two, with a lot of stops and starts. I take my cello out to my car in the parking lot. I should just throw it in the dumpster, but I can't quite do that even though it's definitely dead—beyond repair. I don't even know why I'm getting in my car and leaving the parking lot . . . I didn't think I was going to when I came out here.

My bank isn't anywhere near the newspaper building, but smells like it because there's a photo lab on this street. It's not the one I quit but it is unmistakable, so I always know it's there whenever I pass this way. Earlier in the day, like now, the chemicals are fresher, the snapshots glaringly bad. If I'd stayed there much longer, I might've successfully learned to despise the sharp smell of a new print, the frozen-in-ice look of a glossy surface, the grainy texture of photographic skin-tone. I quit too soon . . . or just in time.

In the bank, when they leave me alone with my drawer, I glance in. The capped eye of my camera stares me dumbly in the face. All my lenses are carefully laid out behind it. I hold my hands together behind my back. I just had to see the long lens, that 500 mm telephoto which looks like a cannon, a bazooka, only far more accurate, pinpointing action one hundred yards away. It's long and black in the very back, wrapped in soft leather, only used once. I listened to the ballgames every night on a radio in the dark—in bed if the team were home, or while printing and developing if they were on the East Coast. Then the paper switched me to nightside, so I listened in my car as I drove to assignments, silently pleading *please, please* when he came to bat, this superstar on a last-place team. I never covered sports—a few of the guys always had those assignments. I didn't care. But one night I was near the stadium, heading back to the office, the game over, a post-game talk show on. I swung into the parking lot. At the wide ramp where the players walked out of the basement of the stadium and up into their special barricaded parking lot, a small crowd had gathered, as I'm sure one did after every game, those who want to touch or hear or smell a ballplayer up close so badly that they'll wait two hours after the game. Portable three-foot cement walls blocked off a path for the players to walk like gods through a throng of multitudes. About a hundred people, if that. I kneeled, my lens on the cement wall, and watched them smile, wave, exchange private words with each other, or walk past stone-faced and marble-eyed. I returned the next night, and the next, and kept coming back. Bought the big lens. Came back again. Sometimes people spilled over the short wall and mingled with the players. I was watching for him, as usual, and as usual the little crowd surged forward when they saw him. He seldom smiled. I don't think he ever saw me. The kid was holding out his mitt and a pen. I barely even knew I'd released the shutter. The kid was falling backwards, the little crowd changing shape. I didn't want that to be the shot I got. He seemed to be the only one who didn't call me afterward to try to change what the long arm of my camera had grabbed and held onto.

•

Windrem fills the tiny upstairs office. He's not a big man. But there's always something swirling around him, at least three feet in all directions. Something confusing that sweeps people out of their desks, drops them at other desks, digging under someone else's arm into a drawer, hardly knowing what they're looking for. The phone rings frequently, and he seldom answers it. He takes a breath, or says "We need . . . ," or "You know . . . ," and everyone's shoulders stiffen or they get kinks in their necks. People lose pencils, can't find typewriter correction fluid, misspell words or get paragraphs out of order. He says "When you're ready to listen . . . ," or "Let me know when you have time for me to explain . . . ," and they're still turning somersaults across the room, addressing envelopes upside-down, saying "damn" when the phone rings, always listening with two ears: one for Windrem and one for everything and everyone else.

We were going to discuss my contract. It shouldn't matter to me what the contract says. But I don't like the *C. Zamora*. It can't be that hard to change it, once I get around to asking. While I'm at it, I think I'll ask for a clause in writing giving me permission to use the camera anywhere in the theater, any time I want. Just in case. I'd do the stills too, but if I'm going to do it, why not make pictures worth looking at more than once. That is, if I shoot any at all. . . .

At least I thought we were going to discuss the contract—isn't that why Harlan said to come up here after rehearsal? I asked about my contract today, backstage, during a scene change, and he said, "We'll discuss it in the office with Mr. Windrem," and not until I arrive do I realize that Windrem hasn't the foggiest notion what I'm doing here or that there is anything about me to discuss.

He looks at me without blinking, then turns to Harlan and says, "I'm taking off. See you later?"

Harlan cracks his knuckles, palms against his heart. "No, I'll probably be heading home soon."

The secretary covers her typewriter and leaves. The two other clerks close drawers, clear desk tops, put on sweaters and leave. Whipping his coat off the back of his chair, Windrem stings my cheek with a button, follows it with a glare of his button eyes, and leaves.

"He'll void your orchestra contract and want you to sign the other," Harlan says. "But regardless, I personally want pictures of this show, and I'll pay you for them if you do some for me."

What would *he* see in my photos? My heartbeat is heavy at the thought.

"How about if I give you an advance for supplies." He already has his checkbook out. "Make it out to Connie . . . ?"

"Zamora, but—Actually *Constance*, but I'm still not sure I'll—"

"That's your name?" he says.

"Yes."

"Legally, or just what you like to be called?"

"Does it make a difference?'

"What is this, February first?"

"I don't know."

"I'll put the second." He bends to write. He fills out the stub first, then hands the check toward me, looking at me, and I look at him, not it.

"I don't want to call you by nicknames," he says.

"Huh?" I don't touch the check.

He stands abruptly. The check is lying on the desk in front of me. "I just can't change anything right now."

"Why?"

"I can't appear to be intimate with parts of you or your life that have nothing to do with the show." He puts one hand in his pocket and, I presume, finds nothing. He sits back down.

I never did make a legal name-change . . . maybe I should've. Then my legal name wouldn't be illegal. Tax and bank people occasionally get confused by the *Constantina*, which is also on my birth certificate and social security—along with the middle name, that other monstrosity, *Fortunata*—chasing me around . . . sounds like someone I wouldn't even *like*. So I stamp *Constance Zamora* on the backs of my photographs, and that's how I get paid, but no one with any amount of brain should get confused. I pick up the check.

"If you do any photos for the company," Harlan says, "make sure it's compensated for in your contract."

"I'm glad you said *if*."

"You took my check."

"If I cash it, you'll get your money's worth."

"If you don't want to, why can't you just say so?"

"It's not that . . . but . . . I haven't done any shooting or printing for a while. Did you know that?"

"How would I know that?"

"I mean, you *should* know, I guess, if you're asking me to. When things got hot, I quit and ran. When a picture really mattered enough to people I didn't know, had never seen before . . . or only from a distance. . . . Usually artists *want* to create controversy, so I don't know what was wrong with me." I also don't know why I'm babbling on like this. He's looking at me steadily, levelly. "So I guess I thought I would solve the problem by finally choosing one of the things my father wanted me to be, a painter or a musician. See, I can still take pictures someday, if I want to, but if I take pictures *for* someone . . . well . . . why should I show anyone else my photos if they won't see what *I* saw?"

"Whatever you decide. Just give me enough time to get someone else. And also, I should've said this earlier, if you decide to do it, do a set for me personally that I can keep *and* a set for the company. But you have to do both or neither. You can't just do it for me. Understand? And don't mention you're doing a special set for me. And if it's not in your contract, get reimbursed by the company for the company's stills."

He leans over his desk, over a little pad of paper he has there to write on, holding a pencil stub which is lost in his hand. I know he has a pencil hidden there because I hear it scratch. I glance down at the check—it's also in pencil. "Here." I throw a pen onto his desk. When he stops to pick it up, I say, "I heard about some tricky ways to get reimbursed."

Harlan puts my pen into his mouth and seems to read the scrap of paper. His eyes might not need to move to read across it. At any rate, they aren't moving. "Yeah, everyone has heard stories about that." His hand finally falls to the desktop with the pen threaded through his fingers. Then the pen rolls free and he uses both hands to crumple the two sentences and their little page. It doesn't weigh enough to make it into the trash can on one toss.

"A guy's company would pay him a hundred dollars a night to go to a convention." We hardly watch each other as I speak, as though it would keep other people from hearing, but there's no one else here. "He knows he can't eat *and* sleep out of town for a hundred a day." I retrieve his wadded-up paper and throw it away. "He can eat for *thirty* a day, which only leaves seventy for a hotel, but he likes the best places. He would have to cough up the rest." This far into it, when now I can't turn back, Harlan is facing me. He's turned his swivel chair toward me. He leans across the desk, bracing his elbows there. He hasn't picked up the pen. "But the guy's got friends in the town where the convention is, so he can stay with them. But his company won't give him the money until he's already spent it. So he buys his own receipt book, and he makes receipts."

The room is quiet. Not a horrified or shocked or even mildly surprised silence. It's the funny sort of quiet where people are trying to figure out what to do next because something unnatural is happening.

"You think that's new?" he asks.

"I don't know. New to me."

Harlan doesn't blink. He doesn't so much as even twitch. As though I've prepared him for it but never gave him the punchline.

"I do have to get reimbursed for my cello."

His voice is still a little husky. "Get reimbursed the . . . regular way."

"You know I will."

I can hear him breathe out, but it's not a sigh. "I know." And he gives me a look.

•

Days later I'm still mostly wandering around backstage with nothing much to do. No one seems too worried about the contract. They got me ready for a costume—measured every line and curve: wrist, arm, biceps, ankle, shin, thigh, waist, overbust, underbust, middle-front to waist, middle-back to waist, waist to low back through the crotch. Not a soul has offered information about my scenes or cues. I stay where they can find me; I shadow Harlan. Now he's in the light booth and they're running a dance over and over to the sharp smack of a choreographer's clapping hands. The orchestra is on a lunch break.

I stay close to these thin strips of curtain which protect the wings from the audience's view, tuck myself inside the folds because entrances and exits whisk past. I can well imagine the scene if I tripped someone and said "I'm sorry" and they asked "Who're you?"

No one, of course. Pretty hard to be no one when you've just sprained someone's ankle.

That's why I still like to be a photographer whenever I want—even if it's not in my contract yet, even times I'm without a camera, like now—if I'm a photographer, I'm *allowed* to be no one. The photographer knows everything and is still *no one*. You look through the lens and have the story laid out in front of you—and yet you don't have to *be* anyone or answer anyone, and of course never be part of what you're watching. When people look at a picture of some place they were or something they once saw, they remember being there, seeing it—but they shouldn't remember seeing the photographer there focusing the lens, or realize they're viewing through her eyes.

The dancing men are in one-piece suits, an extra skin they wiggled into. One has short dark hair, and when he is the only one who doesn't stumble or trip during an intricate part of the dance, his smile really does split his face. And he keeps on dancing, smiling, until the next difficult part—sailing through that one, grinning even wider. So marvelously tall and thin. My heart is pounding as though *I'm* dancing too—faster than I know how.

From the other side of the stage, in the other wing, likewise close to the hanging curtains, hands in pockets, Windrem also watches this smiling dance, then leers at me over their heads. His attention is called away by a blinking phone.

Someone touches my shoulder lightly—I spin around. "What're you doing up here. You scared me."

"Sorry," Galvin says.

Sometimes the backstage wings are as dark as the pit, but not now. Maybe I was right, it's not a bruise. Maybe I didn't defend myself from anything. The dance steps on stage vibrate the floor and the bottoms of my feet—like standing up in a motorboat.

"What's he doing over there?" Galvin says, looking over my shoulder toward the stage, but not at the dancers. I glance across . . . Windrem is off the phone and once again standing in the other wing, smoking.

"Just watching, I guess."

"He needs to *be* watched." Galvin stands beside me and talks without looking at me. "I haven't found out much about them yet—just some rumors about a girl they both wanted. Something like that. But . . . did you know how hard this show was to cast?"

"I thought you said he had a lot to choose from because it was a big opportunity for unknowns."

"It is, but they wanted a few people with some experience for the leads. Minor has-beens or never-weres. But the ones they initially wanted refused to audition."

"Actors refused parts? I never rejected a photo assignment." Until now?

"I'll bet you never had your boss looking over your shoulder."

"I'm not even sure who my boss was." The publisher who paid the lawyers who screamed over the phone at other lawyers? I heard Windrem mention "my lawyer" to someone backstage. "You mean they wouldn't do the show because he hangs around backstage?"

"No, but they'd heard about him. He's sort of infamous, I guess. He even got one of the actresses to audition by having Harlan call her, but when she got here and saw Windrem, she said she wouldn't do the show."

"She told *him*?"

"No. She didn't even want him to see her, even though she admitted she didn't think he knew her."

"Paranoid."

"You think so?" He smiles. "She told me she'd heard that

Windrem once wanted to hire an actress for a play because she'd already done it successfully in Los Angeles—this was when Windrem was back East. But because she'd done the play before this actress didn't want to rehearse at all, not even to learn the new cast. Prima donna bitch, you know." He smiles at me again, and I actually smile back for a second. "Well, Windrem hired someone else for the part, then quietly brought his first choice to one rehearsal. *One.* Just before the play opened he abruptly dumped the actress who'd rehearsed the part and announced that his original choice would play the lead. Of course they'd arranged it secretly and it was great publicity for the show to announce that a famous star was suddenly in the lead. But the girl who'd done all the rehearsals couldn't get hired anywhere else because Windrem let rumors leak that she was incompetent, that he'd hired this star at the last minute to save the show."

In between dances, while the choreographer explains something in a bored East-coast accent, some of the dancers glance at Windrem. But the dark-haired one has his hands on his hips and listens intently to the choreographer.

"Why was she telling *you* all this stuff?"

"I was standing by the door when she came in," he says.

"Huh?"

"She wanted to pretend she was with me so he wouldn't start pressuring her, so we left. Went out for a beer."

"Did you know her?"

"Not before then." He grins again and turns to leave. "Sorry I startled you."

On breaks, at lunch, Harlan sits behind his wooden desk. I know because most days I climb the stairs to pick up my contract and forget to discuss it. No one talks about it. Always an unnatural silence, as though holding their breaths while pretending to look away, unconcerned, as long as I'm holding that paper. I often quickly put it back down without looking at it.

Harlan seems to be waiting for me. He's already looking up, smiling, as I come in. "You look different," I say. I mean, he *is* a little different today, as though he started a new scene before I even read the script.

"I do?" he says. "Maybe I am." He eats a spoonful of hash from a can.

"Is that what you're having for lunch? That stuff's dangerous, it's full of preservatives."

"Maybe I'm becoming a pickle."

Before she goes to lunch, the secretary wordlessly hands me a contract. Probably the same one she hands me every day before lunch. The same one I leave lying around as though I forgot it. No. Today it's been retyped, says *Connie Zamora,* and the position space is blank. A mistake? I look up quickly at Harlan. Suppose I took it home and wrote in *Solo Lead* or *Music Director* . . . or even *Photographer* . . .? Neither of us is laughing, or even smiling anymore.

"Hey, can you type?" Harlan asks. He takes the contract from me, reads it, shakes his head.

"Type? Yes. But you have a secretary."

"I have an important secret mission for you. I don't want anyone else in the cast to know about this." He can't be serious—he's smiling again.

"Me? But I—" I take the piece of paper he's handing me. He still has my contract.

"Type it, please," he says. "But don't show anyone."

"But wait, I— Okay."

I don't need to watch my fingers. This is mechanical copying, words pushed onto paper, not nearly as miraculous as a scene, an action, a personality gradually appearing under chemicals in a darkroom. It's magic, when I think about it, that a piece of chaotic memory can become tangibly real—an idea, blur of motion, streak of light smeared/painted/brushed lovingly onto paper. Having it to hold and look at afterwards should be just as miraculous, but all too often it's just a fleeting magic because someone invariably stamps a name-credit, signs a signature, and the memory becomes *property*. So you have to start over and work on another one. Who was it—Balboa?—who crossed the Mexican mountains and saw the whole Pacific stretched out, as far and wide as his arms could reach while he stood trying to catch his breath, waiting for his heart to stop flopping around, for the adrenalin rush to pass. . . . Then he charged down the mountain, stuck a flag in the sand, paid his glass beads, but never did touch the miracle he'd seen. He made it into real estate. How can I do this—type and not even read what I've been typing? Yet my fingers stop automatically. I've been typing one sentence far too long.

"Are you finished?" Harlan asks.

"No. I can't finish it. It's got a very bad run-on sentence right here."

"Type it exactly as it is."

"Really?"

Harlan comes and leans over my shoulder to see. I try to make myself smaller, staring at my fingers resting on the typewriter keys. "Well," he says, "just fix the grammar."

"I can't. I'll either have to completely reword it or leave it as it is—which is *bad*."

"Then leave it." He stands up but stays behind me. He's rereading the copy he gave me, propped up beside the typewriter. I watch his eyes touch each word, sad blue and guarded. They weren't like this when he came to get me out of the pit.

Then I join him, looking at the original letter I was copying from. It's typed. Harlan said he can't type. "Who wrote this letter?" I ask him.

"Let me check the very first version." He gets a yellow legal pad from his desk with his familiar pencil handwriting. "Here, read this, see if it's better— No, don't compare the two."

But I *am* comparing. I look from sentence to sentence, word to word across each letter. "They're totally different. How can this be a first draft? The second version doesn't share one word in common with the first. Who wrote this first one?"

"I did," he says.

"Then who typed this so-called second version?"

He takes the handwritten letter away. "Someone."

"Not you, in other words."

Harlan sighs. "Mr. Windrem wrote it."

"Does he know how bad it is?"

"Just type it."

I throw my head back. "You mean he wrote this letter to the mayor recommending *himself* to be Man-of-the-Year for *you* to send? Why not use the one you really wrote?"

He sits on the edge of his desk; or rather sinks onto it. "He prefers his."

I feel wild. I touch my hair expecting to find it tangled from a windstorm or wet with rain, or matted with leaves and twigs as though I've been in a fight. "I'd hate to see you sign your name to this."

"It's okay."

"It's not! Why doesn't he sign his own name?"

"Connie, that's enough!"

I finish typing. First only my arms feel sick. My joints are hot water. As he signs his name at the bottom, my stomach flops over, onto its backside, everything upside-down.

He seals the envelope and hands it to me. "Get it out of here."

I say, "We argued about something we agree on."

"We didn't argue."

Thinking I'm going to be sick, I sit on my heels in the cool aisle between loge seats, letter in hand. The young dark-haired man is dancing. No one claps a rhythm or accompanies him on the piano. But he is complete anyway. Not just rehearsing—*loving* doing what he does best. If he had a mirror, he could be an audience for his own dance. A photographer can't—with a mirror you only get a picture of a photographer taking a picture, which is no good because the whole idea is to feel the scene as though no photographer was ever there analyzing light and trying different filters.

When Harlan comes from the office, he walks down the aisle, leaps onto the stage, and disappears into the wing without glancing at the dancer nor at Windrem, across the stage in the opposite wing. Something about the way Windrem is lurking backstage . . . something about the way he hides there, quietly smoking, not speaking . . . something about the way his eyes are glassy, hardly noticing those who pass on and off the stage . . . something is begging me to put him on film.

But why bother? A picture of a man, smoking, leaning against a wall or support beam, in semi-darkness, maybe a piece of curtain behind him. People probably wouldn't know how to look at it, wouldn't know how to look with more than their brain, would want quick *answers*; would turn to a caption or headline to explain it.

A producer watches a play from backstage.

Not the whole story, not what the photographer remembers.

Or someone might add to the caption: "*he looks for flaws the audience would never notice but would feel. . . .*" Or, "*. . . watching the play for the one-thousandth time . . . the intense concentration required by those behind the scenes . . .*"

None of these would be *my* photograph. A photo done right makes them feel what you felt when you shot. Maybe I've never made a picture good enough yet.

•

A chorus of "congratulations," and "you're a star now," and "how many curtain calls d'ya think they'll make you take?" before I'm finally given a copy of the paper. Inside section D, the light stuff, here's a photo of Harlan talking to two actresses, neither is me, but the article starts with my voice and words I never said.

> "It's great, it's my dream-come-true," are the first words Connie Zamora is saying to people these days. "Instead of always wondering what-if, I've got the chance I always hoped for, dreamed of, but thought was too late to come true." Zamora, a 29-year-old photographer, is talking about her chance to be under the lights instead of behind them. That's the whole idea behind The Opportunity Players, a new theater company in San Diego dedicated to giving new talent its first leg up. "Connie exemplifies what we're doing here," Jay Harlan, director of the production, said. "She's a photographer with no stage experience whatsoever. All she had was desire, and a dream. Around here, that's all you need."

It goes on, background stuff, mentions Windrem's name, the name of the show, something about the history of the old theater, comes back around to my name and the remarkable words they say I said:

> "Who knows how it happens?" Zamora said wistfully. "You want to be something, but fear or practical necessity gets in the way, one thing leads to another, and there you are, you've grown up to be something else, but you still want what you've always wanted."

There might've been more, the paper is too far away to read now, as it floats from hand to hand backstage, heads bending over it, scanning the type for their own names, some saying "who's Connie," others looking up with still more smiled congratulations.

"Yes, congratulations," says Galvin, coming into the backstage area with his own copy, "and be prepared. Your colleagues are going to be curious about you. They believe this crap . . . for now. It's quite a coup. By the way, I was just upstairs. Harlan's wisely taking a different route in this morning."

"Why? What's wrong? Isn't this what Windrem wanted?"

"Yes and no. Whose name is barely mentioned? Who doesn't have a single quote in the piece? Who isn't in the picture?"

"How'd that happen?"

"Nothing mysterious. He sent in prepared statements—yours included—but the reporter and photographer who followed up got here late day-before-yesterday. Harlan and a few others were the only ones here. They posed a shot, took some comments from Harlan, and used the prepared stuff for background material. Windrem's hot about it."

"He's admitting that he's mad that the publicity about the play isn't enough about *him?*"

Without my realizing, somehow Galvin has moved this conversation off to the side, deeper backstage where no traffic bustles past, darker, more echoey, and we're whispering.

"No. It doesn't take a bloodhound to sniff it out though. He did say someone blew it—spraying blame around without pointing anywhere specifically—by not sending photos with the prepared material which put us at the whim of a staff photographer, he says. He complained that the picture of Harlan looked phony, didn't do enough for us. You know how transparent that statement is, don't you? But the reason I wanted to talk to you—he's saying we'll learn a lesson from this, we'll be in control of our own press pictures from now on."

"So? What does that have to do with me?"

He stares, then says, "If you weren't so busy slaying dragons. . . . Open your eyes, girl. Who does the snarling dog bite when the puppy's getting all the attention? And you're the only photographer he *has* to control around here."

"He can't control me. Why aren't you warning Harlan?"

"Harlan knows him. He can take care of himself. Who knows where Harlan is coming from, anyway."

Clapping hands, and Harlan is standing in the dark aisle ten rows deep. "From the top," he calls.

Another trip to the bank. I've tucked camera and three lenses into my case. Leave the long one. It's safer here. I want to hurry and leave, but now there's something to sign. I don't care what it's for. But I didn't sign a contract today, when I stopped by the office, slipped in when I saw Windrem wasn't there. Harlan shook his head over it in amazement again today, I presume, because some kind of salary was typed in, but still no job to do. He never even handed the contract back to me after he took it away.

•

Final dress rehearsal. I finally know my entrances and exits, my cues, my blocking. I've been measured twice over, pinned, stitched, sewed neatly into my costume. I have no lines, but know when to smile. And my smile is practically painted on. All I have to do is twitch, and the red, smeared across my mouth, smiles by itself. I'm caked, powdered, and sprayed stiff all over.

Windrem finds me in one of the underground halls where I'm trying to learn to move without breaking the stage makeup. "Getting some photos tonight? You have time between your scenes don't you?"

"Tonight?"

"Get something interesting, no clichés okay?"

"But tonight?"

"Yes, Connie, tonight, as in right now, pronto—how else can

I say it to make it clear? Harlan wants pictures of the run tonight, to study details."

"Harlan—? But I—"

He's not even here anymore.

Neither is my camera. I never told anyone I *would* do it! Haven't gotten the free-reign-with-a-camera clause yet. Haven't even asked. Harlan wants them? Why didn't he tell me?

My dark-haired dancer is in the makeup room. Mine now because we're paired in a scene—I serve him a drink, beam at him, then lure him to greater glories. Actually, we go offstage into the wings where he stretches and I look around, and when our eyes meet, we smile, often the same smile we rehearse on stage.

"Randy, where's Harlan? When do we start? When's curtain?"

"Relax, I don't know. Dress rehearsal never starts on time." He has one long leg up on a barre, swinging his upper body in huge arcs, backward, forward, side to side.

"Well, I'm going home."

"You're not that nervous, are you?"

"See you, I'll be back."

First I take off the dress—silk and lace and rustling satin—leave it hanging on a hook somewhere downstairs. Over my black fluffy underwear, I pull on someone's T-shirt that was already hung on the hook.

Harlan wouldn't stop a dress rehearsal unless forced to . . . would he? No, I doubt the cocktail waitress speeding across town when she should be wagging across the stage would be sufficient to force a production halt. If it were—if he stood arms folded, foot tapping, silence on the set until I came creeping back. . . . No, just a miscommunication, he'll understand. I'm doing what he wants. Why else did I get it out of the vault except to use . . . ? Anyway, I know, something in me knows, if I'm not there, he'll never miss me, never miss me, never miss me.

So why are you crying you little fool dressed like a slut, isn't it what you wanted? He'll *never notice your puffy eyes and blotchy face, the absence of your smile on stage, the quiet breath you would've taken in the wings, your name not on a contract, you'll disappear forever and no one will notice,* he'll never miss you. . . . *But there could be pictures to hand him, for his eyes to touch, a memory to share . . . so afterwards at least he'll know,* you *were there too.*

The automatic sprinklers have come on at home—the kind with arcing jets of water. I slide on my ass across the grass, taking a short-cut to the back door. So instead of dashing through and missing the water, I catch it across the front of this shirt which belongs to someone who hung it on a hook back at the theater and who'll find there now, should he go looking, a glittery black cocktail dress which practically starts and ends at my waist.

At least everything is already packed in the camera bag, no run-around to gather together stray filters or film. I slap the camera bag over my shoulder. My body remembers the weight.

Keys in my mouth, I pull my tripod from my trunk in the theater parking lot. No time to glance at the place where they drew around the body with chalk. All I ever saw was that lopsided outline, the basic shape of his death. I still wonder what he thought during the seconds before he landed here, and what he figured he should do about it.

In the center aisle of the theater, I set up slightly behind an audience of two: Windrem and a white-haired man. Second scene, they're past my first entrance. The tripod is stuck, not lubricated, and Windrem turns to look because the metal whistles as I lengthen the legs.

"Connie, we're not having a wet T-shirt contest."

The white-haired guy turns and stares too. I spit my keys into my hands.

"Hello little lady."

Probably a fitting endearment for a girl with no contract in lacy black underwear and a wet stripe across her shirt. How can I get them to turn around again, stare at the stage instead of me.

The orchestra jumps, a drum roll with cymbal pulls the dancers upstage, but even more importantly pulls Windrem's attention back to the show. I don't have much time. Long-legged men with their bulging tight pants . . . I don't have time to watch. Windrem's stomach growls. I have another entrance soon—I leave the tripod, slip away with the rest of my equipment still hanging from me, and hit the wing face-to-face with Harlan. He says, "Oh. There you are." I keep going, threading my way to the backstage areas, then downstairs, through every little room, through almost every door because behind one of these my costume is hanging.

But I can't find it.

I've got to get some shots or I've got to make an entrance. One or both. I can't do *nothing*. My feet are lead returning back up the stairs. I've never tried to do something and shoot pictures at the same time, never considered doing it . . . but would I have said it's impossible? A stretch, a distracting tug-o-war. Then if the tug-o-war rope breaks, both halves are equally useless, opponents shrug and toss in their ends. Wait, please don't give up on me—!

"Someone found this," Harlan says. He's holding my dress. "And you've lost your makeup."

I touch my wet forehead where the sweat comes away brown, rub my cheeks with the backs of my hands and the lingering tears wipe off red. My next entrance after the dance is approaching quickly. I have my camera on, but it's slung around to the back. There's nowhere to put it, nowhere I trust except its cell in the bank vault. Maybe no one will notice it on me . . . keep my back to the walls . . . why did I ever get it out, what made me think . . . no time to wonder, I'm on now, here goes. . . .

No! I duck back into the wings. Not in a T-shirt. Not wet and streaked with muddy red. I circle behind Harlan, wrapping myself in the shadow of the leg curtains, squat and hold the camera up, press my eye to the window but keep my finger away from the button. I can't hold it still, it knocks against my head, raps my eye socket. Makeup smeared all over its black body.

III

A Snarl of Wires Plugged Into a Whole Wall of Holes

• • •

Once upon a time I might've stayed hidden at home at least a week, but as soon as I left the theater last night, I knew I would have to come back this morning. The only thing scheduled today is a last-minute dance rehearsal to change some of the steps. I'll have to go upstairs to that office. Never missed a photo assignment before, not on purpose. But how many potential photos have been missed since I quit making pictures? This apology, does it mean I'm someone's photographer again now—and that nothing much has changed in the meantime? It doesn't say so in the contract yet, but the contract isn't signed. Probably now there'll be no contract. Unless I can explain without defending . . . or reacting or crying or dying. Last night was just a relapse—I really mean it, I don't want to be a strange girl anymore, isn't that why I've come back here?

Backstage while the dancers warm up—Randy gives me a reassuring smile and a backhanded pat . . . maybe a backhanded smile and a reassuring pat. "They can't fire you," he says.

"I guess not."

The choreographer calls the dancers on stage. Maybe if I wait here long enough, Windrem will come out of the office so I can go up and explain to Harlan alone. A late dancer brushes past me in stocking feet, her shoes in her hand.

Overhead hundreds of poles and a spider web of ropes descend, tied to a long row of hooks. And there's a snarl of light wires plugged into a whole wall of holes. Someone knows what they mean. A sign nearby says "In Case of Fire, Cut Rope." In pencil someone crossed out the last two words and wrote, "*Run Like Hell!*" I try to follow the rope with my eyes—up the wall, along the ceiling to whatever it's tied to, to whatever will fall when there's a fire and the rope is cut.

I'd better go. But I'm taking the long way—out a stage door into the orchestra seats and around the front of the stage. I stop halfway across to lean over the wall around the pit, and—too late to jump back again—Galvin sees me.

"Hi, Connie, what's up?" He's on the podium, no musicians to conduct, following measures in his songbook as the choreographer claps.

"Nothing."

"Didn't you know there's no rehearsal today?"

"No. I mean, yes, I knew. But I guess I should go explain to Windrem about last night."

"Last night?"

"I didn't get any pictures."

He turns a page, writes something in the margin, then looks at me. The wall comes up to my waist and his head is level with my feet. "Did Windrem ask you to take pictures *last night*?"

"Yes, and I . . ."

"That's odd," he says. "There's always a special photo session. Posed. In costume."

"Why wouldn't they want real action shots during a run? Isn't that what Harlan wants?"

Galvin was writing again when I said that, the choreographer talking to him, dancers—hands on hips, standing in a half-circle—watching.

"That's where the accelerando is," Galvin says. I continue my slow tour around the pit, on my way to the office.

"That's just not how it's done," Galvin says before I get very far away. "But then again, who knows with this assbackwards high-school outfit. Oh well, don't worry, it was just a minor publicity gimmick to call you a photographer. I'm sure there'll be other stories that don't involve you. What're you going to say to him?" The choreographer is busy with the dancers, Galvin again looking at me.

I shrug. "He can't hurt me."

"I think it's Harlan he wants."

"It wasn't Harlan's fault." Galvin doesn't look away, so I add, "It was just a little mix-up." I turn and actually hurry through the exit door and run up the steps to the office, pant outside the door, then push it open without knocking.

I think it's a contract on Harlan's desk, on top of a pile of papers pushed to one side. I don't know if it's mine. He's not looking at it. In the middle of the desk is an open script. He's tapping a pencil on the page he's staring at, making a spatter of dots and lines. Then he notices me and points to the chair opposite his desk. Before his eyes return to the script, I can see—and feel—the sting in them.

I have to wait until Windrem does something—leaves or gets on the phone. I'm nearly ready to call him myself, from the extension on Harlan's desk, and put him on hold. But he takes care of it, having to go somewhere or other to negotiate something concerning the outrageous price of something or someone.

Whatever Harlan is thinking doesn't make creases on his brow or twist up his mouth. Maybe if I touched him he would be soft, an anemone, pulling away from me. But I'm the one starting to silently shrink away when he speaks.

"You made a lot of mistakes yesterday."

Why did I come here . . . and let him look at me that way? I can't get up and leave now, but if I slouch far enough . . . I'll slip down below the desk file, lower than the books and papers, beneath the surface of the desk.

"Hey!" he says, catching me before I move. "Hey, didn't you?" There's a smile in his voice but not on his face. "Well?" How can his eyes be simultaneously bright and sad? "Hey, you can talk to me, can't you?"

My mouth opens, shuts, I shake my head no.

"Why? I've never harassed you, have I? . . . have I?" His snarl is chillingly real. I believe it. My fists are tight.

"Do you want to hear what happened last night? I mean why I—"

"Not really," he says. "I know what happened—you missed all your parts in dress rehearsal."

"Not that."

"What else is there?"

"I didn't get any shots for you. Didn't you want pictures of the show?"

"Not at the expense of dress rehearsal. I'll *tell* you when to take the stills. There'll be plenty of time. After the show some night."

"But he said—"

"Now this," he says. The contract. He slides it over in front of me. It's filled in again, *Connie Zamora . . . Non-Speaking*. That's as far as I look, then I say, "Does he mean a non-speaking *photographer*, or what?"

Harlan smiles, pushes the contract aside.

"You know what?" My voice is finally normal.

"No, but I think you'll tell me anyway."

"All that running around back and forth last night—and I didn't even have any *film* in my camera!"

"You'll have your chance." His eyes back on the script.

•

I know I can get him some *better* shots than posed stills and yet still be ready for my own entrances—by shooting from the backstage areas. And it will be something he's never had, a new angle, the perspectives of the scenes will be *mine*. He can remember the show in a way he's never seen it. He doesn't need to tell me—I know when to shoot. When I'm not on stage, he won't know where I am, then tomorrow I'll hand him a stack of 8 x 10 glossies, at least one from almost every scene, and I won't miss an entrance. It doesn't matter if an unsigned piece of paper doesn't say I'm allowed to—it also doesn't say I'm *not*.

Old habits return easily: as I clean and check each lens, I plan the shoot. If I could get behind the sets, in back of the stage, I could use the wide angle and get shots of the whole scene from opposite the audience's point-of-view. The 50 mm might not be much use, but the 270 zoom will work fine from the wings. Call is five o'clock. If I get there early I can investigate some backstage passages, maybe find cracks in the sets big enough for a camera lens to look through, corners in which to tuck myself away, boxes to prop my arms on to steady the camera—I can't lug a tripod around. I could also try some shots from the lighting booth—in the back of the theater, up above the audience, like a balcony. There are some long stretches in the middle of the play when I have no entrances. I could use the big gun from up there. Wrap the whole stage up from that range. The whole theater. My camera case is packed and ready, each lens in a leather bag, side by side, like an armory, but missing the cannon. The camera has film inside, and extra film stuffed in the pockets. I have time to stop on my way to the theater. . . .

It's cool and quiet in the wings when I squat behind one of the sliding sets, which will be pushed on stage in the second or third scene, to test my medium lens—how much of the stage will it get, what's the best setting? So quiet here that no one can sneak up behind me this time—so Galvin doesn't startle me. I can hear his unhurried footsteps, a board creaks. . . . But dammit, I haven't even attached the lens yet. My camera is sightless, a raw hole on its face.

"You're early," Galvin says.

"So're you." I fumble in my bag for the lens, but he crouches beside me.

"I was taking the opportunity to use the office while no one was there." His voice is calm, steady, quiet without any effort to be quiet.

"So?" The cord on the lens bag is in a knot. I have to use my teeth to loosen it.

"I made some calls," he says. "Found out a little more."

"Oh." The cord is still in my mouth. I tug on the knot a few times. It's wet, but no looser. "Are you going to tell me?"

"I thought that was why you came early . . . didn't I tell you I had found a few people I could call?"

"No." Finally the knot gives a little. I wipe my fingers on my pants then finish untying it.

"I thought I did. I meant to. Anyway, everyone has heard the same rumors about the woman, but I also heard a story about a play Harlan directed back East that everyone thought would bomb out, a lot of financial trouble, but his *wife* saved his bacon, bought out the three co-producers, including Windrem, for below their original investment. I don't know why he sold to her—they think he didn't know it was Harlan's wife."

I uncap the screw-end of the lens and attach it to my camera. Then look up at Galvin. "And?"

He smiles. "Well, I wonder how Courtney got Windrem to sell. It may be that the show was really going broke and everyone knew Windrem was a coward. But then . . . ." He touches my shoulder with one finger. "The show was a surprise success and made the Harlans a lot of money."

A couple of doors slam. Maybe the technicians. Voices boom in the basement, coming up the stairs, then disappear down the hall toward the dressing room. Finally I say, "I have to get to work."

"Okay." He stands. "I'll let you know if I hear anything else."

"If you really think I need to know. . . ."

He stares at me, then shrugs and walks away.

Damn. Almost five now. I leave the bag and take just the camera across the center of the stage, my moccasins making sandy, scratchy sounds on the wooden stage floor.

In the right wing, in a dark corner behind a phone booth which isn't needed on stage until the second act— "What're you doing back here, Connie? You're not supposed to be here."

What *now!*

Windrem. Sitting on a stool near the circuit board where all the wires are plugged. My mouth is open but I haven't said anything yet.

"I understand you refuse to sign your contract," he says.

"Well, I—"

"I should've explained earlier—this is a small production. We hope to build with it, but right now we have to save where we can. Only the leads mandate scale. But believe me, we'll try and make it up to you when some profits start to come in."

More voices downstairs, and laughter, sounds almost like screaming.

"Understand? Good. Now go on, you're supposed to be dressing, aren't you?"

"I guess." I look down at my camera.

"Go on, Connie, get moving."

After I go back across the stage and pick up my camera bag, I pass Harlan coming in the door to the backstage area. I smile, but he's not looking at me, doesn't hold the door for me, doesn't pause as I move past him.

A rack with all the chorus and small-part costumes is in the middle of the dressing room. A few dancers are already in makeup, rolling nylons up their legs. I get my dress and shoes and go to the mirror that has my name taped to it. Actually not *my* name, just *Cocktail Waitress*. I rub the black satin between two fingers. They've added red sequins to the bodice. A few come off in my hands. My stomach hurts—it feels like a fist. I leave the dress draped over a chair and hurry out of the room.

Everyone except the leads shares a makeup room—lots of white-light and rows of vanity tables facing mirrors.

"I'll do you next," a makeup technician says to me when I pause beside her. She's smearing Randy's cheeks with red. He's already got his lipstick on.

"Pucker up, sweetheart," Randy says to himself. He bounces a wink into the mirror and back out at me. I hate it and don't want to look: even his hair I hate—it's slick, smeared to the shape of his head, painted on like his putty ears, fragile waxy nose, heavy brows with points. His eyes are far inside the mess.

"I'm going out of this light to check my camera."

"A half hour."

"Yeah. I'll be back."

Still in jeans and a sweater, both dark, and my soft shoes, I go back down the hall to the backstage areas.

Everything is so crucial now. Who among the ticket holders could tell it took fifteen people knowing what they were doing three weeks ago to make that one midnight-blue floodlight wrap the star-lovers in their first kiss. Now, opening night, the technicians speak through wires: each, with headphones, at his station, calmly checking with the others. The set changes wait to be dropped from the back, pushed in from the sides, each in order. Someone knows when to roll the brick wall and street lamp onto the stage. Someone knows when to replace the bar and cocktail tables with a park bench. Someone knows to pull back the panel wall and neon window so the night-time sky and silver foil stars can glitter under a moonbeam spotlight. Everything waits to happen: waits as though we never did any of it before. All this work, all these weeks, yet nothing has started.

Once again I walk across the stage, this time by slipping behind the starry-sky backdrop, and emerge in the right wing in back of the low cardboard-brick wall that's fastened with a board to the unlit streetlamp. This gives me a better view of the stage, a more interesting angle than from behind the phone booth on the up-stage side of this same wing. Maybe it's a good thing he made me leave so I could come back a different way.

But even if I push the film up to a thousand, I'm going to need to shoot virtual statues to avoid pictures of blurs. The backstage light doesn't reach behind the prop wall; from the waist down—camera and hands and the rest of me—I'm in total darkness. I squat, camera between knees and chest, remove the medium lens then set the big one on the hole in the camera body. It whirs and clicks into position.

I swing the lens over the wall, rest the barrel on the cardboard, directing it toward the empty stage. Of course nothing's happening there, so I watch the light meter inside the camera as I pan slowly until I've got the lens pointed toward the backstage area—right in front of me. The wings right now are moderately light. Too early for the rustle of an audience out beyond the pit. Too early even for the hissing whispers of the orchestra. Too early for the thumping of a nervous shoeless dancer backstage. But Windrem is still back here. The right wing technician lifts his headphones so he can hear what Windrem is saying to him. He nods, puts the headset on his stool and slips out onto the stage. I can hear his feet bump all the way across.

Windrem pulls on his cigarette. I can see how long the ashes are. Watching through the camera, this lens works like a telescope—I guess he's actually about 40 feet away.

Stepping back, but not out of my horizontal range, Windrem surveys the light panel—the circuit board where jacks from each set of lights are plugged into the proper hole, wires all tangled, like an old-fashioned telephone operator's bewildering muddle of lines. Behind him I can see Harlan looking at the ropes. He must've just come in from the forestage entrance to the wings. Windrem runs his fingers along a grey cord until his hand is lost in the snarl. He takes in smoke, then sets the cigarette down on a box, reaches and runs his fingers down another cord. Even moving as slowly as he is, I couldn't get a good shot.

The two men seem so unaware of each other . . . but I forgot that this lens smashes everything into one dimension;. Harlan is actually fifteen feet farther away from me. And Harlan, living two hours in the future—the eight o'clock curtain—will be a zombie until time catches up. He has his hand wrapped around a rope, looking up to the rafters where it terminates. The lens puts me right there next to them, as though standing beside them, and as though they continue to not know I'm there. Harlan doesn't budge, doesn't stir. Windrem's motions are like murky underwater action, stroking the light wires. . . . Then he stops. He closes his fist around one large jack. And he freezes too. The tendons in his wrist pull tight. Practically posed.

I release the shutter. Takes a quarter-second to click. The next click is Windrem pulling the jack out. Harlan has disappeared like a dream through the forestage door.

I advance the film to the next frame. Windrem pulls another jack. I'm no longer watching through the lens—I'm taking it off the camera, capping both ends, pulling the drawstrings of its leather pouch. When I look up again, Windrem is gone. People learn to pad around back here on soft soles.

As I pass the light panel on my way out, both sockets are filled again. The cigarette smoke is as visible and irritating as though Windrem were still standing here.

I wish I could dance. I'd love to tap dance down this hall to the dressing and makeup rooms. The tile floor is slick and hard, but all I can do is run on my toes, burst in the door just as Randy is removing his bib and leaving the vanity table.

"Teach me to dance!" Taking both his hands, I hop in a circle around him, my camera swings around my neck.

"What? Wait! Boy, you're crazy!" He grins.

"I *must* be. But I'm not strange. Is it my turn yet?"

"Just a sec, okay?" The technician is putting a finishing touch on a chorus girl. Such blue eye-lids. Randy looks as though he was painted in oils and stepped off a canvas—not one of my father's, that's for sure!

"You're not dressed yet," he says.

"There's lots of time," I take my camera off my neck and start to put the lens cap on.

"No—don't put your camera way," he says. "Take some shots of us here."

"What for?"

"For opening night. Bring out the ham in everyone."

"Doncha think there's enough already?" But, encouraged by his flaming smile, his rosy cheeks, I fix my medium lens back onto the camera. Randy is calling everybody's attention to me. This is the type of photography I usually hate and avoid. I don't know what's wrong with me, why I'm going along with it. Red smiles, shiny eyes, so much color and action, ad-lib dance steps, candid poses of faces cheek-to-cheek, grins, tongues stuck out, no one hides, no one turns his face away. Such willing subjects. I can't stop *laughing*. Too bad my film is black-and-white. By the time they finally get me facing that mirror, I've finished a roll of film, rewound and stuffed it in my pocket.

Now my own eyebrows arch up and out like black wings. Now my own eyelids are too blue, my whole eye outlined. My natural sleepless dark circles buried in pancake, my lips ripe red.

"Careful with your face, dearie, if you're going to take pictures."

"Sure."

Someone at the door calls, "I want all chorus people upstairs, on the barres, loosening up in five minutes." As they go, Randy squeezes the back of my neck. The makeup technicians clean up, the choreographer turns and follows the chorus, leaving Harlan in the doorway.

"Hurry, Connie."

"Okay." I skip through a swinging door to the crisp pile of black satin and red sequins on the dressing room counter under my typed name-tag which still doesn't say my name.

On my way out I meet cross-traffic. The orchestra is filing through the hallway toward the stairs to the basement. I stand aside, waiting for Galvin, but he isn't with them. My freshly loaded camera rides on my lacy hip. Twice I fall off my spike heels.

Backstage is delirious and Randy is marvelous in a pleated ruffled shirt and tight black dancing pants. He'll sit at a table in the second scene and I'll serve him a drink and smile at his leer. Background action.

"I'm gonna grab your ass on stage," he says.

"No you're not!"

"Sure, we'll steal the spotlight."

The owner of half that spotlight, Margie Dean, moves among us like a lithe giantess. The male lead, Eric Something, or maybe just Eric, stays in the right wing. They'll enter from opposite sides and meet in the middle, in the spotlight. Randy tugs my skirt down where the camera strap jacks it up in back.

Harlan is standing in a little nook near the left-wing technician's stool, tucked away near the phone that blinks without ringing, near the entrance aisle. We'll pass close by him as we leave the frantic crowded wings and sail onto the stage—past the magic barrier which I've seen remove Margie's bitchiness on the way out then put it back when she returns. Tonight, however, during the opening chorus number, she and I are alone back here—with Harlan—relaxing and watching. Margie keeps her arm around my shoulder until her entrance after the song, keeping me back out of range until she hits the stage. We move in together, but I stop at the edge and follow her with the lens, keep her in focus and click in rhythm.

"Get rid of it, Connie," Harlan's stage-whisper reaches me. The prop technician has my glasses filled, my tray waiting.

"Where can I put it?"

"Here. Give it to me." Harlan takes the camera by its black body, but doesn't put the strap around his neck.

My nerves remain with my camera held by Harlan in the wings. I serve colored-water drinks under hot lights. Once or twice I even think about the camera. No one'll have picture-proof that I'm out here doing this.

My smile to Randy, the tug of my shoulder that seems to pull him out of his chair, helps end the scene. We leave together into the opposite wing, and while the bar is transformed into the park at midnight, I hurry back behind the backdrop sets. I have a while now to shoot. In a pair of technicians' coveralls I can go get from a nail backstage, perhaps I can even get out into the audience for the clinch and kiss. They're still in their pre-kiss song, which gives me time to pick up my camera, get out there and set myself, check exposure, change lenses—

Dammit . . . forgot to bring my bigger lenses out of the dressing room!

The song builds toward a climax: I have 16 bars left to dash to the dressing room. My ankles wobble over the spikes—this must be what charm school would be for, to be able to run down a slick tile hall in spike heels during a love song in a sell-out opening night without falling, breaking something, or sounding like a horse on cobblestones.

Miraculously the last chord is still humming when I hit backstage again. They lean into the kiss, but there's still no camera in my hands. I head for Harlan.

A technician: "Lights, warning, cue 14." A calm whisperless voice: "Lights, cue 14, ready." As the lovers touch, as I reach Harlan's side, the tech says, "Cue 14 *go*," into the mouthpiece, and abruptly the stage is blazing—the spotlight is *red* . . . and orange and yellow . . . every hot floodlight!

"Shit!" Harlan pushes me aside to get out. He heads for the forestage door toward the light booth. Margie's horribly ugly grimace stares point blank into the red spotlight.

"Kill it," the technician hisses.

The sun burns out.

The audience wonders—you can hear them wondering. But Margie's thin "eeep!" cuts their dull questioning throb, so an appropriate stark silence accompanies the sound of a crash landing: familiar clatter of music stands and crunch of wood.

"House lights. Someone's gone into the pit," the technician commands.

The leading man, Eric, had disappeared into the right wing during the darkness. Now he's out in the audience, in front of the pit wall, still with a stage voice, resonant and deep from his abdomen, saying, "There's a small fire, would everyone please—calmly—exit out the front. There's no danger. Please, slowly and calmly."

The technician behind me barks, "Throw the master switch before it gets to the circuit board!"

There *is* a fire! An orange flame licks its way up a black leg curtain in the right wing. As the master switch is hit somewhere, the house lights die, but the wings across the stage from me remain blazing. Automatically my fingers grope to my hip for my camera. Not there. Where is it? Where's Harlan! The hotline phone blinks. I'm rooted while everyone else dashes about with armloads of props. The audience drains out the front of the theater, crowding and pushing through the doorways. Squealing chorus girls hug their flimsy costumes with bare arms. An actress removes a blond wig, stuffing it down her blouse in one motion—her scene hadn't been played yet. The phone is still blinking—and on top of the phone box, there's my camera. I reach for it, but take the phone instead. Windrem's voice, "Wasn't anyone the hell *over* there?"

"I guess it just suddenly ignited."

Another line is blinking, so I cut Windrem off. Galvin from the pit: "Get us a stretcher down here."

"Okay." I turn to a technician rushing past. "They need a stretcher in the pit."

"Gimme that."

I have my camera in one hand before he pushes me away, so I head across the stage while attaching a longer lens, then click off a dozen heroic shots of a tall man in a tuxedo with a smokey face who is fogging the flame with an extinguisher. He turns his head and coughs, eyes crying, my lens putting me close enough to brush away the tears. *Harlan.* One more click. A cloud of extinguisher fog gets in my way . . . batting it with one hand, holding the camera with the other, squinting through the lens, clicking the shutter but never blinking my eyes, straining for a clearer view of him. . . . The fire isn't as hot as others I've covered, but the fumes stink worse, thick and acrid. The extinguisher fog is cool . . . Where is he . . . yes, it *is* Harlan with the red extinguisher, the only color in the shot—or is my film black-and-white?—becoming dimmer as the flame-light dwindles. I throw my camera back to its place on my hip and move toward him.

"Lemme take it . . . ," reaching for the extinguisher can.

"No, go on, get outta here."

His knees are smudged. A black stain on one cheek. His eyes laced red. I drag on his arm, panting, sucking smoke inside with each breath.

"Connie, *go!*"

"No."

Holding his arm, I ride along as he shoots the flames. Fewer now, and smaller. I shut my eyes against the smoke. I can't hear anything except a giant hiss, and I feel cold blasts against my face. Vaguely aware I'm not even supporting myself. When did we switch? Now he's got *my* arm, his hand tight in my armpit, a vise around my biceps. With the other hand he aims and shoots. My eyes are open again, squinting, but still watching. I went to a 360-degree movie once. Everything but a single frame directly in front of me was a messy blur. I got sick and had to leave. Now this is the same, I raise my head and all around me, on all sides—in back, above right, above left—*everything* vibrates, shimmers, never stops moving, never focuses, all fuzz, greyish whipped with swirls of color. My stomach rolls in agony.

Harlan drops the can, turns and coughs against my hair.

"C'mon."

Back across the stage. I must be walking because no one is carrying me.

"Go on." He gives me a final shove, a little fling. I fall off my heels one more time, land on my padded, lacy backside, camera on my lap, red sequins falling around me.

Almost afraid to crack open the two film containers. One stayed with me in the fire, one was safe in my jeans pocket in my locker. Even in the pitch-black developing closet, there's no chance to slam the lids down after I peek. When the cans are pried open the tender celluloid springs out into my hands.

Why not walk out into the sun and burn it clear? There's no sun at night. It's still opening night. Why not turn on the overhead white light and fog both rolls? I don't know. But I keep the room dark and work quickly. Automatic fingers wind the film onto two spools. I plunge them, both hands up to my wrists, into the tanks.

Everything is coming out perfectly. I remember it clearly. I can almost feel it again—the cold white fog of the extinguisher like swirling snow—as I print a panel of slow-motion movie shots: Harlan in the fire. As though he had been alone in the building, a custodian or night watchman who wears a tuxedo to work, fighting for the life of an old wooden theater and dusty props and faded velvet curtains . . . was he the only one who wanted to save anything? In the darkroom, the pictures still submerged in solutions, everything in the scenes is incredibly obvious.

At 12:01 A.M. it is no longer opening night. Everything is already opened—when I left the theater, the back doors were flung wide with black sick-smelling smoke rolling out. So it's the day after opening night when I finally float that first shot in yellow chemicals, the first one I took yesterday, before the fire, before the red spotlight. . . . Maybe I was surprised when I aimed and shot the cannon and nothing blasted, until it explodes here, a black-and-white image plastered onto slick white paper. It was Windrem's arm I focused on, his sleeves rolled up, tendons popping out, his fist still unmistakably holding the thick jack. I remember his hard glassy face, the set jaw, the glaring eyes. Beyond him, but pulled closer by the brilliant optics, in much gentler focus, Harlan is still there, his face and upper body appearing between the circuit board and Windrem's head . . . holding a rope, his eyes in shadow, perhaps glancing toward the ceiling.

Enlarger jacked to its extreme, I expose the mid-section of the negative. Windrem's hand, still hard but losing clear edges; Harlan's face badly grainy and losing shape. But there in the lower corner, in a dark square below Windrem's fist, the undeniable white of cigarette paper, the grey of ashes. What shade does red glow in black-and-white?

Dried and stiff, I seal the last two pictures in a brown envelope. The photos which *should* remember everything *I* do: that Windrem switched two jacks in the lighting board, producing a lewd red spotlight in a soft love scene; that someone was smoking backstage and left the cigarette on a box beneath the circuit board near a black leg curtain; that Harlan, who doesn't smoke, was standing just fifteen or twenty feet away—but he looks closer. What the photo doesn't say is what Harlan saw or if he knows . . . but how could he have known and not stopped Windrem from doing it? It's only the flat perception of that lens which remembers him as a possible accomplice. Harlan could burn, again, in Windrem's light trick, and doesn't that make *Windrem* safe . . . protected by the same photographer who could accuse him? The same photographer who wasn't there, who wasn't supposed to *be* there. I can't just *say* I saw this, I'd have to use the photo as proof . . . yet if I show this to someone, anyone, the scene could easily blame Harlan too.

But that doesn't seem right—isn't this picture what I saw? Why is it so obvious that someone else could see it differently? Did the camera malfunction? Or that big lens? It warped everything! I'll never use it again. I shouldn't have to explain a picture; I saw this—*this* is what I saw!

But *is* it? Wouldn't I have to use a photographic face-lift to make this picture actually be what I'm sure I remember was happening . . . and to protect Harlan . . . ? What didn't work or what did I do wrong? This picture speaks for *itself*, not for me.

I stand and shiver outside my darkroom at pre-dawn, startled by each rustle, twig snapping, bug crawling, cat prowling, wind sneaking about. If I were only as stealthy and could somehow sneak the picture into someone else's mind—into Harlan's, where from his point of view it's a different image, there's no sight of himself. If only two photographers could've taken the photo together, the two sides of Windrem—our eyes could meet and lock on him, each without catching the other in the background.

•

He sits on a prop box. This is where I knew he'd be. But no longer tuxedoed—which means he didn't sit awake until dawn in the ruins of opening night. Still, he's sitting here as though he knew I'd have to find him today and ask him . . . *somehow* ask him . . . or somehow find out what I should do with the photographs. Maybe a simple word from him, not even an explanation, and I can throw the envelope away.

He watches me as I cross the stage from the charred right wing. Curtains make a fire too quick and not nearly hot enough to even warp the hard plastic jacks filling the circuit board. I keep my camera flung around back. My eyes swollen from sleeplessness, from *rage.*

I know he's watching because I feel him sitting there, like a hot light which I can keep out of my eyes but my skin has no defense against. He motions with a finger—come here—and I stand beside him like a naughty child.

"The fire inspectors were here already," he says.

My fingers touch the camera on my hip. "Yeah? What'd they say?"

"Nothing any of us didn't already know."

"Which is?"

He shrugs. "There was a fire here."

"Is that *all*?"

Does he look at my camera? I think maybe he does, for a second. A funny careful glance at me, at his two hands, at me. "You did a good job last night."

"Are you talking about *during* the show or—"

"I was afraid you still thought you were supposed to be shooting photos. We never have a photographer working during the show—we pose it afterwards. But I was afraid if I told you again right then, it would rattle you."

"Mr. Harlan, what rattled me was—"

"It's ironic, isn't it, about Margie—broken leg." He sighs. "I want you to be able to go out there and feel confident that you'll play a good show, that you'll know every cue, every movement which affects you, and have fun doing it."

There's something about the way his mouth fits together that's almost scary. He doesn't look like he had fun saying that.

What are we talking about, anyway?

"I hope I didn't get in your way. I was *mad*, but it didn't seem to help."

"Perhaps because you're not mad at the right things," he says, calmly.

"It's the right thing." I take a deep breath that tastes of burnt cloth and paint. Suddenly my voice is rushing on: "But sometimes I try to tell myself to do something—I *know* what to do, like how long to burn a hotspot in a photo or if I airbrushed something *out* it would be a perfect shot or to stop thinking about something at the wrong time . . . or to tell someone something . . . and I tell myself to *do* it, but my body won't cooperate."

He folds his hands, rests his arms on his legs and looks at me, and his mouth still fits together that same way. He's a funny color. Is he sick? Should I ask? He says, "I'm always telling members of the cast what to do. I also *know* what they should do, and I tell them, but they don't always cooperate either."

Voices, sounding like stage dialogue, echo upstairs, downstairs, out in dark corners of the house—technicians who punch a time clock are always here. I look down at his knees, at his hands clasped between them. I lean forward, put my palms flat on an empty technician's stool, press my weight down. "But why do you do what *he* tells you to do, don't you know—"

"Connie, no—"

"Well, people may not be cooperating because they don't think you're the one who're really in charge around here, and you *should* be—"

"Connie, you don't know what you're talking about. Someday you'll discover that everything would be easier if people were always cognizant of what they were saying . . . or seeing . . . or doing."

Now the predictable silence. And the silence wonders if we've both really been talking about the same thing. Silence that stops the working technicians ten yards away. They come no closer.

"We're not always, are we?"

"No," he says. "We're not." Then a smile, and time to go.

Time to go lock the prints, camera too, back in the bank vault. To figure out by myself what to do with them. To be cognizant.

But Harlan, instead of clicking, I could've called to you—if you'd only turned and seen for yourself . . . or if only you'd look *now*.

IV

The Darkroom in the Storm Cellar

• • •

My vault is big enough for everything—lenses, camera, envelope of pictures, and a smaller envelope that contains the negatives, cut into strips of five, each strip slipped into a separate tissue-paper folder. My camera bag is empty and lighter but doesn't look it from the outside.

There's a man on the phone—twice on my phone recorder yesterday before he catches me—who says he's from the newspaper . . . but he doesn't sound familiar, and also obviously doesn't recognize my name, or if he does, knows enough not to mention it.

He says, "I understand you're the photographer for the show that had a fire backstage."

"How do you understand that?"

"Are you?"

"Who gave you my name?"

"The theater office. Look—"

"Who was it?"

"I don't know," he says. "Some secretary I guess—"

"Male or female?"

"What difference does it make?"

"Never mind."

"Well then," he says, "what *is* your position at the theater?"

"Why?"

He is silent for a moment. But I know better than to hang up on a newsman. They read into it.

"Let me start over," he finally says. I hear a pencil scratching, and a lot of noise in the background—he doesn't even have a private office. Some new kid, probably, just off the obituaries. "I'm Glen Peters from the *Tribune.* I wondered if you happened to take any photos of the fire—we'd like to run some. We'll purchase them at our regular freelance price."

"Why would you want to do that? It's two days since—"

"Oh, you know, theaters are careful of fires. Wherever there is one, it's pretty spectacular. Even a small one. And . . . let's just say I got a tip . . . people always want to blame someone. It never seems to be an accident . . . does it?"

"What people? Who?"

"I don't know. Wish I did. Maybe you can help me."

"Look, I'm in my darkroom—very busy—you'll have to call back in an hour." I click the phone down before he can say something like "Okie-dokey." I've known enough newsmen.

So I take a sweater, my wallet and car keys, and without having to pause to decide, drive straight to the theater parking lot where I already know the dancers are meeting to caravan to Los Angeles for a master class, where I'll be also—or somewhere in between—in an hour when the phone rings. But I'm not hiding. Does it seem like I am? Look how many people I'll be around all day, you can hardly call that strange or reclusive. Besides, I pushed the shutter release and developed the film and printed the photos and dried them. I could've stopped at any time and didn't. I could've thrown the pix and negs away. And didn't. But that doesn't mean I have to show them to anyone. Does it?

Here they are, waiting for someone to say "Okay, let's go!" A flock of dancers, most of them with tight jeans pulled over their leotards, and as they face each other in conversation, they twist and stretch their bodies. They never stand still.

Randy says, "Hi," and immediately puts one foot on my car hood and touches the asphalt flat with both palms.

I say Hi to the top of his dark, sunny head.

"I didn't know you were coming along." He reaches up with one hand and runs his fingers along his spine to make sure it's straight. "Has it always been your dream to be a dancer too?"

"My dream?" I sure didn't dream about dancing last night, unless you could call that mess a dance.

"Wasn't that article about you?"

"Oh that. Yeah, no, I'm no dancer. But didn't Harlan say that any of us who *could* go *should* go? Anything I pick up oughta help me somehow."

"He said that a while ago—now there may not be a play . . . your chance-in-a-lifetime may've gone up in proverbial smoke."

"No. They won't drop it."

Randy straightens to his usual full height, his eyes a foot above mine, and is as still as he's ever been, just rocking from flat feet to tip-toe, up and down . . . my head nods with him.

"Do you know anything?" he asks.

That's what a detective might've asked someone out here the day they found the body. "I know a lot of things."

"Hey, you know something, don't you."

"Why would I know any more than anyone else?"

"I've seen Galvin talking to you a fair amount. Also Harlan. I'm not the only one who's noticed."

"Is that unusual?"

He shifts his feet into a ballet position. "It usually means something."

I don't say anything, look away, across the spot where the body lay, through the chain link fence, over the parking attendant's booth in the next lot, to a billboard advertising a spy movie.

"Hey, I'm not trying to insinuate or pry, it just seems as if you know for a fact that they're not going to let the show die. That's all I care about."

"There wasn't *that* much damage."

"But Margie . . . and what happened to start the whole debacle anyway? Something was awful screwed up."

"But she's replaceable."

"I wonder how it happened, though. I mean, an experienced actress falling into the pit—"

"The stage was black—"

"Yeah, and *why*?" He has stopped rocking, flexing and stretching altogether. The sun is sharp in his eyes, a crisp reflection back at me. "This *was* Margie's big chance, you know, sort of a comeback after doing a TV pilot that never aired five years ago and never getting another call."

As though given some silent cue, the dancers begin getting into vehicles. Randy holds the door of his little car open for me.

"Don't actors have a disability pension—or a disabled list, like in baseball?"

He's gone around to the other side of the car and says, over the roof, "Yeah, sure." Then we both duck and meet on the inside. "And they put us on waivers when we get old," he smiles, "but they can't send us to the minors if we've had eight production titles." He starts the car and we join the caravan.

"What about Actor's Equity?"

He flashes a look at me. Either afraid to take his eyes off the road, or afraid to really look at me. "What about it?"

"Isn't she, somehow, protected?"

"Well . . . what do you mean? . . . There was no net across the pit."

"Is there supposed to be?"

Another flashed look. "I suppose they could've asked for one."

"Didn't they?"

"I don't know," he says quickly.

With his eyes back on the road, I turn the radio on and watch his profile—his dark curved lashes and fine Grecian nose, calm cheeks, relaxed mouth. Looking at him, normal girls wouldn't be thinking about implications and ramifications and responsibility and the morals of manipulating evidence. Was it a mouth like his, warm and wet and pulling at my skin like a suction-cup, last night, that made me wake, cotton-mouthed and headachy, heart pounding, staring as though in panic through the darkness, out the dark window . . . ? Whose mouth was that? I put the light on and read til dawn.

We park at a big theater complex in downtown Los Angeles and I tell Randy I'm not going in. It costs $50 for a half-day master class and I didn't pre-register or bring any money. He says everyone could chip in a few bucks and probably cover me, but I shake my head. There are trees enclosed in little brick prisons on a patio between one massive theater and another. The whole front of one theater is glass, and three glass chandeliers in the lobby are as big around as boulders A red scroll-patterned carpet without worn marks is being swept by a custodian.

"What did you come for, then?" Randy says.

"I thought it would be . . . different. I shouldn't be doing this. It's for you."

The custodian opens the door for our troupe. He's dumpy and coarse compared to the lithe dancers who swirl past. But he's not old. On the lapel of his khaki jumpsuit he has pinned a painted metal inchworm with a smiling face.

But I stop at the doorway, the custodian and his happy bookworm still holding the door, Randy on the inside, still holding my arm.

"What are you going to do all afternoon by yourself?"

"Sit under a tree."

"Connie!"

"It's okay. I'm used to it. I can take care of myself."

The glass door closes. Randy stands there looking at me, then someone takes his arm and pulls him along with the rest of the dancers. I move away without looking at him.

The first hour is easy to kill, I played like this as a child. Click my heels against a tree's brick wall for a while. Lie down along the bricks and draw in the tree's mud with a stick. Make piles of pebbles and bowl at them with a rock. Clean off a bit of root which peeks above the ground. Wipe the mud off my hand against the tree trunk, but still my palm is dirty. Walk all the way around the theater—the back and sides are not glass. Also walk around the other theater, dragging my dirty hand against the cement wall to scrape it clean. Then I find a restroom and wash my hands without looking in the mirror, and dry them on my pants in back.

And when once again I tap my heels against a tree's wall, the custodian props his litter scoop here and sits beside me with his grinning worm.

I was right—he's not old. And I was also right—he's quite coarse.

We exchange names. His is Richard Wedmann, but I don't tell him my last name. He guesses I'm 19 before I tell him 35—neither correct, but I'm closer—and he exclaims about what a nice day it is, although the bleached sky seems tired of being blue. He says, "I think I know your problem."

"My what? Problem? You don't even know me."

"I knew it after I talked to you for three minutes just now. You see, I've been watching you all afternoon. And I know from what I see. . . . I'm a glowworm."

"A glowworm." It should be funny. I should be laughing like crazy.

"You heard of us?"

"No."

"It's a society," he says. "A social society. We study and learn and practice body language as a means to break social barriers—to more quickly get down to a more basic spoken language. We get to know people better, quicker, closer."

My heels tap the brick wall, one then the other; I watch my legs swinging because I don't want to see his smiling worm pin or his own small eyes set so close together.

"Anyway, I can guess what's wrong with you," he says. "I'm hoping I'm *wrong*, but I don't think I am."

"So what's wrong?"

"I think you need the glowworm society."

"I need worms?"

"I knew from watching you. I like how you dress . . . I was really attracted to you physically—your legs—you're real athletic and compact." His hand with dirty fingernails is on my thigh, squeezing. I remove it, holding his thick wrist. Unconcerned, he goes on: "But I could tell what's wrong with you, and I was a little disappointed—not necessarily in *you* . . . it's just that I'll need to get control of it."

Still holding his wrist, I'm forcing his hand to stay in his own lap. "Get control of *what*?"

"Your problem with men is something we both ought to be aware of if we're going to be able to have a relationship."

"What are you talking about!"

If I didn't have to hold his wrist, I'd get up and go. *Run.* But if I do let go, his puffy, rough, stubby, dirty hand will come back. I do have to stop swinging my legs and brace them against the wall to give me better leverage on his wrist. His pressure against me is increasing. If I could think of just *one* self-defense technique that I could use from this position. . . .

"You know, glowworms believe that people know if they're

interested in each other right away, right off the bat, and therefore it ought to be spoken. Why wait?"

I reach over with my free hand to help the other hand that's holding him back. He's getting heavy.

"So, that's why I'm telling you that you're just what I'm looking for . . . except this problem with men may keep us apart." With his free hand he gently touches my hand which is holding his other wrist. "I'm interested in you, in all of you, so I need to know if you'll ever open up to me."

Our arms begin to tremble against each other, straining in opposite directions.

"You see, the glowworms believe that sex is just as much a way for people to get to know each other as it is a climax in a relationship."

Finally I'm turned all the way sideways on the brick wall, facing him, pounding his wrist against his leg with both my hands.

"Stop screaming, will you?" he says, and shakes my fingers off his arm, throws my own hands back at me. Up I jump, standing on top of the brick wall, kick his thigh, but he doesn't move. His hands aren't even reaching for me. He looks past me with his tiny pig eyes set close over a bony red-veined nose. I'm about to leap off the wall, step backwards and run, but afraid to stop glaring—isn't that what's keeping him in place? Instead I jump out of my skin as someone else from behind slips a firm arm quickly around my waist.

My heart keeps leaping in my throat even when I know it's Randy, standing beside me, his head below my shoulder. I turn toward him—seems like I'm falling—feeling for the ground with one toe. He lifts me down. His hand holding the back of my head, his voice beside my ear: "You'd better get outta here, mister."

I can even *hear* Weird Richard's coarseness as he leaves; even the air rubs rough against him, like scraping a shovel along the sidewalk. He drags his litter scoop behind him, around the corner of the theater.

"Randy, he was so weird weird weird—"

Randy has eyes like a hound-dog, they're put on his face sad like that. I'm holding his wrists, one in each fist, and I can feel his bones, intricately put together, not like the thick jumbled mess in Weird Richard's wrist. And when Randy clasps his hands behind my neck, I still don't let go of his wrists: my own two fists press against my jaw until I slide my hands up his smooth arms as he pulls me closer and kisses me. A dancer's untense mouth, not flabby, not slimy—perfect firm wetness.

His eyes are still sad and his mouth doesn't smile, and his whole body seems to sigh before his arms flex under my fingers, and he presses my ear against his skin, in the V of his leotard neckline. He holds me against the length of himself. And I relax against him without even making a fist. I must be normal after all.

"He had some society that was going to save me from myself."

"Don't they all."

I can hardly hear my own voice, but I can feel his before the words come out. His rib cage swells then buzzes against my head.

•

I never used to use call-screening, never wanted to hear my own voice boom into the room when the machine clicked on after four rings. But maybe it's time. There was a message from Glen Somebody yesterday when we got back from L.A. "You didn't say you *didn't* have any photos. *Please* contact me. It's important."

I have a phone in almost every room. My father had them installed. Business people called all the time, but he wouldn't answer when painting. We just let them ring. That was before answering machines were standard equipment. Sometimes I thought the ringing phone could be my mother. The phone rings. I don't move. Randy's voice on the machine says "I'll pick you up for the party at two."

I break in, "Okay!" He laughs.

What party? I forgot to ask.

As we park on the street across from a beach-view condominium complex, I finally do inquire, "Who lives here?"

"Harlan."

There are lawns like carpets and low iron-rail fences, a meandering walkway through fluffy hedges, and a single huge front door with buzzer signals for each family.

Eric, whose last name I never learned—I also don't know Randy's—is escorting a model-type along the picturesque winding sidewalk. "Maybe he's gonna try to get *her* the lead in Margie's place."

"If there's even a show to lead," Randy says.

"Why are we here?"

"I really don't know."

"Who told you to come here?"

"Gene."

"Who?"

"The choreographer," he says. "Didn't Harlan or Galvin call you?"

"No, you did."

This is not a place where dancers stretch or twist, and they're all wearing real clothes, but still manage to look odd here among off-white wool furniture, deep blue rug, no mirrors on the wall. They wear long black trench coats or cowboy boots under mid-length skirts. Bracing myself against Randy's shoulder, I stand tip-toe next to him and scan the tall crowd. Windrem is not present.

Harlan wears a V-cut sweater with nothing underneath. It's

light tan and he's darker than it is. Except those blue eyes. I've got to start using color film.

The room is unusually still. When one person bites a carrot stick, everyone else knows it. Randy and I stand near the door we just came through. Everyone is looking at Harlan. I hear Randy clear his throat, and he puts a hand on the small of my back. Maybe he doesn't feel me shiver. He doesn't remove the hand.

Finally someone says, "I can't stand the suspense—is this a farewell party?" It's someone in a long black raincoat with a fur collar.

"You mean you guys don't know?" Harlan smiles. "I thought I sent word out that this was a *good* news party. We don't want anyone to leave town or audition for any other shows—we're going to put this show back together as soon as possible. Maybe a month, maybe two. The first tour is now scheduled for early April."

The entire room seems to fill with their red-mouthed smiles. I nearly expect all of them to begin their exercises again, bracing ankles on the back of the couch, bending heads toward the floor or kicking legs toward the ceiling, asking where the mirrors are.

Instead they smoothly segue from their collective anticipation to a casual party, and sag like regular people onto chairs or right down onto the rug.

"Hi, Jay," Randy says to Harlan. They shake hands, but Randy keeps his other arm tight around me.

"Keeping busy, Connie?" Harlan asks.

"Sort of."

"I see."

We remain near Harlan as Eric leads his magazine cover-girl by one languid hand across the room to us.

"Jay, this is Beth-Suzette. She just graduated from Saint Mary's."

"A college?"

Eric clears his throat; Beth-Suzette giggles. "No—a private school. For girls. A hell of a drama department too. I've been coaching there this year."

"Do you have a last name?" I ask her. I'm not sure anyone heard me, but when Harlan faces Beth-Suzette, he talks sideways to me, and slants his eyes down at me too, glinting blue in the corners.

"What's the mascot name," he asks, "the Saint Mary's virgins?"

Beth-Suzette continues to smile but doesn't blush.

"What kind of band uniforms do they have," I ask. "Maybe long white nightgowns?" Randy puts a tight hand on the back of my neck. But Harlan turns and his sharp smile becomes a pungent laugh, hot like too much wine.

After Harlan passes behind me—a mild hand on my arm, just a touch as he moves away—I peel Randy's fingers from my neck and meet Harlan at the ice bucket. It steams when he lifts the lid.

"It's weird," I say, carefully selecting an ice cube—I don't even have a drink—"that Windrem didn't call the whole thing off."

"Why?" Harlan uses tongs to pick up an ice cube.

"After what happened."

"Why should he want to cancel the whole thing?" he says. "Just a few mistakes . . . a little damage."

"*Whose* mistakes? Do you know?"

His eyes are crisp over his glass. Looks at me that way before he adds seltzer water to the ice. A rather delicate look which he was careful not to mix with any other motion.

"Just technical mistakes. We're not giving grades, Connie."

Constance. I hold my ice cube between thumb and finger. Slipping away from me, it runs down into my palm, a trickle down my wrist toward my elbow.

"Well, just in case, if you want to know, I *was* backstage opening night."

"I remember," he says. "I took your camera away before your cue." He sips. "*Most* of us were backstage opening night."

"No, I mean before that. Before curtain. Before makeup. When I still had my camera."

He blinks. He waits. It's possible he could be trying to say *So? Tell me*. But if he already knows, I won't have to tell.

"I know what happened," I say.

He takes his ice cube into his mouth and sucks it, then drops it back into his glass, smooth, clear, no longer frosty. My own ice drips from my elbow. I catch it in the waistband of my jeans.

"So do I," he says. "The technician who set the lights probably just didn't know the board well enough."

"*No.*" I feel myself glaring. "I mean I know what *happened.*" And *he's* forgetting the fire . . . a technical mistake? The technical difference between mistake and accident . . . and being cognizant of what we're doing. I finally leave the last of my ice in a wet hand print on my thigh. "I mean I *know*. But don't worry, I . . ."

He clicks his glass down. "Careful about any claims to *know*, Connie." His voice gets louder as two singers approach the ice and will have to reach between us. "It's foolish to believe everything you read. That's as bad as believing those pseudo news shows about finding Bigfoot. The media is full of bullshit. Even if your uncle does own a newspaper."

The singers leave smiling.

Read . . . ? What does my uncle have to do with anything . . . ? He's in real estate. Maybe, somewhere in the computer, he does own a newspaper. So what?

Harlan turns to shake hands with someone's wife. My own hand is cold.

•

I've waited all day for Harlan's voice on my phone-answering machine. After the party, after the witnesses were gone, I thought he might want to contact me, have me come back, tell me what he wants me to do with the photographs. Maybe his *not* telling me is as good as telling me—*keep quiet, Connie.*

Why? Are you saying it was *nothing*?

The athlete I photographed—he only spoke to me once. After all the lawyers had already shouted at each other and me and anyone who would pick up the phone. "Look sweetheart, you know what you printed? A picture of nothing. All this blown up stink over nothing. No controversy, no exposé, *nothing.*" But a picture of nothing is solid black.

The phone does ring—not Harlan or Glen Somebody. Randy again: "I *know* you're there, Connie, pick up the phone!"

This time without giggling. "Hi." I lay on my back on my bed.

"What's wrong?"

"Why?"

"You sound depressed."

"Just tired."

"What've you been doing that makes you so tired?"

"Sitting around. Doesn't it make you tired?"

"Yes," he says, "but I can't afford to sit around, you know, in case this thing backfires."

"What thing!" I sit up so fast it makes me dizzy. Of course I also haven't eaten anything since the party.

"You know, putting the show back together. It might not make it."

"Oh. That thing."

"Yeah. So I've got to get ready for another job, just in case."

"He said not to . . ."

"I could schedule modeling around rehearsals, if and when the show starts again."

My ears prick. "Modeling?"

"Yes. That's what I was doing before this show." He is silent for a moment. Then says, "My portfolio is out of date, though."

"Portfolio of what?"

"Photographs . . . of me."

Of him. I could touch him with a lens. Press that cool, smooth, convex glass against him. What the hell am I *thinking*—I must be crazy.

"I could help you."

"That's what I thought," he says. "I'll pay you a percentage if I get any work."

"No. Don't do that. I mean . . . no. I've never done commercial work, so I don't want to get paid. I have no experience."

"I think it's easier than news photography, Connie."

"But it's *different.* You probably wouldn't understand. I don't like to shoot a subject who knows I'm there . . . and wants me there."

"What about all those ladies' club awards banquets?"

"Oh God, I just clicked off five shots and got the hell out."

He laughs. "Sounds like you're feeling better."

"Maybe I am."

"In that case, let me be your first subject who wants you there."

First he comes here, knocks on the door, and we smile together. But it's different than looking down into the chemical tray while I tickle a smile onto a face until I have the sharp taste of it under my tongue. The darkroom is one place I alone have control over everything that develops.

I direct Randy to the bank, but go in alone and once again liberate camera and all lenses from the vault. Hesitate, then take the envelopes of photos and negatives and give my key to the clerk: "I don't need it anymore."

"What I want to know," I say, while inspecting lenses, using an air blower to get some fuzz off the purple domes, "or make clear, is: in the pictures, do you want yourself to *know* you're in a picture?"

"In modeling," he says, "it's okay to know you're being looked at . . . in fact, you're trying to be looked at."

"You mean you'll blatantly pose?"

"How else?"

He chooses to dress in white, but I soften him to ash-grey. Using black-and-white, I don't want bold contrast; don't want his clothes to overwhelm what they cover. It's an old trick I'm using: a thicket in the park, gnarled dense foliage, deep shadows, an innocent-looking man.

His modeling *is* posing, but it's never frozen. Randy maintains constant slow-flowing motion. The way I know when to click, I discover, is when the sight of him makes me feel something—like hungry, or scared.

Hand on one branch, foot on a rock, Randy arches his back, lifts his chin. His smooth neck lengthens. I take it. Short of breath already and we've only begun. And like a doe he turns, whiteless eyes, long fingers on his throat; my knees ache and wobble, the camera clicks. I pant, open-mouthed, steaming up the view finder. Can't even wait for it to clear, to drip down the glass, as he turns toward the thick trunk, touches his hips there, holding the tree with the far hand, the far knee bent, also braced against the tree, he tips his shoulders back, twisting, reaches to examine leaves on a twig. Hold my breath—the camera clicks again. Gulp, cock the lever with a stiff thumb, practically wringing the camera dry in tight fists, fingers leave damp prints. And he—still pressing his pelvis to the tree—has a hand now on either side of the trunk, leaning back, drops his matted lashes, drops his chin, looks down to where his body touches the tree. Swallow hard and take that . . . and the next, as all he moves is his head, opens his face at me, mouth parted, a smile in his eyes.

"Stop. Wait. You didn't take that, did you?"

"Yes."

"Oh no," he says. "It looked like I was humping a tree. I realized you were taking whole-body shots, so I looked to see what you were getting down there."

"But it was good. I liked that one." I untuck a shirt tail and push the tip into the viewfinder to dry the dampness. He turns all the way, puts a shoulder against the trunk and folds his arms. Cocks his head a little.

"I'm sorry, Randy. You want me to come in close?"

"Well, yeah, whatever. I don't mind. One thing they pound into our heads in modeling classes is this takes two people. You can only take what I give you. And I get back what you think is best."

I've had time to change lenses, cap both ends of the one I've cleaned and removed, replace it with a bigger one. He smiles, full dimples this time, lilt in his eyes. I've come right up next to him without moving, squeeze and the camera pulls his laugh inside.

Randy sends a peculiar nod to my left, and I look over, not through my lens, at a bare-chested man with a tripod and a Roliflex. He says, "Hi," touching his two lenses with a soft rag. Looks like a diaper.

"What're you doing?"

"He's good." A nod back toward Randy.

"He's mine."

"You have an exclusive contract on him?"

"I'll tell-ya, he won't sign a model-release for anyone else."

"So who's publishing?" The man shades the sun off his nub-front camera, looks into the series of mirrors where he's got Randy.

"No." I move in front. "Get your lens off him."

"Move outta the way."

"He's mine."

"I'm not going to use him up."

"You're not going to touch him."

From behind, Randy slips his fingers on my neck under my

strap, lifts the camera over my head. "Come on." He swings my bag onto his shoulder.

"No, Randy, I hardly got started."

"Don't worry."

Randy turns to go, but I do take my camera back. I don't like the way he's dangling it.

We finish that roll, and two more, at the beach, with Randy bare-torsoed, then a towel wrapped around his neck, and eventually back into his shirt. I am slow—probably slower than someone more experienced. Keep thinking I have to clean and dry my lenses, both ends—it seems I'm close enough that he's steaming-up the filtered end of the lens, while I keep fogging-up the view finder. But I want to keep clicking, nearly motorized, because he is better without waiting in between. I keep him going until he's sweat-shiny. And I'm far more tired than I ever was after a day at the newspaper.

Dried, cooled-off, he says he's hungry. The evening breeze chills my neck where my hair is wet. I have no appetite, though. I swallowed something—maybe gritty, salty air, my own saliva and sweat—with each shot.

He chooses a Mexican place—not near the beach—where the booths are red vinyl, the tables black plastic, the walls covered with laced-together reeds. While Randy puts away an entire combination plate, I dabble in vegetable soup, stopping often to cool my fingers on my water glass and press them on my hot temples or the soft places under my eyes.

Randy says, "Isn't that Ron Galvin?"

"Where?" I look around.

"Don't stare. Behind me, to your right. Don't look now, wait a minute."

He watches me dip my fingers into my water glass, make a raccoon mask with fingers on upper and lower eyelids. Some extra water drips like a cool tear down one cheek.

"What're you doing?" he says.

"Getting ready to look. My eyes're tired."

It's a blond man, but all the lights are amber here, everyone is fire-colored. There is a yellow bug-candle on their table, flickering an expression onto his face. The girl has her back to me.

"Isn't that *Margie* he's with?" Randy whispers.

"Maybe." I'm not looking anymore. I hold my water glass against the side of my head and shut my eyes.

"It *is!* Can you see a cast or something, or maybe crutches under the table?"

"No."

"Open your eyes."

So I do. Our own yellow bug-candle winks in his eyes. All amber like the printing darkroom. And it's so warm here. All the ice in my glass has melted.

"He's married, you know." Randy's eyes crinkle. "Hey, you know what I heard? There was a story going around that you punched-out Galvin for getting too friendly. Is that true?"

One quick glance at Galvin. He's not looking over here. He has a glass of beer and a basket of chips on the table. The beer is half gone, but he isn't eating the chips. I could hear him if he did.

"No."

The waitress brings our bill, then goes immediately to take Galvin's order. Randy scrapes his empty plate. "So it's not true about you and Galvin? You two were always talking."

"He'd just been telling me some places where I can have my cello repaired if I want to." Maybe when Galvin finds out more about Windrem, I'll know what I should do with the pix—maybe *he's* the one I should ask.

"That *is* her, isn't it," Randy says. "Margie, I mean." His eyes brighten. "Hey—why not get some pictures of them!"

Attached at my shoulder, my camera bag sits beside me in the booth, but follows me as I start to slide out. "No. It's not them."

But at least I do imagine sitting in my kitchen, maybe it's a sunnier breakfast nook than I actually have, with a greenhouse window, butcher block table and chairs, coffee steaming and Randy looking at me through it, every once in a while, over the rim of his yellow pottery mug. And I touch his wrist with manicured fingertips, still feeling the detail of his fine bones, how he fits together so well. Perhaps I need him there across the table, maybe wearing only shorts, hair jumbled over his forehead, dark eyes and solemn mouth which laughs when he smiles, in order for me to say, "I'm sorry I seem so strange, Randy . . .," or, "There's something I may need to tell someone. . . ." But it's as though I don't know how.

Side-by-side in the darkroom—actually he's behind me, looking over my shoulder—we print a set of his photographs. He wants me to narrate what I'm doing, but gives up and breathes silently on my neck as I only hum or answer with a one-word moan. I move back and forth, tray to tray and back to the looming enlarger, rubbing my thighs against the low table, leaning all the way over it, then straightening, feeling him always behind me.

By the time I get several done—stack the best prints in the fixer tray—I am satisfied enough to at least mutter, "Good, good," as I expose, dodging dark places, burning flat brightness. Sometimes I need to use my fingers in the chemicals to touch skin-tone onto his face, his shoulders and chest. Other times I want his sweat to shine, heave a breath out in relief as I find I caught sun sparkle in a drop that trickled all the way from his scalp to his neckline. I complete the last few with Randy's hands on my shoulders while my fingers rub him under developing fluid.

"Done. Magnificent." I'm a little hoarse, still slightly breathless.

"Are you okay?" His hands tighten on my shoulders, rubbing my neck with his thumbs.

"Oh. Yes." I sag back slightly, still looking at the last print I slid face-up into the clear fix solution: His hips against the tree, looking down, as he must also be doing now. I feel his voice puff against my hair.

Standing quietly for a while, the only movement is my hand rocking the fixer tray a little to keep the chemicals moving over the prints. Randy says softly, "I never thought I'd see you so relaxed. You're always so hyper. . . . It's nice."

"Yeah. . . ." I feel his hand smoothing my hair on the top of my head.

"Wanna go out and get a cup of coffee?" he says.

Since everything is in slow motion now, I can wait before answering. As though drugged. "We can go upstairs for coffee." Perfect. Like a dream.

Up on the shelf above my enlarger, where I keep my chemicals, is the key to my father's metal World War II footlocker, now under the darkroom workbench, not so different than under a bunk in the barracks in France. I get the key, then squat down to the footlocker, my back pressed against Randy's shins because he hasn't moved a step. This is where the envelopes of pix and negatives are now, along with a hundred-dollar bill I keep here for emergencies, and keys to the house and car. I have the large envelope in my hands, hugged against my chest, biting the tip with my lips. I can feel the thick crispness of the prints inside. I could spread them out on the table—while he spoons sugar into his coffee—and watch his eyes grow wide and not even have to explain when he looks up at me again—

"When will they be ready?" he asks. His voice way up there, no longer whispering.

"What?"

"My prints—when can I have them?"

"Oh. . . ." I shut the footlocker and stand again, carefully because there's still barely room for me between the workbench and Randy. I still have the envelope, held in both hands between us. "I still have to wash them. Then tomorrow I can dry them . . ."

Randy is trying to pull the envelope away from me. I let go, but he just places it on the chemical shelf, takes my arm and starts to guide me to the door. Wait, not like this, still need to think—

"No, Randy, I'd better not waste any time. Sorry, but I forgot . . . I, uh, have some more work to do down here."

"Leave it for tonight."

"No!" I shake my arm, knocking his hand away. "No, I'm really sorry, but . . . well, the timing is crucial for your photos. I have to get them into the wash water, you know. . . ."

He looks at me for a long time. I'm not looking back . . . but I know he's watching. His feet don't move.

"Okay," he says. "Call me when they're ready." Then he turns and feels his way carefully to the cellar door. He doesn't know about the stairs and trap-door directly into the house—the darkroom is in the storm cellar, but I've never been forced down here by the weather. When he opens the cellar door, a gust of fresh air comes in.

After he's gone—I hear his footsteps outside going past the ventilation holes—I latch the cellar door from the inside, then sit slumped on a stool in the dark without even the yellow filter light on. I don't know how long. Not long. I hear Randy's car in the driveway, backing out, then the gears shift, he accelerates, and he's gone.

Hold my breath a while. This is something I used to do when I was an amateur: give the prints extra time in the fixer just to make sure they're not fogged and ruined when I turn the white light on to clean up the mess and prepare the water bath. I set the timer for an extra five minutes and again crouch down to the footlocker, this time in the dark. No trouble finding the small envelope of negatives. Before the time is even half ticked away, I go ahead and flick on the fluorescent overhead light and begin scanning the negatives, holding them over my face, looking up through them, remembering in each where I burned under-developed places, where I cropped troublesome spots. Looking at the fire this way, the flames appear black and the spray of the extinguisher makes the negs seem flat.

I put the negative strips away and break the seal on the larger envelope. The last time I saw these pictures, I didn't have the fluorescent light on. It was almost dawn and I turned *all* the lights off before removing the prints from the drier. It's much lighter this time. If I were someone else, outside of my darkroom, would I look at the photo and say, *yes, he did know what Windrem was up to that night* . . . ? How quickly would I say it? How long or closely would I have to look before I made the conclusion? But I can't be someone else, and . . . Harlan, it would be easier if *you* told me . . . how much did you see? Why won't you say anything about it? Why would you protect him?

The newsman on my phone machine yesterday—or this morning . . . or two hours ago?—said he's still interested in some photos. And said if I'm under contract with the company, he'll print them anonymously, if I preferred that. I'm not deciding anything right now . . . just checking. The timer still clicking—until it stops.

V

The Cellar Isn't Well Ventilated

• • •

I seldom do use the stairs and trap-door which opens into my bedroom, because I often leave the developing trays when I'm probably near death. The cellar isn't well ventilated and the chemical fumes can be overwhelming. After turning off the light, I creep slowly to the door, feel for the latch, then burst out into the night, gulping gallons of dark air. Living on a hill is supposed to be peaceful—the stars go forever, and the valley below likewise, thousands of porch lights and window lights with spaces of black in between.

My heart beats dangerously hard as I read in bed before going to sleep, like a stiff finger tapping my breastbone. I can even feel the *echo* of my heartbeat, a little off, like watching someone else's turn signal while hearing your own clicking, first nearly together, then one follows the other, downbeat, upbeat, then nearly the same again, closer, closer, until they throb together once, twice, three times, then separate once again, one heavy, one lighter. And I feel it all over, especially on the inside of my head, behind my eyes, and inside my mouth . . . my *gums* pulsate, and my tongue. And when I open my eyes, I *see* it, my muscle jumping, something under the skin, all over my arm, like there's something alive in there. Then when the pulse is lower, not just my head and arms anymore . . . when it's down thumping between my hips and the mattress, bumping on the inside of each thigh where they touch, then I think maybe my heart isn't trying to kill me.

My forehead down on the pages, tears blurring the words . . . am I reading this scene in my head? Am I falling off the bed . . . ? Or rolling over, limping as I fall, and aching, all over, a single hard ache. I'm lying on something bumpy like rocks or boards . . . or music stands and chairs all up-ended and broken apart after I landed here . . . where did I fall from? The stage? The rafters? The second story? The light booth? Randy down on one knee beside me . . . or Galvin? . . . or Harlan? . . . probably Randy . . . says something unremarkable to me: "Are you weird in both ears?"

This need not make sense. I smile in my sleep, knowing it doesn't have to.

"You know, you men don't have a corner on the hernia market." Is that what aches? I thought it was my back . . . or the back of my head. . . .

I see his smile, flaming laughter. "Hmmm. I hear business has been poor. Nobody wants one."

"You know what I mean. No. Don't help me up. I hurt. I don't want to move."

"Okay." So he joins me. The length of him lying beside me.

No! Go away. You're not allowed in the orchestra pit during rehearsals. Are you? Are you?

I have my back to him. He's humming all his songs right into my ear.

"Go up and sing on stage. The audience can't hear you."

Is he humming or moaning? I'm not sure how asleep I am. . . . It's a different song than the rail-faced, narrow-hipped boy at my junior high bus stop who announced to a crowd, "Connie's got nothing to offer." A beardless, sweet face said that and leered. Yet

I can only see Randy's face—it could've been Randy standing on the water meter which marked our bus stop, cock-of-the-dome, knew what he wanted, I didn't have it. I practiced my cello and close-up photography on bugs in the backyard after school, a thirteen-year-old phenom with a camera, already had what she needed to know.

It doesn't have to make sense. But now it does. Somehow. I watch someone else—maybe someone named Constantina—who rolls over to face whoever I had nothing to offer at the bus stop. She grins all over inside. Randy wraps her like a blanket, like deep warm water, dark waves and bubbles, lacy plants and tiny tickly fish—moving against her on the outside, blowing bubbles into her with hot breath . . . getting hotter and hotter, begins to sting like sunburn, abrasions, gallons of iodine. . . . It still burns after I wake and find no one here, the wetness all my own. It *doesn't* make sense. Jump up and slug the wall and silently cry cold tears, sucking on bruised knuckles in my shadowy bedroom, still lit only by the reading lamp which I yank from the wall and hurl across the room.

•

His dance class is downtown, a studio over a deli-grocery. Some people still shoot those corny photos of old men in their equally old small-town groceries—complete with a soda fountain—on a busy downtown street that grew up around the store. Shoot it down a dark aisle where customers line a bar counter under hanging cheese and bunches of dried onions, peppers and garlic. The shot *I'd* like to get is when dancers come downstairs after a lesson—they seem looser and longer than when they went in. The sidewalks and sign posts and mail boxes become props as they glide down the street.

Of course I have my camera. It's always around me, the last few days, hitting against the front of me or slung around back, riding my hip; and I have photos ready for him. Plus I tossed the photographs of Harlan into the back seat.

He is surprised to see me—spots me waiting on the sidewalk, comes straight to me, stands there, staring, not smiling, too close.

I step back, already uncapped, set and focused, and say "Hi" from behind the camera. And click—his smooth unhurried face against a blurred background of contemporary action. He smiles, tilts his head and laughs.

"What're you laughing at?"

"I don't know. You. That camera. My *posing* for you." His laugh stops, but his lips twitch. And his dimples remain. "If I get a job, I'll owe you a cut of my salary."

I drop the camera to its place in front of me, below my waist. "That's not the reason I brought the camera."

"I know." He says it like a written line, spaced, punctuated.

People crowd past on the sidewalk, and I step closer to him. Perfect stage blocking. So he drapes a long arm across my shoulders, his hand dangling limp next to my neck. I look sideways at it. Fingers separate. Poised. I take his hand and squeeze the fingers together. Then look at him on my other side. "Does an actor ever stop posing?"

"Does a photographer ever stop looking for poses?"

"Maybe I'm ready to." Who said that, her or me? Which one of us is the strange girl? I know what I have to do to find out.

Suddenly I can hear him breathing, and see the rise and fall of his rib cage. "Let's go somewhere," he says.

We begin to walk—awkwardly attached. I pull his hand farther over my shoulder which tightens his arm on my neck, hook my other hand by one thumb in a belt loop on his other side. My camera swings out and bounces back against me.

His apartment is the kind that doesn't have near enough unshared walls—there are other apartments, adjacent, using the same floor or ceiling, on both sides, top and bottom. Only one side, the back, doesn't have anyone living on the other side of it. He shows me his small living room window from the parking lot.

"It's a mess," he says.

The mess is perhaps a wet glass near the sink, the magazines piled too thickly on the coffee table and a few on the bar counter—*Photoplay, New Yorker, The Atlantic.*

He actually has furniture too, a light tweed love seat and delicate wicker chairs. "Are these yours?"

"It didn't come furnished."

"And they're *yours*?"

"Of course."

"You *bought* them?"

"No, I stole them. What'd you think?"

"I mean, you went in a store and picked them out?"

"Yes I did," he says. "Something wrong?"

"No."

He even has a lamp with an amber glass base, a magazine rack stuffed with still more titles, and no dust. He has *no* dust. He has a real wood stereo stand, polished and varnished, and speakers like trunks or chests, huge, in the corners. "I like this." I stroke the silky wood.

"It's knotty pine."

"That doesn't make me like it less."

"No, I'm just telling you," he says. "It's a style of wood furniture. You act like you don't have any furniture of your own."

"I never notice it. Is this a 10-speed? Why do you keep a bike in your living room?" It's against the wall, under the window, behind the stereo.

"Where else am I going to keep it?"

"It's so clean—do you ever use it?"

"Of course."

"I have a bike . . . why don't we take a ride sometime?"

"Sure."

"Wow, this must be almost new, no scratches, have you ever used this nifty hand pump?"

"Not yet."

"Do you know how?"

"Connie! *Dancer* doesn't automatically mean mechanically inept. Stop listening to stereotypes."

"I didn't hear any. *My* hand pump broke. I need to use the restroom."

"In here."

Down a short photo-walled hall, black-and-white Gene Kelly, Nureyev, Randy—an even younger version with pale ears sticking out of his haircut.

I wash my hands. That's all. The mirror is huge. Everything is put away. The toilet cover matches the rug: soft violet. I leave my camera bag and both envelopes of photos—Randy's in one envelope, Harlan's newly sealed in another—behind the door.

He is behind the bar, standing, reading something on the counter, holding his head up with his hands, his jaw cupped in his palms. I sit on a stool and face him across the bar. "I didn't mess it up. Wanna go out and eat?"

"Let's make something here," he says.

"Here . . .? You have anything?"

"Let's see. . . ." He doesn't even look in the refrigerator or cupboard. "I've lettuce, carrots, avocado, tomato, bread, cheese, pickles, sardines, potatoes, probably a frozen steak—I usually do—eggs, milk—"

"Okay, stop." I look down at the *Sunset* magazine—sunny photo of an airy high-ceilinged room, dinner on the table. "I'll make a salad."

"No," Randy says. "I will."

"What'll I do?"

"Whatever."

I come around the counter into the kitchen. He has already taken the lettuce, two kinds, from the refrigerator and is washing it in the sink, feeling up the spine of each leaf with his fingers under the stream of water. Then he tears them, breaking off pieces gently. He fluffs the growing pile in the salad bowl occasionally. When he picks up the carrot, I don't think I can bear to watch him tickle the skin from it, so I turn to the refrigerator myself.

Skip the pickles and eggs—no sardines, please, we'll both be tasting them all night. I realize I'm grinding my teeth and make myself stop. My jaw aches a little.

The cheese is okay, mild cheddar . . . bread, mayonnaise, Randy's got the lettuce, I guess I don't need it. I kick the door shut, lay the bread out and smear it with mayonnaise. Randy is holding a slippery peeled avocado in one hand, surgically slicing it in swift bright movements with a knife. I push the dull mayonnaise knife through the cheese, making it crumble, so I cut thicker, cover the bread with cheese, cover that with more bread. Randy turns as I'm sucking mayonnaise from my fingertips and licking it from between my fingers.

"It's funny," he says.

"What is?"

"You're immaculate in your darkroom."

I look at the two rough sandwiches. "Precision is important there." Intricate control. It takes time—I give as much detailed care as a photo demands. Food I just plonk together and swallow. To get back to the darkroom. Sometimes even eat with the sharp smell of chemicals still on my hands.

He cuts the sandwiches in half with an enormous knife. "So, let's see. . . ." He puts empty bowls, the salad, the sandwiches, napkins, glasses, forks on the counter, moving lightly—yes, even dancing—around the kitchen . . . pours water, has tiny square ice cubes in a bucket in the freezer. "What am I supposed to say next?" he says. We sit at the counter. "Tell me about yourself."

I chuckle. A horror-movie laugh. "You know about me."

"No, c'mon, all I know is you're a photographer. And you're in this play for some reason." Randy holds a half sandwich in both hands with his fingertips, looks at the ragged cut edge of the cheese. "I hardly know anything about you."

I could answer, "As much as I know about you." But for some reason I stuff those words back inside with a bite of bread and cheese, wash them down with water. Take a deep breath, as much air as I can, even more, then let it out slowly . . . slower . . . slow *down*. . . . Slip a cool avocado slice between my lips. "I guess you know my professional side."

"Why *are* you in this play?" he says.

"I just am. Why is anyone anywhere?"

He chews lettuce thoughtfully. "Well," he says, swallows, drinks, "Was the article true?"

"First I auditioned for the orchestra. Shortest career as a professional musician ever recorded."

"But," he runs his finger around the rim of his water glass, "music is as competitive as theater, how'd you get so lucky?"

"I don't know. Well, yes I do—this play conflicts with symphony, opera, and both large theaters are also doing musicals, so no one else was available. I don't have professional credentials, but I *have* played all my life. I auditioned for a job, and got it"

"You mean you didn't know Ron Galvin beforehand?"

"What makes you think I did?"

He shakes his head, smiles with his mouth full, chews behind the smile. Finally he can speak, "It just seems so impossible."

"Improbable. . . . You wanna hear improbable? Maybe it is just luck. The story of my life: I've been taking pictures since I was eight, a homeowner in my twenties—with a little help from my father's heart attack—a photojournalism career without going to college, unemployed at 27, worked in a lab about a year, then unemployed again for a few days, then an orchestra job, now I'm in the cast, but maybe unemployed again—they *say* we're not, but I don't think it matters because . . . well, I can always sell photographs." Quick mouthful of water, let it trickle down my throat. "And that brings me to *now*—here I am."

"I read all about that. I was surprised."

"At what?"

"Your many talents."

"Well, I really can't act."

A block of silence interrupts and we stare into our plates.

"Your family live in the area?" he asks. He can't be interested. People don't ask questions like that for interesting answers.

"No. I don't have much. An uncle or two. Never see them. Don't know my mother. More luck: when my father died, he left me fairly loaded."

"I wouldn't call that luck."

"He was a strange guy. Painted the most god-awful pictures. . . ."

"So," he says, "if I know your professional history—which apparently started when you were eight—I know *you* pretty well?" He inspects some lettuce on his fork for any sand specks which might've escaped the waterfall earlier.

"Everything else just seems sort of unnecessary." Bread sticks in my throat. I smile. "A guy at the newspaper who followed me around, once asked me why I bared my fangs when he came close to me."

"Did you answer?"

"Yes. I said, 'That's self-defense—and it's working!' "

He laughs with his lips on his water glass, then stops to drink. Afterwards his smile glistens.

"You're different, though," I say quietly, and just let that lie.

Randy finishes eating in silence. It's not really out of character when a little later I seem to continue the same conversation: "There are other sides of me, I think." Following me around like the guy at the newspaper.

"Well . . .?" His nostrils flutter, barely a movement, testing the air, perhaps, for the first signs of musky heaviness. The tip of his nose and thin nostrils are almost clear, like new skin, like baby skin, always scrubbed without a shine and without a line. I'm sure he smells nothing, now.

"I have to use the restroom."

"You know where it is," he says.

Again I pass the younger Randy, with the same nose, posed on the wall. Again I only wash my hands. The sink is still wet from my last visit. Sit on the toilet, covered lid down, and dry my hands on my jeans, palms down on my thighs, then push my hands down over my bent knees, down my shins, untie each shoe and line them up against the wall, close under the toilet. Reach behind the door without looking and take the camera bag and both envelopes of photos, then pad sock-footed across the hall and onto the plush wall-to-wall carpet in his bedroom. I can do this. The queen size bed is made tight. I have to edge closer to read the titles of the books on the headboard. *Party Jokes, How to Win Friends and Influence People, Success Because You Want It, Tom Sawyer.* Two fringed lamps stand like pillars on either side of the bed. Slide closer, feet pressed flat on the rug—it stands up around my toes like grass, my footprints are two snail-trails. *Dress Right in 1989*, and one just like it for 1990. But he's dressed in a leotard much of the time. Right now, in fact, under his jeans. There's a closet, a long one, covers a whole wall. Slip closer, my knees nearly touching the mattress, put my camera bag on top of the closest pillow, the two photo envelopes side-by-side on the bedspread. Down on the shag floor near my feet, the magazine he'd read last night, perhaps slipped off the mattress as he slid into sleep. Face down on the floor. An ad for wine on the back—warm and bright, two blurry people in front of a fire.

"Here you are." He tosses his leotard and tights—which he's obviously no longer wearing under his jeans—onto the bed, then stands behind me, wrapping his arms around.

"Did you ever have you nose fixed?"

"What?" He laughs. "God, no! Why?"

"It's a nice one." I tell a man his nose is nice while he stands behind me, close, pressing against me, and all I can see are his hands, long-fingered and flat on my stomach.

"I have something to show you!" I break out of his arms and grab a photo envelope. Pull out the prints— "Whoops, wrong batch, just a sec. . . ." Unzip the camera bag and wedge the envelope of Harlan's pictures in beside the lenses. Doesn't fit well. He's so close, behind me. Zip it closed, as far as it will go; one corner of the envelope still sticks out. So I take out my camera, reposition the lenses until the envelope fits, then zip it, move the camera bag over to a chair beside the bed, and the camera too—without a lens cap, must've come off in the bag, or I left it somewhere, which I often do—put it on the soft seat of the armless chair. "Now, finally! The moment you've been waiting for." I pour his photos onto the bed, spread them out so they all show. The light in here makes them purplish. But there's not even the slightest possibility that he, nor anyone else, will misinterpret them.

"I saw them all when you developed them," he says. "Thanks again." He's winding his watch, then doesn't put it back on—lays it on the bookcase headboard. He goes to the other side of the bed, sweeping up his dance clothes as he goes, and drops them on the matching chair on that side, one black arm swings free and dangles down to the floor. He's not wearing anything from the waist up, just like the photographs at the beach which I'm staring at down on the mattress. "C'mere, Connie." He kneels on the bed, grabs my wrist, pulls me across the mattress.

"No, wait, the pictures, they're getting ruined."

"Put them away—I saw them already." His voice is still gentle but he's pushing all the photos off the bed like sweeping crumbs away, except the one or two I'm lying on. My knees and feet hang over the edge of the mattress. "Okay," he says, "come on, there's plenty of room." He laughs and grabs my upper arms and yanks. Before my arms come out of their sockets I'm all the way on the bed, scrambling on hands and knees rather than letting myself be dragged, then fall flat on my stomach, roll over quickly, hands and arms flailing, sit up, feet back on the floor, backing away, hands still up as though he's going to throw a basketball at my face. What's wrong with me . . . calm down . . . it's okay. . . .

Still on hands and knees on the bed, he's no longer laughing, nor smiling. "You have no right to act so surprised at this, Connie." His eyes dark, not like the darkroom itself—like the sky outside.

Slowly I drop my hands to my side. Panting, as though it's the first air I've had for hours. But it's not cool nor quenching.

He has one hand extended toward me. "Connie?"

"Okay."

What would the meter say about this light? Why is it so purple? Gingerly put one knee, then the other on the already messed-up bedspread and slide to meet him in the middle. Like an understudy he must help through the scene, he pulls me down to the mattress. Stretched out on our sides, our heads propped up on our hands, we face each other. I can see his pulse on his upper lip, sweat on his brow, in his hairline. The camera would zero in on that—that's all it would show. Think of it that way and I'm okay. He sits up, his knees close to me, touching my side. No, he should be with Constantina, the one who's supposed to be playing this scene, where are you when I need you? I thought she was right behind me. I must be crazy—there's no such person.

Randy stays close, kneeling, hands flat on the mattress on either side of my head, dips and touches me once, lightly—a stage kiss that won't smear makeup.

As though timing himself, he is deliberate, sways a little, sighs, and settles, sinks down next to me, knees still beside me on the bed, his two hands cup the dome of my head, pushes his face against my neck, kisses behind my ear. Sounds much like the whir-click of a slow shutter release. His body is still. Just the slow movement of his mouth down my neck. Not an open mouth, but not a closed mouth. I can't see; my neck aches to tell the difference. My muscles jerk with blindness—or suffocation—straining to back up and see what's going on here. Randy lifts his head, like air rushing over me, through me, I see his dark eyes, his brooding mouth. "What's wrong?" he whispers.

"Nothing." My throat works on the word, but only my lips say it.

"You wanna leave?"

"No." Yes, but I can't, I shouldn't—to break the reclusive cycle, the hermit's just got to take the plunge, go farther faster, quickly get as close to another person as possible. . . .

His eyes are sad, stay on me. With another sigh he settles again, pushing against me. I feel his perfect nose on my neck, he kisses my collar bone, I think he opens his mouth on it, but nothing feels wet. Again I can't see him, and it's strange to not see someone who's so close . . . I saw him in the darkroom while he was close behind me. . . . But now, I can't see—*can't see*—only the hump of one shoulder just beneath my chin. I strain to lift my head, to look down the slope of his body, but he crosses to the other side of my neck. I can't *see* him. On either side of me I gather handfuls of the bedspread tight in my fists. It's like I'm caught on the wrong side of the camera now, without a button to stop the action. How can I take a long look, a close look, a careful slow look and know what's going on? With a camera in front of my face, I could see this, frame it, follow it, click it . . . but . . . could I really *stop* it? A tiny flame becomes a wildfire, and no miracle of light and timing and silver emulsion can put it out. Still, at least it wouldn't be *me*. Wait, I can do this, I have to, what does it say about me if I *can't?*

He swings one leg over me, moves his chest across mine, his mouth on my throat and shoulders. I twist under him, suddenly, without warning, bring one knee up and he jerks, grunts, and our heads knock together. His fingers are locked behind my neck. My arms crushed between us, my palms flat on his chest. He rubs against me; our hips and stomachs scrape each other, his arms tighten, my face is crushed against his shoulder, his collarbone across my nose, and our legs are tangled. Afraid if I move mine, it'll be his. One of us shudders. He is tight, all his muscles, *tight*—his hands clamped on my neck, his elbows hard against me, his chin hooked over the top of my skull, his breath is short and hot on my scalp. But I'm blind, caught in a pose I can't even *see*. Where does he end and I begin, which is which, if I wiggle my right toes will they be the ones pushing into my left calf? I have to see again, *have to*, so I pull against his shoulders, chinning myself, groan and dig in and flex the way I used to strain in P.E. class to lift my chin over the parallel bar while my hands sweated and slipped there. This can't be right, can't be . . . my lips pull back against his skin and I drool a trickle down his chest. How could this happen—with his limpid agile body, grace threaded into every joint—that together we're so tight and hot and rigid and tangled and clumsy. My teeth scrape his collar bone, his belt buckle snags in the fly of my jeans. My eyes *are* open, but my virtual blindness rushes over me like something cold and hot, sharp and thick, fast and strong and out of control.

One arm free, I swing it up over my head, across the pillow, the first thing I touch, a book, a hardback, grab it, raise it and bring it down on his head, a dull thud. But it works—sort of—he rolls away, not *all* the way away, one arm still across my stomach, my shirt in his fist, one leg still thrown across my thighs. His other hand is on the back of his own head, his face buried in a pillow.

If his eyes are open, I know what he's seeing—his dark dancing clothes jumbled on a chair, close enough for him to reach, one limp sleeve hanging. He's breathing deeply, slowly. My body seems to sigh, the subsiding feeling after the climax of panic. I turn my face away—that's all I can move, still on my back—but once again, suddenly, immediately, my legs are cold and rigid, my heartbeat in my throat, not enough air to breathe. I'm staring into a soft, drowsy clear blue eye—my camera watching from the chair. It's never supposed to be turned this way! I should be far away, brought up close to the side of the bed only by looking through the lens. I should be *observing* this dry clench on the mattress—Randy and someone else, anyone else—far enough away to be its narrator. What went wrong, what should I do . . . all I can think of is try to pull away and reach the camera, cap it, turn it floorward, or transfer it to the other chair to bury it in Randy's empty dance clothes. Then maybe I won't remember this mess, over and over, later.

His breathing is even slower and deeper, and I feel his body loosen a little, his arm and leg sag more heavily over me, his hand on my shirt gives up, lets go. My own hand is still holding the book. I open my fingers to drop it, but it just lays on the pillow above my head. All I can reach of him is his neck, so I put my hand there, patting him a little.

And he sits up! Jerks me upright with him. One hand on the back of my neck, a fistful of skin and hair. And his elbow locks. Pins me at arm's length. My teeth rattle—it's him quivering, all the way down his arm, shaking my head. His nails begin to cut into the back of my neck. My fingers dig against his, trying to get under his hand, to peel him off me. "You two-faced bitch," barely audible, coming from his mouth . . . his eyes tight shut, his hair falling forward. I sock the inside of his elbow with my other hand, an awkward swing across my body, trying to break his braced arm. But *all* of him crumbles, his head falls into my lap, his arms loosely around me, "I'm sorry, I'm sorry," crying, sobbing against me. I have his face in my hands, trying to throw his *head* away from me but his whole *body* falls off the bed, and I step on him as I grab my camera and bag and stumble for the door.

•

Smother myself in a pillow . . . but I don't stop breathing. Air squeaks between my nose and the pillowcase. I bend my knees and let my shins thump flat on the mattress, one then the other, faster, then both together, harder, bouncing my head and chest and stomach off the bed, land nose first and lie still until I drool all over the pillowcase and sheets. Roll to my back, stare up, one arm flops over the side, fingering books on a low table, a dusty water glass, the telephone. Clever fingers creep to the message machine, press the button . . . rewind . . . but not all the way to the beginning. Catch someone in the middle of a message, ". . . want those photos . . .," then fast-forward a little, ". . . investigating the fire . . ." reverse, ". . . those photos, any photos, Miss. . . ." Click off. Roll over, all the way, off the bed, feet clump on the floor, hollow thump, heavy enough, perhaps, to make me crash straight through the floor to the darkroom, land feet-first at the developing trays where I never did make my own copy of Randy. Maybe I'd better make new prints of the ones we bent and wrinkled on the bed. I don't know which they were.

He's suddenly underexposed and hard to paste onto the paper, a grey shadow I try to scrub into focus in the chemicals. My fingers shrivel, sting around the nails, and still I rub, stroke, scratch, prod, pinch the faded image. A chemical burn spreads across his face and arms, the tree rots yellow.

That one I drop on the floor, grind it there with my feet while

I expose another. Give it more juice this time. Blast him onto the paper. All stops open. So in the chemical he jumps out, flashes, dark hair and pasty skin; I watch without moving. Too much contrast, then grey creeps over the paper like fog, like the mist which came off the sea at twilight, blocks his eyes, discolors his skin; thick, thicker, gray, now black, billowy smoke, not glossy opaque: flat, hazy, dense nothing.

My dripping hands flicker and twitch under my eyes. Or is it my eyelids fluttering? Gone my technique, my clean procedure down here, my darkroom control. If I had a camera in my hands, I'd probably break it.

I dump the chemicals, spattering some out of the sink against my white lab coat. Re-mix. Re-set the enlarger. Print a perfect set of Harlan, moving against the fire, shooting from the hip.

How long have I stared at that last print of the fire as it slowly settles in the wash bath? How long does it take a photo to sink in water? I wonder if it's better than the first set I printed. Clearer, more glossy, a fantasy fade-out toward the edges.

I pull white gloves over my stained-yellow hands before I look through some other negative strips, organized by frame-number, an earlier roll of film; pass backwards through the dressing-room shots—clowns performing for an invisible circus audience, but *I* was the only one watching—back to the first frame on the roll: the circuit board backstage.

While I expose the image onto paper, I run the light a few extra times over certain places—Windrem's hand, the cigarette—and really burn still more light on Harlan's hazy eyes.

In the chemicals, those three places pop out first; they seem to come up from underneath the top shiny layer of the paper—the hand, the cigarette, the eyes—so by the time the rest of the picture starts to appear (the jacks and circuit board, the curtains, Windrem's pug nose), Harlan's eyes are already darkly staring out of the shadow—but at what? His own hand on the rope? The rafters? Windrem? The cigarette? *Me?*

I drop it into the fixer without looking at it any more, swish it around, set the timer and sponge up a few drops of chemicals that are starting to crystallize around the trays. My nose and eyes burn. When the timer buzzes, transfer the photo to the wash, but by the time it finishes its slow drop through the water to join the others at the bottom, I'm already flat on my back on a cot I keep down here, my jeans unzipped. . . .

Of course it's Randy's scene I'll have to re-make—improve—with a script this time to remember the plot order and where I went wrong, where I lost footing . . . develop, dissect, re-expose, perfect . . . with the smell of chemicals, my dry skin, dry eyes, dry mouth, dry brain—no humid fever here, no steamy fire . . . like Harlan extinguished backstage . . . Harlan and his steam pistol. . . . No, it's *Randy* I have to see, his dark painted mouth, black-lined eyes, red-flushed cheeks, smooth pale skin. But there's no makeup counter. No mirror. Just me staring, glassy-eyed, through yellow light and floating dust. The darkness shimmers, like looking through dirty windows, through water, at all the plans I must've made without knowing, like someone else planning for me, or like watching another person's plans: the top of his head beside her on a pillow . . . thick soft hair, hers to arrange, to touch and imagine it feels the same for him as when his fingers follow the bumps of her spine, from her back all the way under her hair to the beginning. He's hers to roll toward at night, to drowsily recite a scary dream, to trace with a finger the slope of his body asleep—turned toward the wall—and edge closer, wake him with a hot kiss on his neck, a hand inside his pajamas. . . . *Hers*. . . . Won't ever be *me* who pushes my fingers into his nut-brown straight hair, who holds the sides of his face, feels those sharp cheekbones with my thumb, touches a dimple with my tongue . . . *who is he?* Where did *Randy* go? Lost in the senseless struggle, the absurd *tangle*, the way it always ends up . . . fighting and kicking and getting nowhere, getting nothing . . . falling off the stage without a single protest, crashing into the pit, and Harlan up there, hands on hips, saying he's sorry . . . *he's sorry!* Tell me what you're sorry for . . . my reclusive life? My contract? My cello? The fire? Margie's leg? The red spotlight? My unzipped jeans? My arms hanging limp over the sides of the cot? Randy? *The photographs?* You haven't even seen them! But you're the hero in every one—even though *I* was there too . . . isn't that how it's supposed to work . . . ? The photographer who's not really there. . . . For every picture of tragedy, of danger and torture, holocausts and hurricanes—someone was *there* doing his job to release that shutter. But the world only sees the photo, not the photographer. Don't worry—only *you* showed up the hero . . . *look* at my image of you!

But my dripping hand doesn't come out of the water bath with any of the fire pictures. Sitting on the edge of the cot, still unzipped—helps ease the stomach ache—holding a soggy print of the circuit board. The background is grainy and his eyes a little too fuzzy . . . but they don't seem to be staring toward the rafters as much as they seemed to before. Harlan, if you saw what he was doing, why didn't you stop him? If you're afraid of him—maybe *I* can help!

Drop the wet print back into the water and run—holding my pants up—to the door, almost fall down outside, have to stop, leaning against a tree. The air is too fresh and my head is filling with it, panting, spitting the chemical taste out of my mouth and throat, then run again, dash across the dark lawn, thick, slick and wet, to the back door, into my kitchen, straight to the spice rack where most people would keep cinnamon and nutmeg, swallow a few pills and fall into a chair, my head on the table, frizzy hair over my wide-open eyes.

The phone ringing. Lemme sleep. The sun is hot through the kitchen window. Took the last pill, the one that worked, somewhere around five . . . I disremember. My head won't lift off the kitchen table where I seem to be, where I haven't moved from, where one of the phones is and rings in my ear, probably many more times than I hear. I lay the receiver on my boulder head. It's Glen Something. Eight:thirty. He's hard at work.

"Miss Zamora, did you call me and leave a message?"

"Huh? No."

"Well, someone did. Look—I'll pay top dollar for any good photo of that fire area. You know what I mean? A photo that says something about it."

"Waddaya wan'me t'say?"

"So you aren't the one who's left these messages about a fire-department investigation going on and that the director of the play extinguished the flame himself and that possibly he's the one—"

"Waddaya want? Wait a minute. I'll get back to you. No, I'll be right down."

The receiver falls out of my hand, my head remains on the table.

VI

The Painting of a Boat in a Fog or Mist or Sandstorm

• • •

Without the finesse I use threading light through my camera, I push my car at a crack between two monster recreational vehicles. "We'll fit in," I say, but I feel it—a horrible screech.

"No!" But too late. It hurts to look at the wound in the bright blue metal. Hurts because the sun concentrates deep there and bounces back at me, in my eyes. A glaring mistake.

If it *were* up to him, which he says he knows it's not, he wouldn't want them published. Harlan is glancing through a stack of glossy prints, a flip show where the actor barely changes position, takes forever to lift an arm, take a step; but plunges so savagely, or desperately, into the fire as I lunged likewise, or desperately, after him and found the sweat-tears on his sooty skin.

"They're so good," he says, "you deserve to have them published." He lingers over the last scene. "Photographers will always have to shoot and run. That's why they're alienated and live in huts or shacks or darkrooms." He laughs. But is it funny?

I've brought him the set I printed last night, the ones I instinctively exposed longer—a few seconds is all it took—and used higher contrast paper. The sharpest, most vivid image is the action in the middle and the surrounding flame, but toward the edges it fades out like a Hollywood dream.

His mouth twitches slightly on one side, perhaps wanting to smile just a little at himself in the pictures. I prop myself against his desk. "I've got others too. All from opening night."

He hands the set to me. It takes me so long to reach for it . . . I have to look at my arm and force it to move, direct my hand to reach for the pictures. He puts them on the desktop and says, "What you do with them is up to you."

"That's not what I wanted you to say."

"What did you want?"

I have a side-ache. I ran in from the parking lot and up the stairs. I wish I hadn't dented my car. "Mr. Harlan, this is just an example of how much *better* I can make it look than what other people may be thinking. If they could see what I saw. . . ."

He smiles, but doesn't look at the pictures again.

I'm clutching my side with both hands. "And . . . you're a hero in these pictures . . . maybe that's a good idea, who knows? Maybe someone will be so impressed they'll send money."

He looks at me: lank, damp, dirty, two-days hungry and still several sleeping pills dopey . . . and orphaned. Orphaned, finally, seven years after my father died.

"I guess I wanted for you to tell me . . . if your version is different. . . ."

His lips part. His breath is slow. Not drawn in . . . it's a silent sigh. A heavy release. The bars are down. What's he going to say? Hurry and say it!

But Windrem bashes through the door. "Any coffee? Oh, Connie, I've got a check for your cello. Jeez, Connie, you look like hell."

Harlan shuts his eyes. Then turns away.

"I never even gave you an estimate for how much it was worth."

"Well, I went out and priced some on my own."

I spin away before he can hand me a check which I might take—nearly surprised that warm tears touch my cheeks, tickle the corners of my nose, my mouth, even dangle on my chin. And I actually sob in a watery voice, "Who put all the RVs in the parking lot?"

"What—?" Or maybe Harlan didn't say that. Just his eyes.

I keep Windrem at my back, lean front-on against Harlan's desk. "I destroyed my car on one."

"You wrecked your car?"

"Destroyed." The word is long, drawn-out, slurred, tremolo. I shake silently, eyes shut. As though the collision is happening now. When did it happen? When *did* I become weak-kneed and mushy-spined and fuzzy-eyed? My chin falls to my breastbone. This is just so ugly. He'll probably be gone when I'm through.

"How big a dent?"

I lift my face and bat the water away. He swims there in front of me . . . the same way he swam under chemicals last night.

"Like this." A foot long. Then I pass my knuckles across my bee-stung lips. A few more jerky breaths.

"The best thing to do," he says, "is to sulk about it as long as possible. Get into a real blue funk."

Everything's getting clearer. "It's only two years old."

"And now it's lost its virginity."

Together, and slowly, our faces begin to break. Still leaning against the desk, I take the photos and hug them with crossed arms to my chest. I feel my face heat up and watch his—a plum ripening on time-release until it splits and spills its purple insides. I'm seeing and feeling the smile at the same time, like a print I'm developing in the dark. I *know* the elastic tautness of his smile-muscles because mine are the same.

Harlan says, "Did you want to take your contract home and look at it?"

"No hurry." Neither of us move. "But don't worry, I'm not quitting."

"I hadn't considered the possibility."

Near the door, hard not to notice the table that holds the coffeepot, dirty cups and spoons, box of lumpy sugar, torn-open creamer packages, crumbs, coffee stains. The baton and stack of music look out of place among the litter of garbage. Musical scores from other shows. Each stamped with Galvin's name and address. Glance back at Harlan—he's writing something with a stubby pencil. I write Galvin's address on the photo envelope then slip out the door.

It's nowhere near the newspaper offices; in fact the opposite direction—out toward the college where I've heard he teaches part-time. That's where I'll look for him if he's not home. A small house on a street without shade trees, but with a few tall lonely palm trees, the leaves way up. They may as well be telephone poles. The front lawn is overgrown, devil-grass threads through the shaggy bushes in the garden. I don't hear any music playing inside. The doorbell works.

The woman in the doorway has short straight hair, lots of freckles, bony legs, painted toenails. "Can I help you?"

"Uh, yeah, I need to talk to Ron Galvin."

"You've come to the right place—are you one of Ron's students?"

"Um, yeah."

"Come on in, I'll get him."

"No, it'll only take a second—I'll wait here."

She's already gone. It can't take long to find him in this tiny house. If she comes back to the door with him, I'll say, what do *you* think my cello is worth, Mr. Galvin? But she isn't with him when he comes. He's wearing jeans and no shirt.

"One of my favorite students!" He stands in the doorway without shutting the door. "Come on in, Connie, Patricia won't bite you."

"No."

"Okay." He smiles and leans in the doorway. A car drives past. The street isn't very far from his front door. It would only take me ten minutes to mow his lawn, though I haven't done mine lately either.

"So what's up, Connie?"

"Huh?"

He laughs. I think it's a laugh. What else could it be. "What did you want?"

"I, uh, wondered if you found out anything else."

"I didn't get the impression you were very interested," he says.

"Sorry."

He combs his hair with his fingers. It's kind of wild, like he just got out of bed. Maybe he did. Did I brush my hair before leaving the house? I'm not sure. Can he tell? "I've been talking to people who have worked with them before," he says.

"Like who—Margie?"

Galvin takes a step onto the porch and closes the front door. He didn't move quickly. I had enough time to back up. "Margie never worked with Harlan before this," he says. "No one in this company has, except Windrem."

"Oh." I take one more step backwards.

"People say that Harlan had a string of shows or several shows that went under quickly after that one surprise success. A lot of the failures seemed to have had production problems. A disproportionate number."

"Like what?"

"Sets that didn't work, stuff like that."

This time when I step backwards, I step down off the porch. "Is that all?"

"Well," he says, "people lost money on him. He stopped being bankable."

"There must've been something more."

"Why do you say that?"

Another step back, another step down. "I don't know . . . *you* thought there was . . . was he blacklisted? Do they *do* that anymore?"

"I didn't say that, Connie. He didn't work, that's all I know. There might be something more—I haven't found out yet. Some of the people I contacted called him a disaster-area."

I stare at him. I have to look up. He still has one hand on the door knob.

"So they blamed Harlan?"

"That's what it sounds like." He pauses, looks down for a moment, then says, "Why Windrem's giving him another chance, I don't know. I think it's a little strange both that Windrem asked Harlan to do this show and that Harlan agreed. But if he fails here too—a two-bit operation like this, and it doesn't look good for him right now—he may as well go back to sponging off his rich wife for good."

I turn and head down the sidewalk to my car. The dent is on the other side—I can't see it from here.

"What's the problem, Connie?" Galvin has followed me, but stopped at the edge of his lawn. I can't see his feet. How does he know he won't step on a snake or something in that ratty grass?

"I have an appointment I'm late for. I forgot how important it is!"

Was I shouting? This is a pretty quiet street. He laughs and waves and turns back to his house.

The car is hot and by the time I get to the newspaper offices, sweat is running out of my sleeves and down my arms, my shirt sticking to my back, my pants damp where I've been sitting.

The newsman, Glen Peters, passes through the photographs much quicker than Harlan did. From my angle, as he flips them—each image hardly lasts before it's already the next one, and the light glazes the slick surfaces—it's alive and the fire cackles.

"I'll take all of them," he says.

"No. Only three." My voice is feeble. He stares at me. A newsman's face, never surprised, just staring now at what probably is a white-skinned, bony-faced, bruised-eyed, mop-haired photographer. Wondering, perhaps, how it is I have the strength in me to stand up. I don't know either. I haven't seen myself lately. With both hands I'm holding the back of his wooden desk chair, the top of it pushed under my ribs. "I mean, just run three in a panel. It'll be enough."

"I offered to *buy* them all."

"Only three." I lean over the chair, find the middle three in the stack of photos. "Here. These are the heart of the action."

"I want this one too," pointing at the last one. It looks like the lens was pushed right up against Harlan, his face a distorted grimace, white teeth in smokey, grimy skin, his eyes frantically squinting, the corners creased a thousand times, streaks of sweat through the dirt on his face, wet trails through the soot, even including one hard bright drop frozen on his cheek.

"No."

"What?" he says. "Why?"

"There's no release on this photo."

"Pretty lame, honey, you know as well as I do a release isn't required for news."

"It isn't news anymore. It's evidence—"

"Of what?"

"Huh?"

"What were you saying? Evidence?"

I spread the three out in order in front of him on the desk. "These three." In the middle shot a cloud of extinguisher fog billows like a tornado around the flaming curtain. The last fleecy edges of the white dissipate just barely before they could've touched Harlan. He is flinching—turned and buried his head in his free arm. For a second. For as long as it took me to click. But in the third frame, the most aggressive one of these three, he's leading with his upstage foot—so he never turned his back on the camera, just like he told us in rehearsals, undaunted, leading *into* the action. "They tell a story," I add.

"Yes, but—"

As he looks at the three pictures, I gather the rest of the stack. By the time he turns back to me, the extra photos are gone. You have to be careful with newsmen. They're so nosy and suspicious—their promotions depend on it. That's the reason they're so interested all the time. He shakes his head. "Okay . . . is ninety dollars enough—thirty for each?"

"I don't care."

"May we mail the check?"

"It doesn't make any difference."

"Let's see . . . you're got your address stamped on the back. And is this how you want your credit: Constance Zamora?"

"No." My head is heavy. I talk toward the floor. "No credit . . . *he* knows. . . ."

"Pardon?"

One full breath, one solid line, shaking my head, "No photo credit."

He grooms his moustache with thumb and index finger, brushing the hairs outward. Then he touches it with his tongue. "You're a strange girl."

"Maybe so."

He sniffs. "Well, we'll probably run them tomorrow."

I watch him print the run date on the backs in black ink.

"Oh—" He caps his pen. "We write our own captions here, not the photographers—not even our own staff photographers do captions."

"You don't need to explain."

"But if you can *tell* me anything. . . ."

"Go ahead, write your own caption, I don't care."

He turns, but I grab his elbow. The chair between us tilts. He catches it and pushes it out of the way. "Mr. Peters, make it simple, please. I mean, just describe what's there, don't try to read anything else into them."

For a moment he stares at my hand, a white claw on his arm. I let go, let my arms dangle limp at my sides.

"Okay, is that all?" he finally says.

"Probably. For now."

"What does that mean?"

"Nothing. That's *all*. Damn!"

The air-conditioner has dried my clothes. I feel like cardboard. Three desks away from him, and he's still talking: "You'll get the check this week."

"I don't *care*," and I don't even turn around to shout it at him.

Nobody to share my newspaper with. No one to keep the pages organized for. I spread it all around my breakfast coffee. In underwear and undershirt, I kneel in a chair and prop my sleep-warmed head up with hands and arms.

> Jason Harlan, director of the stalled musical production at the Guild Theater, fights back against the fire which halted their opening night performance a week ago. Harlan was able to control the flames before the arrival of firefighters, limiting damage to backstage curtains, miscellaneous props and general smoke damage in the backstage areas. However, cause of the fire is still under investigation. No one was hurt.

I don't know how that creep Glen Whatever managed a perfect caption. Perfect. I can hardly believe it. But, then again, why did I worry, how could anyone see anything else in these pictures? Presumably abandoned, left by himself in the fire . . . Harlan didn't run away. A storybook prince, firebreathing dragon—is that going too far?

But he really wasn't alone—*I* know it. And he should know it too. When he gets his newspaper this morning—or his wife hands it to him—he'll open up and see this. She'll come lean over his shoulder and admire his heroism and kiss his neck. But *I* was the one who stayed with him in the theater. He'll remember I was there.

Yet the phone doesn't ring.

Except a television man who got my number from that Glen Peters. The one thing I didn't tell him *not* to do.

So I bring a phone downstairs and plug it in the jack in the darkroom while I print another complete set of the fire photos, even though it might scream at me any second when Harlan calls. It might make me spill chemicals or drop wet prints on the floor, and I know how much control I need to make the fire brighter, the background darker, Harlan in a spotlight created to look like it's all firelight. But *I* threw that light on you, Harlan.

To the TV newsman I give the same three photos plus two more, but again hold back the last one of the set. I might need it later. This guy doesn't offer me money and I don't ask for any. He interviews me—sort of—and writes with a scratchy pen while I answer in a slightly raspy voice. How/where/when/why questions. Mostly I say, I don't know, I don't know. This is short and painless. No one says, "That's a wrap."

I drive home along the street where Randy has dance lessons. Maybe he'll be walking and need a ride. Maybe he'll be late somewhere and welcome a lift.

He's not on the street.

So I watch the local news on TV alone—I can stretch out and use the whole couch. As usual.

They flash my prints on the screen like a black-and-white slide show, or an old school filmstrip with recorded narrator for guided viewing.

1.

Screen shows still B&W shot of stage-right fire from on-stage angle. Man in black, back to camera, completely outlined by the flame directly in front of him.

VOICE OVER:

It seems no one could determine just how or when the backstage fire started at the Guild Theater last week. Just as mysterious to the responding firefighters was the fact that the fire was completely extinguished by the time they arrived, five minutes after a three alarm call.

2.

Change photo to still B&W scene of man (in black) profiled to camera, fire extinguisher under one arm, puff of white emerging.

VOICE OVER (CONTINUING):

Part of that mystery was uncovered yesterday when a production staff member produced a set of photographs taken during the fire. It seems the director of the aborted production, Jason Harlan, found a fire extinguisher and fought the blaze.

3.

Change photo to still B&W scene of man with extinguisher. Extinguisher steam overtaking the flame. Man is protecting his eyes from the chemicals. Slowly zoom to man's head down against his arm.

VOICE OVER (CONTINUING):
Harlan answered firefighters' routine questions about fire prevention procedures in the theater, approximate time of discovery of the flame, and estimated backstage damages. However, he took no curtain calls for his apparent lone scrimmage against the fire and did not offer information on how the blaze was halted.

4.

Change photo to still B&W shot cropped close to man's face, thrust-forward chin, hard, nearly fierce eyes.

VOICE OVER (CONTINUING):
Threatened by the loss of his production, Harlan had perhaps more to lose than the actors and actresses, stagehands and technicians—none of whom stayed to help smother the fire, the cause of which is still under investigation by fire authorities.

5.

Begin to slowly zoom out, showing man leading with upstage foot, stepping toward the fire, still shooting the extinguisher.

VOICE OVER (CONTINUING):
Harlan has been a director for several Broadway and Off-Broadway productions in the past. His first opening-night since coming to the West Coast may've been a little out of control, but obviously not too hot for him to handle.

The news probably continues. I turn the set off, smile at the ceiling, lying back on the couch. If Harlan were here I'd be sitting up, but the celebration is almost the same. I've taken him farther, with more momentum, than anything else I've ever held onto with my camera. Yeah, the athlete's picture was also on TV, as was I—staring stupidly into the lights—and the lawyers, and his agent, and anyone else who thought they had something important to say. But this is different—*obviously* different.

I stop smiling, slowly let it drain off my face, when I realize I'm tired of it. My muscles can't hold it. And the phone doesn't call.

A picture of Randy is still on my darkroom floor. No one would be able to recognize him, but *I* know it's him. Bent, wrinkled, stepped-on, dirty, torn . . . finally I pick it up and throw it away. I need one more set of fire pix. I have to be careful, can't make a mistake because I only have six of the super-gloss high-contrast papers. I haven't yet been paid by the Opportunity Players, and I haven't taken that check for my cello, and I haven't cashed the check I got from Harlan. This time I'm burning in new highlights—a spark of reflected light in one eye, ash smudges on his formal black pants. I whiten his knuckles on the extinguisher hose, intensify those rigid jaw muscles. In the last one, with the enlarger pushed farther up, cutting out some of the smoke and flame, I catch the shine of the wet trails on his neck, the brittle gleam of the single drop standing still on one blackened cheek. "I know you knew I was there." My voice surprises me.

•

This time I want a credit, says Constance Zamora to the *WorldView Magazine* representative.

Actually I say, "I want my full name in the credit. No initials or anything."

He nods, framing portions of a print with a collapsible cropper to see how close he can get to the face and still keep some smoke or fire in the picture.

I look down at the print—the glow of energy in Harlan's skintone, the swell and strain of his facial muscles, the tear, and trails of others.

"It was from the smoke," I say, and touch the wet place on the photo with the tip of one finger.

He mentions some amount of money before he leaves. I don't care. I do have that check from Harlan (I don't remember how much), and a check from the newspaper (don't remember where I put it). Also that reimbursement from Windrem—I could go get it if I wanted it, and leave my splintered cello on his desk.

Now all I can do is wait for the magazine. Six to ten days, he said. "I'll wire the pix back East and see if they can find a place for them."

I made myself dizzy trying to blow the dust off the kitchen table, an even layer, coating everything lying here: some spoons, a coffee cup—never washed because I keep using it, or thinking I will—salt and pepper, a hot pad, envelope of pictures, cloth napkins, unopened mail—advertisements and bills—a plate with bread crusts. Clutching the back of a chair, I wait for the lightheadedness to pass, then go get the fan out of the closet, turn it on high and hold it over the table. The dust flies into the air but doesn't fly away, so I set the fan on the counter, still blowing, then push everything on the table to one edge, except the photo envelope. Somewhere I have a magnifying glass, a junk drawer by the stove, dig it out, return to the table, sit in the breeze.

What were you looking at, Harlan?

Everything else is obvious enough—*no* one could look at this picture and say Windrem's hand isn't on the jack, that he wasn't backstage, that it wasn't Windrem at all. Could they? Of course not. I'm *sure.* They got the fire pictures right, didn't they? What would they say about this one? *Producer Hal Windrem, a perfectionist in every aspect of the theater, has an eye for detail as he inspects the lights before opening night.*

Wrong! All wrong! Maybe that's what *he* says. Tell them, Harlan, what did *you* see?

Hal Windrem, producer, teaches his reckless director about the light board.

No! Harlan, can't you speak up? Isn't it important to you?

The director can't say anything about it when the producer decides to change the lights.

That can't be true!

Avoiding a fight, avoiding trouble, avoiding everything except a disaster, director Harlan pretends not to notice what producer Windrem is doing.

Was that it? But, Harlan, if you saw what was coming, what made you not do anything about it? Look, *I'm* doing more to help you than *you* are, but you don't seem to notice. Don't you understand—you're not guilty . . . are you?

I've lost count . . . How many mornings in a row have I fallen out of bed and dragged myself to this table for a lonely breakfast—crackers and cold coffee—with this picture. Is the kitchen light bulb fading it? Is it covered with dust? Are my eyes growing a film? Cataracts? Do I need glasses? Should I look at the picture through a camera? Set up a tripod with the 500 mm lens and look at the picture from across the room, hiding behind a chair, from outside the window?

Why am I so bored?

How long ago did I jump out of bed every morning—alone—and find something to do or do nothing, read a book or stare at the TV, not have the phone ring for days . . . and usually feel fine, not give it a second thought. Was that so strange? What's wrong with me now?

I spend a lot of time sleeping until it seems I'm immune to the pills one at a time, so I try two. Sleep is like a fever. Hours and hours, and days and months, it seems, of opening magazine after magazine, stacks of thousands and rows and miles of stacks. And every page blank.

Conscious vegetation is almost easier:

7 A.M. Coffee. Television. News and kids' shows. Hard to choose.

8 A.M. Coffee. Television. Exercise and interviews. More coffee, please. I'll have to make a fresh pot. Thank you.

9 A.M. Coffee. Television. Roasting a duck at this time in the morning?

10 A.M. The sun is high enough. But it's cold. Sit in it anyway. Eyes closed. Radio. Babbling. Music. The ads wake me up.

11 A.M. Shed shirt, shed pants, bathing suit already on underneath. Flip. March is too early for sunbathing, isn't it? Radio. Like white noise. Not too chilly anymore, except when the breeze blows.

12 P.M. Flip. Block the sun from eyes with a book. Careful of reading matter. Don't want to start those *other* dreams and contradict my desire for a conscious coma.

1 P.M. Return inside, soft and mushy as sun-ripened fruit. Television. Hungry? No, too much trouble to fix. No, it's no trouble, really. No, please, don't bother.

2 P.M. Drive downtown. Drive back. Why? I don't know. Randy had a dance class from noon until two. I forget which days.

3 P.M. Sit-ups. When I was strong I could do 100—break five minutes—100 more. Now: five during each station break. Game shows. Soaps. Can't figure out who's who. Only approximately one kiss per show. But everyone's exhausted. Drained. Me too. Enough exercising.

4 P.M. More television. Cartoons. Reruns. Stare without laughing. Problems climax and clear up in half an hour. Simple.

5 P.M. Et cetera.

6 P.M. Ditto.

7 P.M. Likewise.

8 P.M. Continued. Add warmed-over coffee. Also maybe some bread. It's not too much trouble. A little stale. Forgot to shop again. Ice cream in the freezer. Left over from summer. Ate it, alone, on hot afternoons. Where was I the 4th of July?

9 P.M. Bathe. Warm water. Notice flaccid body no longer so pale. But I tan yellowish-red. Swim suit line and shocking white below it.

10 P.M. In bed. Already? Eyes opened. Television. I could run one of the cameras. Take the film of Harlan's first movie. But I wouldn't stop rolling when he says, *Cut.*

11 P.M. Television. What's on? Doesn't matter.
What's this show about? I don't know.
Is this the news or a cop show? I don't care.

2 A.M. Off the air. Video-taped dreams. . . .

Every day, every day, every day. Until the day the thick, slick magazine arrives through the mail slot. And the pages are not blank. And it says Photo Essay by Constance Zamora. And the photos are end-to-end, over four pages, laid out on a negative-strip design, complete with sprocket holes. And the title does not overcome the photos in size.

> *Theatrical Director Fans His Own Flame*
> As panicked cast, crew and audience departed a flaming theater on opening night in San Diego last month, director Jason Harlan stayed alone to fight for his production. From left, Harlan. . . .

Photo Essay by Constance Zamora. The photographer who wasn't there.

They inverted the last shot. Had to—otherwise he'd be looking off the page. It made his right eye left. His face still snarling, still flaring, still tight and extreme. Except he cries from a different eye.

I press the magazine to my face. Smell the ink, the paper, the slick chemicals. Where I breathe, the page gets damp. I cry into it and crumple it in both hands and bite off the corners and chew them, and sleep, still holding it to my face.

The phone rings.

Of course *all* the phones are ringing. The closest is in the kitchen.

First I knock the receiver on the floor—sit in the chair and gather in the cord until I have the receiver in my hands again.

"Connie? Hello? Jay Harlan. Did I wake you?"

"Did you see it?" My voice cracks and wheezes. How long has it been since I said anything?

"I did, but the reason I'm calling—"

"Wha'd'ja think?"

"Connie, just listen—we'll have time to talk about that later. The cast is getting together at my house again. Can you make it?"

"Sure. Why? When?"

"Tomorrow. I know it's short notice. We have a couple of the girls in the office on the phones trying to notify everyone."

Suddenly my heart is beating, as though it hadn't been.

"Connie—are you still there?"

"Huh?"

"Listen—it's going to be sort of like a press conference. Windrem asked the paper to send someone over. There's going to be an announcement. I thought you might help me out."

"Okay. . . ." I'm still holding the magazine, rolled into a tube, looking around the kitchen through it. "How?"

"I figured you'll know what the reporter will want," he says. "Keep him satisfied and away from me."

"But what about . . ."

"See you at three tomorrow, okay?"

"Wait!" I'm staring through the magazine at a slow drip coming out of my kitchen faucet. "Hello?" No answer. I put the phone down carefully so it won't fall again.

I have to lie down on the kitchen floor, put my cheek on the cool linoleum, ignore the grains of salt or sugar or sand, the crumbs, the dust, and let my pulse slow and my breathing regulate.

•

Moving quickly, I'm able to arrive at the door the same time as the newsmen. I waited in the car until I saw them already going up the garden path, two of them—one with a camera bag, two units and a flash strobe. The other isn't Glen What's'sname. My own strap cuts into my shoulder. Once again it feels heavier than ever.

On the inside the photographer mumbles, "Which one is he?" Their coats and ties give them away. Maybe Harlan has staged the room this way—a clump of lanky dancers between himself and the door. I take a round-about route to the couch where Harlan is, walk up to him like a crazy actress leaving the dark wings and charging on stage long before her cue, but before I have time to stupidly blink into the lights, the scene takes over. I'll have to improvise. I haven't seen Randy yet.

Harlan says, "Connie, you haven't met my wife . . . Courtney."

I don't meet a wife, it's a twin, a female counterpart, except she's light-haired: streaks of orange and yellow and chestnut. His darkness is highlighted by a pale mask across and around his eyes. Branded by sunglasses. But he and she both have a direct look—her green-gold eyes and his deep-water blue—both pointing at me. He says, "Keep them away from me, please."

"What're they doing here?"

"Connie, wake up—I told you they're here for Windrem. Let's just keep it at that."

Someone's cigar smoke pushes my face away. Some man is sitting on someone's lap in the corner, a long bare leg with sandaled foot shows between his legs. Can't see the rest of her. Can't hear well at parties, and vision is a kaleidoscope. Breathing isn't free, but give-and-take.

"Connie?"

"Yes?"

"I'm simply requesting no publicity . . . concerning me."

The strobe goes off. Hurricane-style conversations organize

and swell, interest peaks and dissipates, then the voices are separate flurries of life again.

"Oh, I understand now. It was probably some newsman's fault in the first place."

"What?" He's sort of smiling. I think. Maybe it just looks that way because of the white mask around his eyes. Take a picture of a bandit in a black mask, or the Lone Ranger or Zorro, and in the negative the mask is white.

"You know how newsmen are." I smile too, I think. "It was a reporter who wrote the caption for my picture of that athlete."

"What're you talking about?"

"I'll bet something like that happened to you once too—someone blew things out of proportion."

"Like just a few weeks ago." Now he *is* smiling.

"But this time I made sure it came out *right*—that was the whole purpose, so no one will think you're a disaster-area again. They won't blame you this time, even if—"

"Connie, I don't think you know what you're talking about. I know *I* don't."

"Yes you do . . . bad press . . . but for once things came out right. If I could be *sure* every photo was done well enough to touch the viewer directly . . . well, I'd publish more pictures. I mean, I'd publish pictures more often."

"Connie, I don't think you understand. . . ."

"But I do. . . ." Sounds like an owl. What would an owl be doing here? An owl's a predator. Here's a tray of fancy cold-cuts, if I was hungry. Several people abruptly shriek. It's their way of laughing, I guess. The cameraman's flash goes off again.

"Don't sit down—" Harlan pulls me up from where I have sunk onto the off-white arm of his couch. I don't remember when. Randy came in with the last flash, and is grinning and batting his eyes near the doorway. His front teeth are a little crooked. Makes him look even younger. A boy I knew once. A boy I never met. Harlan jiggles my arm.

"Connie?"

"Huh?"

"You okay?"

"Uh-huh."

The crowd folds in around Randy's thin back as he moves into the party.

"Connie?"

"Huh?"

"Okay, listen—it's really very simple," Harlan says. "Windrem wanted them here for his announcement."

"Okay. . . ."

"So they're here. But I don't want them around me. Explanation enough?"

"Do you have anything to eat here?"

"On the bar."

"That stuff's carcinogenic."

"Good. Just what you need. It'll give you some energy."

Mrs. Harlan returns, or did she ever leave? She leans across the couch to straighten a picture on the wall. It's as though a party brings weather indoors—wind and sunshine and heat and ice, so the painting was blown askew . . . a picture of a boat in a fog or mist or sandstorm with a featureless man in it. If he can't see out, likewise I can't see through, and he's all one shade—black, which is no color at all, caused by an absent sun.

"It's just a little awkward, that's all," he says. He has a drink in one hand—actually an empty glass with half-melted ice cubes and a piece of lemon or lime. Did he have it the whole time? I didn't see him drink from it. "It was bad enough that I knew about the new money first, before him. He's a little jealous. But it's simple—he wants the publicity, let *him* have it. It's *his* news now. Make sure *he* gets the credit—"

"I think she understands, Jay," his wife says, her hand on his arm.

"Connie?"

"Mr. Windrem makes his announcement then they leave. Right?"

"Can you see to it?"

I move through the crowd with no sense of the show in progress here. Five or six people stretch their necks over someone's shoulder to see a strip of black-and-white photographs in a magazine spread. One voice says, "You mean you haven't seen this yet? Harlan's a hero."

You can't let the scene carry you, Harlan told the cast just before opening night. *You* carry the scene by having a clear sense of the show. There's only one center of the universe on stage. You all come here from various separate, individual lives, but you have to give all that up during the show. Here you share the *same* universe and it has the *same* center. Whether at any given point it's you or not, you have to have a sense of what that center is and play the *one* show. Otherwise each cast member has his own private show—that's only in real life. We're in the theater now.

It's taking forever to cross this carpeted stage to where the newsmen are role-playing, smoking, looking bored, checking F-stops and guide numbers.

"Everyone, may I have your attention over here!" Windrem is behind the bar.

"Get to work," the reporter says to the photographer. He lifts the strobe and kicks it off.

"Here, everyone!" Windrem claps his hands. Someone next to him whistles, splits the conversation-choked air, and broken sentences fall into a pile at the foot of the bar.

A show has a rope of sense that must be followed, Harlan said, and at any given point you may be hanging on or hanging from that rope, or tied up *in* it. But you have to know when you're *not.*

"Leave as soon as he's done," I tell them.

The photographer says, "Who're you?" and the other, "Don't worry 'bout it, kiddo."

Innovative theater could be two shows on the same stage, completely unrelated. Or an unraveled rope with a knot at the far end to keep it from becoming separated all the way. A subplot that falls off the stage and moves up the aisles.

"I have some news I think you're all going to like," Windrem announces.

"Showtime," says the reporter.

"Now . . . oh, wait, is Galvin here? Ron?" Windrem scans the room. "I wanted him to be here. Damn!" He takes one more look around. "Okay, I'll just go on. You all probably saw the photo story in *WorldView*. I don't think I need to describe the contents. Some of the local publicity on the unfortunate accident has verged on embarrassing. Yesterday, however, a new patron came out of the woodwork, so to speak. She loves theater, thinks no one should be deprived of it, and has therefore donated enough to complete the reorganization and start the production rolling again. Our first tour is still scheduled for early April."

"So 25 more artsy-fartsy deadbeats are off unemployment," the wry photographer mutters and holds his camera high with a wide-angle lens to catch everything in the room at once.

No surprise here—it's not the first time publicity of misfortune brought sympathy and gifts. Admit it, it *worked.* Why hasn't he said that: it worked, Connie . . . thank you. No, the thanks aren't necessary. But *say* it: it worked!

Harlan's wife says, "Thank you for coming, gentlemen."

"That's *it?*"

"Yes. Thank you." She opens the front door.

"Wow—where are we going to find a local-page top-story, *now*?" the cameraman says.

"Maybe we'll find a traffic accident on the way back."

The scene shift now is abrupt, but really merely a new filter in front of the lens: same set, different lighting—hot red or symbolic green. I'm not the director. But Harlan's in an overhead shower spotlight with a skirt of people around him. "Wait now, here it comes," Mrs. Harlan says.

Windrem, lost his hold on the rope, fights his way to us. I'm leaning on the closed door. She's next to me. He says, "Did the press make it?"

"Oh yes, they were here," she says.

"They left already? Jeez."

"They probably didn't need to hear any more," I blurt, of course without thinking, and, of course, try to make up for it by continuing, "I mean, with all the previous publicity—"

He glares. I shut up. Then he drops his bullet eyes to my camera bag. Unopened.

"I don't suppose *you* got any shots."

"Of what?"

"Naturally not. But I know you journalists." He spits the word at me. "*Timely* means releasing information when time's right for *your* career."

"I'm not a journalist. I'm a photographer. Why're you so mad?"

"Just remember—you're under contract with this company. And that's *me*."

Before I can inform him that I'm not, he goes to refill the empty glass he's been holding. At the bar he digs his stubby fingers into an ice bucket then pours from a bottle. Drinks long. Randy is next to him, leaning over the bar, talking to someone in the kitchen, his legs crossed, his weight on one foot and the other foot balances with just a toe touching the floor. His pants pucker where the belt holds them around his waist. Windrem smacks his glass down empty. "What does the word *produce* mean to *you?*"

Randy turns toward him. I don't know where to look—anywhere else—the floor, the ceiling, the walls, the windows, the misty painting. Harlan sits on the arm of a chair, glass—full, again?—dangled by one hand between his knees, his wife with him now. She touches his hair.

Windrem says, "Nothing? Naturally. Well—*produce* means to bring forth, to cause, to create. I create a production—and thanks to incompetent help it falls apart. *I* create a solution. The producer *produces* the theater, the props, the paychecks, the music, the lights, the audience, the applause, yes—even produces the *director,* and all the rest of the fags!"

Randy puts his beautiful lips together, a pert little smile which is not a laugh. Then he does laugh—a puff of air—and he shakes his head. I dodge and duck through the happy cast members, stuffing their faces around the buffet table, to Harlan, who is still watching Windrem, who is now alone at the bar. Together—Harlan, his wife, and I—we watch Windrem finish another drink. Then Harlan pours the stuff in his glass into a plant. He stares at me. The white mask around his eyes not as distinct anymore, his eyes not as blue—grey and sharp, glaring. I try to back up but my shoulders are already against the sliding glass door. He says, "Tell your friend Glen Somebody at the paper. . . . No, bad idea. It's over. No more story."

Something's wrong—sound is dwindling, light fading, the sun outside found a cloud or fog or is setting, the atmosphere shrinks away like water draining out of a lake, leaving wet rocks and flopping naked fish. I mean, a party shouldn't be this *quiet* all of a sudden—except Windrem's voice is still loud enough. "That's right, this may as well be a puppet show. Your fearless director may have *your* strings, but who'd'ya think has *his?* A goddamn puppet. That's all."

People get out of his way as he heads for Harlan. Mrs. Harlan disappears, a stereo is turned on or turned up, Harlan turns his back, but Windrem squeezes in front of him, a finger up, pointing between Harlan's eyes, his voice still hard, but now low. "Next time tell your friend with all the money I don't need it. I can take care of my own goddamn production—without you or in spite of you!"

How long ago did I leave? I can still picture my last look at Harlan—posed, rigid, silent, Windrem's finger in his face. . . . I had to leave because Harlan just sat there. But I wish I had put my ear to his chest to hear his heart and therefore know that at least someone else on earth is alive.

My car's still in the sun, and the sun's in the dent—that same dent which hasn't healed yet. Your fault, I've told this car a thousand times—your fault! They were standing still and *you* were running.

We glare at each other.

I can't sleep. The windows are open and there're *birds* singing—at midnight! And a full moon. And my wisdom teeth, which no longer exist, ache in the back of my mouth. And the house moans. And toads belch. And in the valley a rooster crows. When the air dares to move, the trees whisper. And I, with my face buried in a goose-down pillow, can hear it all because I can't sleep. I've got the crumpled magazine beneath my pillow—I'd be staring at it if the pillow were clear. But I can see it anyway. The smoke, the soot, the white extinguisher fog, the calm man gravely working—they probably were drops of sweat and not tears at all. I don't think Harlan cries. At least during the fire he wasn't a statue, he wasn't concrete, his eyes weren't flat opaque glass—he was alive. I know it. And he knew I was there. Maybe he let me stay because he saw more than the burning curtains, the smoky backstage, the jet-stream of the extinguisher—was he already seeing where *I* fit into the picture? Bait to lure and catch new money. Then why didn't he ask me to publish the pix right away? He let everything smoulder a while. It was almost too late. That doesn't seem like good planning. He *couldn't* have been planning *any*thing—he was an opening-night zombie. The fire pix don't show it, Harlan, but the other one does, backstage, Windrem and the circuit board—where *were* your eyes looking? Everywhere? Saw everything but nothing registered because you were then too, like tonight, preoccupied with your own private show. What happened to your show-sense? You're supposed to know what the center of the show is—the center of the universe, remember? We're supposed to share the same universe with the same center. Remember? You were supposed to *know what happened.* And now no one else can know because I have to protect you.

A scream outside, on the road below the house. Not human or dog or coyote. Immediately recognizable—four tires . . . no, *eight* tires, two cars. They gun those babies like cannons and fire from the rear like machine guns. Is this like sleep—or lack of it—during a war? I roll over, flat on my back, with my eyes still pressed shut, gripping the sides of the mattress. I don't even try to get up and watch because it'll happen anyway—one car has its howl stuffed back down its throat as it meets the other head-on in the middle of the wrong side. They wring each other out, wrap each other up, fold the metal like paper, crinkle it and toss it over the side of the hill like all the other litter—the beer cans, the bottles, the mousey mattresses. Metal splashing against rocks that are hidden under the tall grass. There's no softness in the weeds, no comfort anywhere except the silence afterwards. Even the crickets are listening. So I should be able to sleep now, because I didn't lie here waiting for them to crash— I *hoped* they would.

VII

An Old Camera I've Forgotten How to Use

• • •

Since we're all going into a reprise of getting ready for dress rehearsal, I presume that's why I have to see what my contract says once again. Will it seem like something's missing—a big hole instead of a line filled in? Will I no longer be going up to his desk every day or so? Is the freedom-to-shoot clause I wanted more or less important now? Windrem's secretary left a message—I was home but didn't answer—to go see Harlan about my contract. Has anything changed? I'll go up those flimsy steps to the theater office, and they'll still be handing me a contract so I can check to see what it calls me. Perhaps they'll still be discussing costume fittings and dress parade, dress rehearsal, ticket sales, and hotshots and big-bucks who'll be in the producer's box for opening night. And possibly nothing else has happened since the day before our first dress rehearsal. We could splice today's scene to our early rehearsals in February and simply snip off the extra loop of time in between. It's not dishonest—editing and time warps are part of photography. A photographer sees something interesting and takes a picture. Then the film is souped, the neg dried and cleaned, the chemicals prepared. Finally the scene is flashed out of the enlarger like a memory, with the blacks white and the brightness dark. And the photographer can crop out bad composition, frame it, intensify it, filter it, clean it. But you forget about all the time that passed after the original observation, all the way up to this vivid reacquaintance with it.

They're frozen when I enter, or they freeze on my entrance. I close the door softly, the room is dim, and I can hardly see anyone. Slowly they take shape: Windrem, on a corner of his desk, smoking, ashes all over the desk top, falling into the typewriter, but not on him; and Harlan, behind his desk, languid, almost drowsy, like a boy rag doll someone threw there.

When I reach his desk, Harlan raises the end of one eyebrow to look at me sideways without having to move or turn his head.

"Hi."

"Hi, Connie." He puts his hand on the back of a wooden chair beside his desk. I sit in it, facing Windrem. Harlan also faces Windrem. The two of us, like an audience.

But I turn to tell Harlan, "I came to sign—"

"That damn bitch," Windrem says.

Harlan puts a hand on my arm and answers him, "It's just talk, Hal. She won't waste her time with a lawsuit. Besides—"

"It's just bad P.R., no matter who's right." He drags, then sizzles the cigarette in a muddy half-cup of coffee. "Can you imagine holding the show eight weeks for her to get out of a splint? Don't get any ideas—you *are* starting rehearsals *today*. No postponement, by her or her agent or you."

Harlan doesn't answer. Again. Just sits there.

Windrem picks up some paper, the white copy of a contract. "I'm gonna ask my lawyer just where in this document it even implies that if this show is presented by this company any time in the next five years we have to use her in the lead." He lights up. "I knew she was gonna be bad business. Goddamn prima-donna bitch. I should just tear this thing up right now."

Harlan's chair screeches back and he stands. "There's too much messing with contracts here altogether."

The air is breakable. I make both hands into one fist and close my legs tight around it, bend my neck and stare down. Finally finally finally. But . . . everything slows . . . there's no crash.

"Well," Windrem says, "I'm just gonna call him for lunch or we'll go for a beer and chat. Just see what he has to say." The snaps on his briefcase click. "I'll be by this afternoon. Running the understudy in rehearsal?"

"Yes."

"Good. Now, Connie! Your contract is here. This is getting ridiculous." A look back at Harlan, "You said you'd take care of it, I mean it, get it done—*today*." Back to me, "Okay?" The door slams, Harlan breathes out, pulls his chair back and sits again. He seems to be staring at a pencil on his desk.

"So . . . do you have my contract?" I say but the pencil doesn't allow his eyes to move.

"Your profession has to do with perception, right?"

"Which—photography?"

"I'm going to give you a perception test, see how perceptive you really are."

"Okay."

He looks at me. His eyes are inky blue. "How many pencils do you see here?"

"Just one."

"Are you sure? Look closer."

"How many do *you* see?"

"Three."

"No. No. Just one."

"Wanna make a bet about this?"

"Okay."

"Will you give me fifty cents if I'm wrong?"

"Yes."

"Okay," he says, "I'm wrong."

I pick up the pencil and tap it on the desk. The rubber end

bounces without clicking. I hardly know where to look, as if I'd pressed the button and the shutter didn't click-release on an old camera that I'd forgotten how to use, then foolishly turn it around to stare into the lens when all it needed was to advance the film.

"I fail the test I guess."

"So you probably didn't see what you think you did in here a while ago."

I hand the pencil to him.

"Rehearsal's not for another hour or so," he says. "You're early."

"I came about my contract, remember?"

"Too many things to remember."

"That's okay. Are we in makeup today?"

"No." He leans back, hands folded on top of his head. For a moment he looks like a demure slit-eyed cat in the sun. He says, "How're you getting along with the cast? Been around theater people much before?"

"No. They're okay." I watch his eyes get wider. "Sometimes they're a little different, but I've heard the same thing said about photographers."

His laugh brings him forward again, leaning his forearms on the desk. One is alongside mine. He is gold-tan while I am yellowish-olive and my fine hair between wrist and elbow is longer than his.

He says, "I have a story for you. When I was in college I had a summer job loading bricks and cement on construction trucks, me and a bunch of Spanish-speaking guys. They never spoke to me, nor I to them, but they were always jabbering among themselves. After two weeks I wanted to break the ice, so I took a brick which was already in two pieces and covered the split with sand so it looked whole. Then I went YEEAAHHH and judo-chopped it so it cracked like an egg." His mouth is in tight control as though this has a funny side which I can't see yet and he doesn't want to give away, beyond the picture I get of Harlan, not too much younger, stripped to the waist, muscles discolored by sweat and dirt. His damp hair flies and his raw eyes strain. He puts twice his weight and three times his heart into hitting that brick. "Well, those Mexicans gathered around while I stood dusting my hands, and one said, Howju dodat, man?"

"You spoke the same language."

"Sort of, but I'd never known. I could see I'd broken some sort of barrier. They were even a little afraid. So I broke the next barrier—I told them how I did it."

"You told your secret? Didn't that ruin it?"

Hands behind his head, he leans back again and looks at me smoothly, as though looking out the window at a simple scene, with nothing else to think about. "It was sure better than them talking about me, trying to figure me out, suspecting I was related to the boss and might be . . . up to something."

Is he waiting for something? Still watching that same scene, looking for a sign that it's real life, like a cloud blowing across, or a sunrise. Without looking down, I check to see if my fly is open.

"I guess Windrem wants you to sign your contract now, huh?"

"Maybe so, he mentioned something about it, didn't he?" I smile because he is.

"He was going to have his secretary give it to you, but I said, 'If Connie wants the thrill of bargaining, she should at least get a chance of negotiating with the boss.'"

"That's right!"

"So he said I could do it."

"I guess that's okay too."

"Ready?" He leans forward, picks up a pencil, but doesn't write, and has nothing to write on. "Here's the final offer—sign or quit."

"Some offer. What does the contract say?"

"I don't remember.

"Well . . . okay, let me see it. I'll sign. Unless . . ."

"Unless what?"

"One thing. My photos are always mine."

He stares at me and I shiver for a second before I'm suddenly hot and sweating.

"I can't find it," he says. "So I guess you can't sign anything right now. But you could still choose to quit."

I don't know whether to leave because he's staring at me or wait for him to stop staring so I can leave. I need to distract him . . . point to the window and shout *look!*, flip a lighted match into the trash can, spill coffee all over the floor. I stand, still being watched. I dig two quarters out of my pocket, toss them onto his desk, saying, "You won the bet." One of them rolls into his lap and when he looks down to get it, I head for the door.

The whole makeup room is lit up. Every mirror is surrounded with rods of fluorescent light. All of them are turned on. But no one is talking. No songs. No laughing. No shrill giggle.

From the hallway I can only see two mirrors in the middle of the front row of makeup stations. With each step through the entry passage, I see one more mirror on either side. But no person, no makeup trays, no hair-spray, no towels. Clean counters and empty mirrors.

The first row of makeup stations, down the middle of the room, is double-sided. The mirrors are back-to-back and people who use those stations sit toe-to-toe although they can't see each other. When I come around the end of the double-sided row, there's another half-row, the mirrors mounted on the far wall. But the people who usually use them never feel their backs are turned on the rest of the giddy room because they can see almost all of it—inverted—in their mirrors. But now only the back of Randy's head is in one of those lighted mirrors on the wall. Down the row, each mirror holds a different angle of him.

At the same time those mirrors on the back wall have a reflection of his face in the mirror he's looking into. The wall mirrors mirror the mirror mirroring his face. In the wall mirrors I can see him take his eyes off himself and look up at a reflection of me that is, in reverse, coming from the wall mirror into his own. And I am actually standing right beside him.

I move around to behind his seat where the back of his head nearly touches my throat, and we meet in only one mirror.

"No makeup today."

"Oh."

He has his tray out already. And there's water in the pan. I lean over him to set my camera down on one side of the counter and reach for his sponge on his other side. Dip it into the water, but need both hands to swirl it in the pancake base. I watch the sponge and my hand holding the cup of makeup . . . have to lean way over, my chin over his shoulder, cheek-to-cheek. When I lift my head, he hasn't moved, eyes in the mirror. So I watch him there, feeling steady, hold his hair off his brow with one hand and brush the pancake onto him, cover his face—the lightness and darkness, microscopic lines and crinkles and the faint blue possibility of a beard—until he is all one shade, and still he doesn't move. And I also remain steady, although I keep my left hand on the back of his neck while I brush maroon cream eyeshadow on his lids, all the way to his eyebrows. He hardly flutters as I paint the underside of his eyes with thick strokes, making points on his temples with the upward hint of a smile. Still I watch in the mirror and don't falter at being inverted.

"You're going to be a theatrical mask." And I press the reddest lipstick to his mouth. At one corner I sweep the color up and at the other drag it down nearly to the edge of his jaw.

"It looks like blood dripping out of my mouth."

"Just look at the smiling side." On that side I color the highest part of his cheekbone with matching red rouge. But for the other side I use character shadow, and using my own fingers, etch dark lines under his eye, around the corner of his nose and downward toward his mouth. And under his cheek I make gaunt hollowness.

"I'm scary."

"No," I say. "You're all right."

Still, we talk into the mirror. I reach for my camera, crouch a little and brush the lens near his ear. This is what I have through the optics: Randy the way I made him up, and me behind a camera which looks over his shoulder.

I take it that way. With no flash . . . we're steady enough.

"What's that for?"

"To remember us by." I stand to his side, but he doesn't turn from the mirror.

"What're you going to do with it—sell it to the newspaper?"

"Why would I do that?"

"To prove there's nothing wrong with you. Maybe just to prove it to yourself."

"What's that supposed to mean?" I don't need proof—my finger didn't tremble on the shutter release. I focused easily without having to bat my eyes to clear them first. "Do you think there's something wrong with me?"

"There's certainly nothing wrong with *me*."

"I know that, Randy. I know it. I never said there was."

"Well . . .?"

"Well, what?"

"C'mon, Connie, dammit, don't play games. You know what I'm talking about." He is leaning on the counter, leaning toward the mirror, as though *that's* who he's talking to, and *I'm* the reflection. And maybe not a very good one either—not in a mirror but in a window or a puddle. But I'm not going to tap his shoulder to make him turn and look at me.

"Y'know, Connie, I've been thinking . . . maybe that strange guy in L.A. was right."

"How could some weirdo I've never met before be right? That

guy was *crazy*. A sleezeball. Couldn't pick up women with his looks or personality so he tried cheap psychology."

"Calm down, Connie. Forget it."

"No, wait! You hardly know me—how could you know anything about whether or not there's something *wrong* with me. Who're you—or anyone—to decide what's right or wrong about me?" I'm panting. Did I stop breathing a while back? Randy carried on this whole scene in the makeup I designed. I haven't stopped staring at him in the mirror but I just noticed the makeup again. He looks a little older . . . not much . . . not enough. . . . My hand is on his shoulder, his shirt gathered in my white fist. He doesn't shake his shoulder to get me to let go. Was I shouting? The room is softly buzzing. The fluorescent lights or the air system.

"Let's just drop it, okay?" he says. He smiles. At least I think so. His teeth show in the makeup. "What're you doing here so early, anyway?" he asks.

"Is it early? I don't remember. Oh— I had to go to the office. Take off the makeup, okay?"

"I should make you do it for me!" Randy dips two fingers into his cold cream and covers his face with it. He uses a circular motion and his colors blend. "What were you doing in the office?"

Something about perception and a secret? Or a secret perception? Contracts. A secret contract? Breaking barriers and contracts? Finding out what's wrong with me?

"My contract, probably." One of my knees halfway buckles and I quickly grab the back of his chair behind him where he can't see that my brief strength ended where the scene should've. I boost myself onto the counter to sit there and cradle my camera in my lap. "I'm in better shape than Margie, I guess." My legs shiver. "I may not have any contract, yet, but she's getting hers torn up for threatening to sue Windrem."

Randy wipes cold cream from his eyes and opens them, practically black compared to the foamy cream covering his skin.

And he looks at me—direct with no mirror in between. I have to be freezing to be shivering this hard.

•

There's nothing to eat in the house. I still have three cases of imported canned fava beans that my father bought, two gallon-jars of hot peppers, and a half gallon of taco sauce. He liked to stock up. I'm not hungry. I might throw up. I could eat some bread and throw it up. What the hell for? I don't even have any bread. How long has the phone been ringing? Drag myself off the couch. TV's on, but no sound. I'll use the phone in my bedroom. Might as well go to bed anyway.

"Hello?"

"Connie Zamora? Hi. Glen Peters."

"Yes, I got the check. Thanks. I'll cash it soon. Sorry to mess up your checkbook balance."

"What? Oh—very funny. Anyway, I got your message."

"What message?"

"You know, about the fire insurance claims."

"Huh?"

"You don't know anything about it?"

"It's late—"

"It's only 6:30."

"Is that all? Damn."

"Listen, Miss Zamora, do you happen to know why the claims were withdrawn?"

"Huh? Who told you that?"

"Look—I've seen the work of drunk photographers, and yours *isn't,* so why doncha cut it out and just answer the question."

"Wha'd'ya mean, why're you asking me anyway? How'm I

supposed to answer it? You want an answer whether I know the answer or not? Whether I *want* to answer or not?"

"Which is it?"

"Every time I talk to you I wonder why I've never hung up on a reporter before."

"Now's your chance."

I don't answer, but also don't hang up. I can hear him drinking something. Probably coffee. His 15th cup. Newsmen.

"Look, Connie—"

"*Constance.* Why ask *me*—ask the insurance company. And why should we worry about a paltry fire insurance claim. We have a big new backer."

"I know—but no one's ever *heard* of your new backer. It's an alias."

"A what?"

"Not real."

"How could it not be real—they're going to be paying us . . . finally. Rehearsals have started. We're going on tour."

"Your schoolgirl act isn't going to make me forget why I called."

"Why doncha go back to obituaries, creep."

"And *you* can go back to trying to slug men in the face when they so much as smile at you."

It's dark in here. I never turned on the light when I came in to answer the phone. I can't hear him breathing or drinking anymore. I can't believe I haven't hung up yet—or put the phone down without hanging up and just leave it. Harlan smiled at me today. I didn't hit him.

"That doesn't have anything to do with it," I finally say.

"Goodnight, Constance. I believe you implied you were going to bed. Sweet dreams."

When I lower the receiver from my ear, feel for the phone on the dark floor, gently push the button then ease the receiver into the cradle, Glen Somebody has already, long ago, hung up.

My head is hanging over the side of the bed. If I throw up it'll go all over the phone. I won't throw up. But if I'm going to, now's the time, quick, while no one's watching. . . . Why was everyone watching me all day? Even What's'sname Peters was staring—through the phone—as though I'm some sort of fascinating zombie he calls to stare at when his day is dull. Next time it rings I won't answer. Let whoever calls talk to the machine and stare at the mechanical static and never know if I'm home or asleep or maybe out doing something perfectly normal. . . . Maybe I'm dizzy because I'm hungry, and because my head is hanging over the side of the bed. But I can't eat. Maybe I would eat if someone prepared something for me and spoon-fed me, but without looking at me, letting me wipe my own face after each bite. I've never had that done for me. I've also never done it for anyone else. I could've, I suppose, when my father was sick. Instead I called an ambulance. I could've made fava beans with hot peppers and taco sauce, as a final request. I would've done something if he'd asked. I would've *gladly* brought all his sickening paintings to the hospital, if he wanted . . . maybe even mount the portrait of my mother across from his bed. He didn't even ask the doctor what the hell was going on. Neither did I. My uncle took over. Does he own a newspaper? I thought he was in real estate. Maybe he runs a chain of family restaurants. Do they have a spoon-feeding service? Only for total weirdos and I don't qualify . . . yet. Is that what everyone's looking at lately, waiting for me to become a hermit recluse again before their very eyes? Did they think I was going to do something for them to stand around and gape at when Harlan shouted, *Connie is that contract signed? Last chance tomorrow!* Everyone stared. I saw what the dead man couldn't—everyone's eyes on him, open to the public. I *tried* to sign, remember? Didn't you remember? You wouldn't let me sign it. What were you talking about? That damn contract—give it to me then. I'll sign it! No one thought it was strange at all that I stood on the smoky stage and took pictures of the fire—no one even knew I was there. I thought *you* did! Why are you staring *now?* What're you trying to do—see into the lens to how the camera works? Watch the shutter open and close? Harlan, *please* . . . I don't even remember what I'm trying to tell you . . . you remember me being there, don't you? Do *you* think something's wrong with me too?

•

I'm glad we're in makeup today—everyone's facing a mirror. I do my own face, quickly, barely looking, change into costume, wait in the wings. Everyone's too busy preening and stretching—no one saying, *What's wrong with your contract, Connie? They trying to rip you off? What're you asking for anyway? Isn't a non-speaking role a standard minimum? What's wrong with you?* Maybe they've found something else to talk about today.

As I exit after my first scene, Harlan yells, "Connie, slow down, you're supposed to be leaving *with* Randy, what's the matter with you?"

"Maybe he's not her type," someone says. They all laugh.

Luckily they get stuck in some solo numbers. The understudy's voice is thin, doesn't blend well with Eric No-Name. The orchestra's too loud. I have a long lunch break, but the secretary in the office says I'll have to come back after rehearsal because Harlan's got my contract and she doesn't want to dig through his stuff.

They're both occupied with the phone—Harlan listening and writing, and Windrem dialing. I'm relieved to rest beside Harlan in the chair, fix my eyes on the near corner of his desk. A rough climb up here. When Harlan finally says a few words—thank you, see you next week, goodbye—Windrem still has made no connection. But he hangs up at the same time. Maybe I slipped in like a ghost to sit in this chair and no one noticed. That would also be a relief. At least after Harlan shouted in rehearsal, and they all laughed, I was in the wings on the other side of the stage, and they might've even forgotten what was so funny. Just like the dent on my car—other people never think about it, so why should I?

My contract is right here on his desk where I can see it while I wait for him to hand it to me. It's different than the last time I saw it . . . when was that, before the fire? Now: non-speaking extra plus a clause about PR photography—all photos to remain property of the company and its producers. No, he knows I won't sign this. My photos are my photos, period.

After his usual drag on the cigarette, the usual swallow of coffee immediately afterwards—his mouth might taste like the muddy dregs left in the cup where he dunks live butts—Windrem says, "You know, some asshole cast or crew member told someone else that I was out to finish Margie Dean off so she'd never work again."

"What—?" Harlan sounds sleepy.

"Yeah. Something like that. I got two calls from cast members at home last night, and I'm damn mad about it. That kinda stuff really burns me. I'm gonna find the person who started this one and get rid of 'em."

I blink and leave my lids down, look straight down the front of my shirt to the floor.

"What would prompt anyone to start something like that?" Harlan asks.

"That's what I'd like to know. I'm burned and I'm going to find the person and get rid of 'em. I'm sick of it. Of course it's all screwed up—taken from a private conversation between you and me, something about me destroying her contract to deny any responsibility the company ever had for her. Bullshit, and when I find the person who took that conversation outta here—do you have any idea who it would be?"

Although I haven't moved, haven't breathed a breath that could be heard, haven't thought an outrageous word, Harlan puts his back against his padded chair and flashes at me with his eyes. Practically points.

"No . . . ," he says. "I don't remember who was here when we talked about that."

All he has to do now is think. I close my eyes, waiting.

"Neither do I . . . too many people in and out of this place right before rehearsal. I'm going to make it off limits." He drags, sips, breathes the smoke out of a pursed mouth. "You hear the cast talking about this, Connie? Know anything about it?"

My eyes are raised but not my head. "No, I—"

"This happened to me once before in another production, some jerk was at the door when I mentioned we couldn't afford something or other and he went down to the stage to announce that the company was broke." He's still looking at me, but with flat eyes.

"I didn't hear any of them talking about it."

Harlan's mouth makes no move to smile or frown or be anything more spectacular than a mouth. In fact, there's no line anywhere giving out any information, not even on his forehead because his brows aren't drawn down over his eyes, which are, after all, just eyes. No muscle on his face has to support an expression for someone else to see. He's not the lead in *this* scene—but am I?

"Why doncha ask the people who called you," I say, but don't look any more at Harlan. All they need is half a memory.

"I will. I doubt if— Well, I'm going to find the one. I'm really burned." He talks the smoke out of his lungs. "Oh, Connie, you forgot to take this check for your cello again when you were here yesterday."

It doesn't even click. All he had to do was think.

Harlan's palm with two quarters is face-up on his desk beside my elbow. "Want some coffee?" His voice is low. "I'll buy if you'll fly."

I don't look up or turn around to face him. Head down, hair all around, I see only his hand, a little bit of the desk, not even much of myself. "No thanks."

"Will you still fly?"

I take one of the quarters out and his palm closes on the other and draws away. All he had to do was think. I sneak a glance at his face, to see if he's thinking.

Reading a letter, Windrem doesn't flinch as I leave to buy coffee. But I don't know where. There's no vending machine in the building and no other coffee maker except the one already full in the office where we were when he asked me to go out and buy coffee.

Click.

But I don't turn around. All the way to the taco stand on the corner where the coffee cup is so thin I have to hold it by the lip to keep from burning myself. Either this coffee or Windrem will get a little cooler before I return.

Or both. Windrem is gone. I set Harlan's coffee down next to his own steaming mug and sit in Windrem's chair. We face each other. He watches me while he pours from the paper cup into his mug. And watches me over the rim as he drinks. I blow out a tremendous sigh. He was probably, after all, thinking.

"You know, this stuff with Margie and all the rest doesn't surprise me," he says.

"It doesn't?"

"No. I tried to tell Windrem, it's really nothing to worry about unless he *makes* it that way."

"Oh."

Harlan moves with staged casualness. He picks up a ruler, stands, walks around his desk, sits or leans there against the front edge, legs straight to the floor, his feet beneath the chair I'm in. With the ruler he fans the air, blurry-fast like a propeller, and lets it hover over my leg.

"Do you think this would leave a welt?"

"Do you think I deserve a welt?"

His mouth says, *no*, without a voice. Then, "Do you remember who was here when Windrem and I spoke about Margie?"

"You know who was here."

Maybe my lower lip has begun to swell. It's throbbing, and he says, "Don't sulk. You know what you need to do, I think."

"Well. . . ." I bat my eyes to clear the haze.

"Connie, I don't think you belong here."

"You told me to come up here today."

"I mean in the theater, in the company. You're fine on stage, it's not that . . . and it's not your moonlighting as a photographer either, although that can be . . . distracting. There's a lot of gossip in theater companies, and this one is no exception. I'm not surprised at *what* I hear—but it *does* surprise me that a good deal of it is about or related to you. That's what tells me you probably don't belong here. If they think you know something about . . . management . . . , they'll try to find out."

I've never heard fluorescent lights buzz so loud, like a hoard of bugs—bees or wasps or grasshoppers. . . . I can't think. What did he say? That I'm a strange girl? No, that was Peters . . . did he slip it into an article on the gossip page? Is Harlan still looking at me? My eyes are shut.

"So maybe," he says like a voice in the background, "we're gonna hafta stop filling the air with psychological admonishments and start beating some people up."

Like the first sigh of wind which will become a blizzard, it must be him moving toward me, hooking an elbow around my neck, tightening and pulling me up from the chair, yanking me backward against his hip, his knee against the back of my legs, making me unable to stand on my own, holding me off the floor, my arms flail, but while I am still unbalanced, his words blow into my ear, "Tell what you know about this, Connie. Then quit." I'm spinning . . . sitting back down, probably while he returns to his own chair, his desk between us again.

Did any of that really just happen?

His face shadow-dark, he sits with bright eyes and watches me like a movie. Screen actors should be able to look out and see themselves being watched like this.

"Do you want your contract?"

"Yes."

He sighs, opens his top drawer, then slides the paper across the desk to me. It's the same one, giving them ownership of my pictures, any pictures I take here. It also says "guaranteed," that word clear amid a blur, and my name . . . at least it's not Constantina, but how could it be, nobody here knows about that. *Connie Zamora.* If I sign Constance, will it still be legal? I take the pen out of my shirt pocket.

"Wait a second." He pulls the contract back. "You know, quitting on your own is better than being fired."

I rub my eyes and discover I didn't take my makeup off after rehearsal.

We walk together to the parking lot. After stopping, he reaches out, but past me, and touches the dent on my car.

"So this is how you destroyed your car."

"Yes. I scratched my car and lived."

His eyes brush my face. Or maybe it's a breeze lifting my hair off my brow. "Barely," he says. "Get some rest, Connie. You look dead."

"That's my makeup."

"No. It's not."

•

Did you and I make an unwritten agreement? If I prove I belong, that I'm as normal as they are, you won't make me quit? Wasn't that it? And when you said, "What do you want, Connie?" I didn't say anything. I was afraid I might cry. Could I ask for a clause to make you stop thinking something's wrong with me? You said, "Maybe you won't need a contract at all. We could just pretend you signed one. Think about that." I understand now . . . you said it was my last chance, didn't you? You shouted it from the loge seats, the echo distorted your voice, but I heard you . . . didn't understand till now, but I heard you . . . Yesterday? I've got to stop understanding what I heard *yesterday* all the time and start getting things as soon as I hear them.

The time when you would've called me a recluse, I always said I was self-sufficient. But what ever happened to my prized independence? I never *wanted* to wake in the morning and see anyone else there, took the last available parking space and let someone else get the ticket, the scratch, the collision. The hard-boiled life. Did I ever really have it? I could've laughed in your face. *Not belong? Me? Who cares!* Could've laughed in a lot of faces. . . . In Windrem's, when he offered me a contract for less pay than his lowliest office clerk and took ownership of my pictures for himself. Why *shouldn't* I quit? Please don't make me! I'm going to try. Look at me, I'm going to not be reclusive, I'm going to be a normal single adult on a beautiful day. Anything strange about this? A photographer without a camera astride a white racing bike. In order to touch the ground I'm stretched to my full height and then some, with the straight brace pole between my legs. Puts me on my toes. Tight blue pedalpushers down to just below my knees, striped knee socks, white windbreaker, white helmet—in case I crash—maybe I look a little outlandish, it's the best my wardrobe could do, but I can play the part, give me another chance, you'll see. I can do it. I got it wrong with Randy, didn't I? I have it clear in my head this time. Ride to the park, meet someone, smile a lot and laugh, use glowworm language and let him be chilled-out or whatever he wants to be . . . whatever he wants to do . . . then say I liked it, thanks, and go home. Do you doubt I can do it? What were my choices? *Tell what you know then quit.* I can't do that. You knew I couldn't—you wouldn't really want me to tell what I know. Do you know what I know? Obviously you knew I wasn't quitting because you said, "Try to fit in and not give anyone else anything to talk about, okay?" And smiled, shaking my hand. That was my other choice, wasn't it? That was my unwritten contract.

I'm all set, helmet on, about to mount and ride off . . . but my tires are flat. Last night when I thought of using my bike—I couldn't sleep until I had a plan—I forgot about the tires. They've been flat for at least a year, maybe two, since I bought the car. Before that I had my father's car—a real tank, hard to park. But I've had the bike even longer, hardly ever went anywhere, never had to fill the tires. They've just gotten old. Randy's are newer—that's why he's never used his handy little pump. But Randy's newer too. Did you know that, Harlan? Almost all of them are younger than me. They don't know. Unless someone told them. But Randy's bike is even younger than he is. It doesn't need to be pumped up. He'll let me borrow the pump.

I'm only going to give him three rings, then hang up. His apartment isn't that big. What if he's in the shower or asleep or. . . . I don't care, three rings, that's all.

"Hello?"

"Randy—you're home."

"I was just leaving."

"Oh, glad I caught you—I need to borrow your hand pump, could I?"

"What for?"

"My bicycle."

"What're you doing with your bicycle?"

"Filling the tires, could I borrow your pump?"

"Well, I'll stop by on my way to dance class and help you."

"I can do it myself."

"That's okay."

His face is bland—bending over the pump, pinching the tight tire, then facing me, helmet under my arm.

"There you are," he says. He leaves first, taking the pump with him, and I watch him go. He doesn't look back. I wanted to be the one to do that. Let him exaggerate *this* story. I hope he does. I don't mind. Just so the next time you hear them talking about me, Harlan, it won't be about someone who doesn't belong.

It is a quick couple of hours to the park, pumping hard, some of it uphill. But I'm no more tired than I was the last few moments in the office yesterday when you and I shook hands over a contract I didn't sign. Cross-legged on a bench at the goldfish pond, I take fleeting glances at people wandering around. Probably much like the parade you have to endure when you're auditioning a show. Do you ever wonder what they're thinking? How they have the audacity to try? But you always have to pick someone out of the mess.

A hissing near my feet. I twist to see the tire swelling, the flesh-colored part getting fatter-and-fatter, growing outside and over the metal rim. I watch and feel the explosion in my face. This isn't part of the plan. I never even got started. I sit and stare . . . what was I thinking before the tire blew up? There's a lump moving slowly down my throat. Someone across the pond screams, probably immediately after the tire burst, a short scream. I reach down and feel the tire, pinch it between thumb and finger, as though it's not obvious enough already that the wheel is settling to the ground, grinding the rim against the sidewalk.

Now what? I'll never get home. Not without help. But who can I call? I don't even have my own phone number memorized. I know Randy's, but of course there's no one home in either place. Wait a minute, who was I going to call at *my* house? My mommy hasn't been home longer than I haven't. Leave a message on my call-screening machine? *Constantina, are you there, come help me!* For that matter, what number did I think I was going to give the guy I eventually find here—social security, serial number of my bicycle, the size of tire I need, the recommended number of pounds of air, Randy's phone number? All the numbers I ever knew are jumbled somewhere between one and ten. All of them can be found somewhere on any camera—I used to know what F-stop and speed to use just by looking at the scene . . . I could still do that, like today—F-11 at 250 straight in front of me, but to my right it's more like F-8 at 125. . . . You and I shook hands over many unsigned numbers yesterday . . . what was it we agreed about?

And I don't have any money to make a phone call anyway. Not a quarter with me. Not two cents.

Yesterday you told me getting paid in cash would be easier if I wanted, and I didn't even put a quarter in the slit pocket of my air-tight pedalpushers.

Helmet under one arm, I lead the lame bike along the sidewalks. The metal grinds. The rubber squishes. I've stopped counting the number of people I've passed who don't notice the flopping tire. Would you have noticed the dent in my car if I hadn't told you? Would you have thought there was anything wrong with me if they hadn't talked about me? Just by looking at me? Staring at me? Would you have come to the same conclusion anyway?

I can't call Randy. Still no quarter. But his dance class isn't too far away. This isn't the story I wanted you to hear, Harlan, not what I wanted you to see—that he found me coinless on the street outside the delicatessen when his dance class was over. One glance at me, "You're not *crying*, are you?" He would think I'm ashamed. But . . . am I ashamed of anything? I'm not ashamed that yesterday I couldn't tell what I know then quit, but maybe should be ashamed I therefore agreed to consider taking cash out of Harlan's pocket instead of a contract. A secret contract . . . it *should* be easier, like no one knowing I'm even there. Contract for a recluse. But a clause said to look like I fit in. I'm confused now. You looked at me like a father and shook my hand.

I am down by the shuffleboard and horseshoe places, where the harmless old men play. And there are three old ladies on a bench, their backs to me—I'm behind the tree which shades their heads and silver hair. When they turn, feeling me there, I pretend to be watching the skill of their men on the courts. Pretty soon I know I've watched them too long to ask. A guy with a backpack passes me, but before I can ask him, he says, "Did you know that helmets can cause a broken neck if you have an accident?" He exposes a mouthful of broken-off teeth. Not just chipped—broken to the nubs.

"What were you wearing when *you* fell?"

I can nearly see you shut your eyes and shake your head as you hear about this. I know, I know . . . *nice going, Constance.*

But nothing happens. Was it my last chance to have something happen? Maybe it would've been even better—what you said I *needed*—if what happened today was to get beat-up and *my* teeth broken off. . . . I could've smiled, showing the nubs, proving there's nothing wrong with me anymore, so probably no one would look twice, like the dent on my car that every repair shop says no one will notice.

On Sixth Street, the border between the park and the beginning of downtown, Mr. and Mrs. Tourist, an instamatic in her hands, but that's okay, and luckier still, one of them speaks first: "Are you a bike racer?"

Is everyone blind? I say, No—but if I were I wouldn't go far today, and point to the tire, tell them I have no money, and a quarter flashes in his palm. I remember your palm with a quarter—two of them—yesterday. You got rid of Windrem when I left, didn't you?

Quarter in hand, I leave the park on a street which turns off Sixth and heads downtown. I stay on the curb, keep my bike in the gutter. When the metal rim rolls on the cement, my joints hurt. Mostly, though, the tire rubber is on the outside of the rim. It's a horrible slit.

I prop the bike against the newspaper stands outside the first corner liquor store I come to. What if he's not home? But he answers after two rings.

"Oh. You're home. Didn't you go to dance class?"

"About four hours ago. What's up?"

He's smiling and doesn't understand how my tire popping like that could be such a crisis. He arrives quickly after I called, but our roles are confused, pages cut from different shows, or two players without show sense—neither player knows what lines the other will have, so we divide the purpose of the scene: He as a man bringing home his tangle-haired skinned-kneed sister; me out cruising, proving something . . . proving nothing. . . . And for the people on the sidewalk, the audience, even you, Harlan—if you were actually seeing it rather than hearing and believing dressing-room and backstage stories—another show altogether. Randy crouches to examine the tire and I stand over him, not watching his hands but the back of his head, his soft brown neck and fine hair and a new tender-white crescent line of skin exposed by a fresh haircut. Did you find it, Harlan? You could have flipped back and shown me—as you used to in early rehearsals—and described the purpose of the scene, told me that what I forgot was the character's original motive, then started the action at the beginning again. I don't care about them, but I didn't want *you* to have the wrong idea.

Our shadows are long in my driveway; they flow in front, ripple up and over the back of my car, the back windshield, the roof.

I stop here while Randy goes on past to put my bike in the garage. On his way out, up the driveway to his little car which brought us here, he says, without stopping, "You're sure blowing this out of proportion. Aren't you going to go inside?"

When he's gone, I embrace my car. With lips up against the hot metal and my fingers tracing that concave place, I say, actually out loud, You're not going to stay shiny new, but will still function. You have to. You're just more careful next time.

VIII

A One Way Street, No-Stopping-Anytime, No Merging Traffic

• • •

On the map the tour is a one-way loop, all the way to Canada and back, never going south on the same road used previously to go north. And it's not quite first-class—by bus. Harlan says we won't see him much—he and Windrem go in a luxury sedan—just at the shows and in the hotels, sometimes, if they're not somewhere else. The costumes, props and sets also travel alone, arrive at each theater before we do, looking a little more worn-out each time, a little more flimsy.

We're supposed to get to each hotel at around three or four after an all-day drive, eat and shower, then off to the theater. But that's only the way it's planned. When we run behind, we bus straight to the theater, into makeup, onto the stage. This sort of thing blends until each performance is like having the same dream every night. We arrive lethargic and out-of-phase, and likewise also receive luke-warm appreciation from the audiences. If Windrem growls in Harlan's ear about it all day in the car, I have no way of knowing or finding out—this time the photographer really *isn't* there—which somehow feels even worse than actually seeing Harlan sit like a statue, not doing *any*thing to shut him up. Especially the day—yesterday or the one before—when a portion of the road was closed and the detour long and twisty so my stomach soured with dizzy worry that for sure we had lost Harlan forever. By the time the car zipped past and I saw his palm flash and his amused smile that showed no teeth—my relief was near agony, like puking, and I shut my eyes against a pillow and cried silently with sea-sickness. So I've acquired yellow pills that hand me over to a dumb stupor from departure at seven until the lunch stop. My head rolls back, my limbs float deliriously in warm liquid. I stagger from dream to dream, bus to show. Sometimes I am somewhat awake all afternoon and watch the intensity come into Randy's eyes as the distance between bus and theater shortens. That's about as close as I get to having any show-concentration, even though I know thinking about the show is what I'm supposed to be doing, not sitting here picturing the way Harlan will fix his eyes over the steering wheel, opaque and expressionless, as Windrem chews on his ear about sloppy performances.

Of course *after* the show, in thick evenings, when allowed to be together, cast, crew and brass swill beer and grow blurry together under yellow bar lights in Monterey or Redding. By now, this is all so almost normal.

Normal—yes, I must be on the right track now. Never the center of attention. How could a non-speaking character ever upstage the stars, the lead dancers and singers, the comics, clamoring and competing all day on the bus to top each other? I blend in now. I have someone in the seat beside me. And I have a contract . . . if anyone asks I can verify that I reached an agreement with management. They won't ask to see the document that doesn't exist. Who can tell which beat-up old car on the freeway at rush hour is the one without official registration, the one whose owner lost the pink slip, the stolen one. . . . I like to drive at night because I *know* no one can see into my car windows—

can't tell if I'm singing along with the radio, scratching my ear, talking to myself, crying, or staring at people on the sidewalk as I pass.

The bus stops at gas stations, but seldom to fill up. It's so the cast can empty their tiny bladders. Lines form outside the restrooms. I need water for my afternoon pill. The drinking fountain is between the two lines standing outside the continually flushing toilets. The water tastes faintly of beer . . . maybe it's rust. The doors on either side of me creak open and slam shut. "Hey, Connie!" Someone grabs my arm, jerking me away from the water, making the pill go down even more quickly. . . . Galvin, grinning, walking away from the crowd around the restroom. And I'm following him.

"Enjoying the tour, Connie?"

"Huh?"

He laughs, stops at an incredibly dusty red car, his briefcase in the back seat, a suit bag hanging over one rear door window. "Haven't seen you for a while," he says. "I expected you to at least toss a timid hello into the pit as you pass."

"It's been hectic, hasn't it."

Just a chuckle this time. "I thought you'd be interested in the last stuff I found out."

"Why should I?"

"C'mon, Connie, those were pretty good photographs, but you didn't give them to the newspaper just because you needed ninety dollars!"

"I haven't even cashed that check yet." Also the one Harlan gave me—it's clipped to my negative drying line. "You moonlighting for the IRS? Don't worry, I'll declare it."

"Hold it, Connie, I didn't go there to check up on *you*—you know that. I called all the people I could think of in the East, so I thought I'd find the reporter who came to the big announcement to see if he'd done any background research."

"Had he?"

"No. I don't think so. He was too busy to talk to me, so he directed me to the guy who bought your pictures. I asked him a few questions, found out he knew less than I did, and I left." Galvin unlocks his car, takes off his windbreaker and tosses it in the back seat. "Anyway, it's not much, but a lot of people seemed to think there was a girl . . . a story about Harlan suspending a production and holing-up with some girl until the show had to fold out of lack of interest, just die or whatever." He sprays his windshield and starts wiping it off. "Windrem had something to do with that show too—lost money or something."

"It can't be true!" I'm holding Galvin's arm—the one that was wiping the windshield with dirty paper towels. "I mean, if so, why would Windrem want him again for *this* show?" I let go of his arm and he sprays the window again. The bus honks. Randy leans out the window and shouts something.

"Who knows? But I don't care anymore. I think I was expecting too much. Nothing I found out is important enough, and it's too expensive to keep asking—leave that job for the spies, secret agents, reporters and talk-show researchers." Again the grin. "I still don't understand why *you* want to hang around this third-class production."

"I'll bet it doesn't keep you up nights, wondering." I turn and hurry back to the water fountain and get another pill down before returning to the bus.

Randy is comfortable. He sits by the window where he has propped a pillow against the glass. His corduroy shirt smells clean and is soft even though I often wake with patterns pressed into my cheek. The bus hasn't started moving yet. I wasn't the last one they were waiting for. A few women shout something at Galvin's car as he drives past the bus. He waves. I can see the back of his head for a second, then he's already on the road, in line at a stop-light, waiting to get back on the freeway, and I can't see *him*, just his car.

"He's smart," Randy says.

"Huh? Why d'ya say so?"

"Driving alone instead of being stuffed in the back seat of Windrem's car."

"Randy, have you heard anything about Harlan and a girl?"

He stares at me. I think I'm not talking very well or very fast—each word seems to come out by itself. The bus shifts gears and starts moving. Someone jumps on late just before the doors close. Randy glances up, over my head, as the late person goes down the aisle. Then his mouth moves.

"Huh?"

He laughs. I think that's him laughing. Also his voice says, "Go back to sleep, I'll talk to you later," laughing . . . I can hear him smile. He gently pushes my head back against the seat and over against his shoulder. I wish he would leave his fingers on my face for a few moments more. But he doesn't. I can hear him humming. I feel it. I don't recognize any melody. . . .

At least I know I'm always awake during the show . . . standing so motionless backstage for so long. I stand—or sometimes squat—in the wings, then abruptly realize I've been staring out at the show as though I've never seen it a thousand times before. But in a way I haven't seen any of it. I'll be awake all night, I know, unless I take another pill when I get back to the hotel, but first the bus will take us somewhere to eat. Randy says, "Just a sec.," and goes to the back of the bus, but doesn't return to his seat before we pull into a parking lot near a pizza parlor, and I've already joined the thick current of bodies moving down the aisle to get off the bus. Where are we, Oregon? Sometime this afternoon the bus stopped for an hour to get a permit to use the highways. Do we have a permit to invade this pizza parlor, laughing, shouting, singing, talking as though delivering monologues, most of us—not me—still in makeup? Men in red coats keep checking identification, staring at licenses, rubbing thumbs over photos in disbelief.

When the bus arrived, Harlan had already been here long enough, with a pitcher of clear yellow beer, so that maybe the stone-faced audience, in a hurry to get home, doesn't matter to him too much anymore. And in a little while it's even funny. "I know what you're doing," he says to the rapt attention of mostly leading players clustered around him at his long table. "You're not in love with the show. You've got to play the show like it's your sex lives . . . or maybe you *have* been, and what's going wrong *is* your sex lives!" He stands and climbs out of his place in the middle of the bench, walks down to refill his mug at another pitcher near the other end of the table, tugs my sweater as he passes. "Connie," he says.

By the time I manage to work my way out of the crowded table and bench, Harlan is already alone at a corner booth. For a moment I just stand beside the table. We haven't spoken, really, since our last negotiation. He takes the cord of my sweater in both hands. Looking down, feeling the material with his thumbs, his brown hair is very straight and is only one color brown without any woodgrain of blond ash or deep mahogany. "How're you fixed for money?" he asks.

"Money? Fine."

"Oh. I hoped so." He holds the cord by the end—straight out—with one hand, pinches it in the middle with the other hand, between thumb and fingers, then slips his hand up and down the taut line. "Because I don't know if . . . I don't know *when* you'll get paid. I'll get it for you somehow, but I'm a little strapped now."

"Huh?"

"I don't know why I'm telling you." He looks up finally.

"It doesn't matter. *He* can pay me when we get home. I'll tell him, now I've done the show so he'll have to pay me something."

"No. Listen, Connie. You're not listening." I watch his hand sliding up and down my sweater cord, which feels like a lasso around my waist now, pulling tighter, tugging me closer. Then he keeps holding the cord with one hand and lifts his mug to his lips with the other. Looks at me over the rim. I might be sinking to the floor, but move—not quickly, it's all so blurry—around the table and slide into the booth on the bench opposite him, his hand and my sweater-cord under the table, still joined.

"What's he gonna pay you? And when?"

"Well . . . I have other sources for money. Money's not a problem, you know. I can always sell photos—"

"No, that's not the point. And forget those pictures." My sweater cord tugs slightly. "I wish you had quit before the tour."

"I couldn't."

"I don't understand why."

"Maybe I don't either, but it doesn't matter."

"Yes . . . it does . . . maybe it shouldn't, but it does." He drops his lashes and seems to look into the beer as he drinks. His throat moves, then he puts the glass down half empty. He drinks so quietly.

"I never do anything just for money. I mean, money isn't the first reason, or the second . . . ever. I just always figure I'll get paid before I go broke." I notice his neck is damp. "I'm not going to let Windrem get away with anything. *Anything.*"

"Don't play against him, Connie."

Constance. "He can't hurt me. I never told you about the other pictures I have—"

"Don't tell me." This time he drinks with his eyes closed tight. Wipes his mouth with the back of his hand, no longer holding my sweater cord. I have to lean forward to hear him because he won't raise his eyes. "It's over, behind us, let's leave it that way." His voice is rough in his throat, but not a whisper—squeezed tight by the muscles I can see working up and down from here. "Believe me, I don't need any more publicity."

"But you don't—"

"Connie, leave it." He lifts his chin, his eyes clear as the beer. "Probably everyone's blowing everything out of proportion. Me too." He inhales and sits up straighter. "All I was going to do is warn you that you may not get paid for a while. I'll take care of it somehow, but I don't know when. I'm talking too much, though. I'm trying to tell you without telling you, but I'm not getting through to you, am I?"

"I guess not."

"I don't know what's wrong with me. . . ." He smiles. "You know, this is what a tour does, as soon as we're hardly fifty miles from home, everything gets . . . out of proportion. Know what I mean? There's no every-day reality to keep things grounded." He wipes the water off the outside of his mug with the back of one finger. Turns the glass, then wipes more water away. "Some things that should be important can shrink away to nothing. Troubles at home . . . it's like they're not even there anymore. Other things . . . minor, stupid things . . . they get blown up, huge and looming and you can't get them out of your mind. The way insomnia makes everything seem out of control. That's what a tour does. What I'm saying, I guess," he watches himself finish wiping the condensation off his beer glass, "is that it shouldn't bother me, but it does. Is it only me?" He looks up, smiling again, "Can other people really feel perfectly normal, even happy on a tour?"

"They seem to be, don't they?"

"Connie, listen, because I'll probably only say this once." His foot touches mine under the table, then moves away. "It was a small thing, just one minor publicity maneuver, you knew this, to promote the idea of the Opportunity Players. But the idea—*his* idea—was to get the publicity and move *on*. We could say we had to streamline the play and cut your part completely out. We *added* that part just for the publicity, it wasn't in the script, so it could easily be cut. That first contract you never signed, it was phony, just to go along with the publicity gimmick. Only the leads have personally negotiated contracts, only the leads are union. That *phony* contract said nothing was guaranteed and the part could be removed any time without warning. We would've already gotten the publicity stills, so you'd be gone, paid for what you'd done then let go, before tour."

"That didn't happen."

"No." He drinks. Thinks. Looks at me when he's through. Smiles. "Because you didn't do publicity stills, you did something else. But without a contract at all, it still would've been easy enough to cut the part out and let you go. Except after the fire publicity . . . it would look like we had something to hide if you were fired. Also, in case you had any more photos, he wanted to make sure you couldn't release them. So he decided to get you to sign a contract that gave him control of your photos and let you finish the show just to secure that clause. You figured that out, didn't you?"

"I didn't like it but I didn't know *why* he wanted to own them."

"Just think, Connie, we've dragged you along on this tour, someone who might know. . . ."

"Let me tell you what I know."

"No." He picks up his glass again, forgetting, I guess, that it's already empty. "We dragged you along on this tour purely for the sake of image. And here you are, away from home, alone. . . ."

"I'm not alone."

"Yes you are. You always seem alone, I don't know why." He laughs softly. "Instead of all this being over quickly for you—a quick two-week job in the theater—here you are, for everyone's sake but your own. But I just wanted you to know why I didn't want you to sign that contract. It was more important that you have the freedom to leave. I wanted leaving to be *your* idea. You could just go away and forget. The little publicity trick we used you for was cheap, I agree, but wouldn't've hurt anyone. But then . . . well, I've said all this. I'm saying too much. You can still walk out, you know. I won't hold you to any handshake agreement. I'd buy you a bus ticket home right now if you wanted. How else can I get out of this funk? Do I just feel guilty about what we're doing?"

"What do you want me to do?"

"Nothing. I guess. Go home, but I don't think you'll do that. Maybe I can warn you about this, though—although, again, don't get this all out of proportion—but if the cast finds out that what they read about you in the paper wasn't true, that you're what they call a trust-fund dilettante, that you worked for management—for publicity, nothing more—and potentially took work away from some aspiring young thing, one of their own, they'll want to kick your butt."

"Huh? I've made friends with them."

"Don't play dumb, Connie." His foot touches me under the table again. He looks at his empty beer mug. The foam on the inside is slowly moving toward the bottom, leaving a crust on the glass. "This isn't a union production, but actors can always pretend—pretending to be like the big boys, playing grown-up . . . the contracted stars pretending they don't know everyone else is bush league, but they'd *all* make a big show of solidarity against a management shill, if that's what they perceived you to be. Pretending, but dead serious. They may seem to befriend you, sure, and maybe some of it's even genuine, who'm I to say it isn't? But you're a prime candidate to know something they don't know . . . because of the rumors floating around about management, which only causes more rumors. The whole thing snowballs, you know. Why they think they need information, I don't know . . ."

"All I know is—"

"Forget what you know, or what you think you know. Let's just get through this, okay? Let's just get through each day and finish the show and then it'll be *over*, the show, the tour, everything else, okay?"

"Am I too drunk to know what we're talking about, or if we're both *not* talking about the same thing?"

His mouth tightens on one side, and he nods, then he laughs and reaches across the table and takes hold of my face, his hand under my jaw, fingers pushing into my cheeks, holding me like a grappled fish. But gently. "Or I am," he says, laughing. "Or both of us are. God, I hope so!"

I think, when he lets go, my head will fall to the tabletop. But it doesn't.

•

I already took a pill, an hour ago, drinking from the abstract-art fountain which I never would have found if not for the sign—DRINKING WATER—bolted to the pastel wall above it in the art deco lobby of the hotel. I don't remember where we are. Or were. It's light out now, makeup washed away, not another performance for twelve hours. But everything is still unnatural: the air-conditioned interior of the bus; the rough crushed velour of the seat; the diesel engine pushing us forward, holding us together; the bright sunlight on the lines on the pavement flashing outside the window. I'm covered with a thin blue flannel blanket, usually stored with all the other thin blankets in the overhead compartments during the day, taken down only at night. But I took mine into my room with me, and still had it bundled in my arms when I boarded this morning. My skirt is imitation wool. A dress code, so no pants. My nylon slip is full of static electricity, bunched up and clinging to my upper thighs. My pantyhose is slightly twisted. My bra is too tight. I can hear Randy breathing. Soon I'll only hear myself breathing. As though I'm someone else too. When the pill works. Soon. Soon . . . everything will be natural . . . warm . . . languid . . . sleepy . . . loose . . . coming in waves . . . I'll be someone else . . . what's her name again . . . ? Her limp body making the numbered, mechanical seat more comfortable than the solitary darkroom . . . indeed, as wholly comfortable as a rumpled bed where *she* lay without moving after he got up, dressed, and left. But her mind has already started to thicken, her joints to loosen, and the heaviness is starting to hold her like cupped hands under the blanket, her hands are deadweight on her lap. Eyes closed. Her hands move down her legs, slowly, find the edge of the skirt, her fingers slip beneath the rough hem to touch the silky tight pantyhose. Then her hands ease back up her legs, up her thighs, bunching the skirt up higher, slowly . . . slowly . . . slowly is the only way she can move . . . finds the elastic top of the pantyhose and the elastic of her underwear, slips one finger, then two, then her whole hand inside. Both hands inside, pressing her palms into the skin on her stomach which feels much different than the shiny nylon covering her legs. Warmer . . . more supple . . . slightly damp. . . . Her hands begin to move back down her legs, keeping the pantyhose elastic on her knuckles . . . pause . . . a supreme effort, in the dark, feels like she's shaking the whole bus, bouncing everyone out of their seats. Her eyes open a crack to see that the blanket covering her body barely moves as she lifts her butt off the seat, pushing the pantyhose down past her hips. Pauses, panting, her thumbs resting lightly in the soft spot where her legs meet her body, sometimes a nervous spot, a jumpy sensitive spot. She can feel her sleeping heartbeat right there. The guy beside her shifts slightly . . . Randy . . . a breeze from the pages of his newspaper. One leg at a time, she bends her knees until she can reach her foot, under the blanket, slips her boot off, peels the pantyhose and underwear all the way off . . . reaches behind her back to release the snaps of the bra which then falls like an untied ribbon around her waist . . . Still feeling that breeze. She opens her eyes. Her entire left leg is uncovered, thigh to ankle. Puts it back under the blanket, back into darkness, and finishes pushing the wadded up nylons and underwear between her hip and the edge of her seat. Finally, she can shut her eyes again . . . breathe deeper . . . settle her limp, drugged, unrestrained body back into the seat. . . . And her hands return to her legs, under the blanket, under her skirt, fingers moving up her thighs, grazing her drowsy skin, feeling her pulse again, thick, slow. . . .

Something shifts and I almost fall over. I guess I was leaning on him. He just moved a little. Sitting close like this on a bus, you see the other person's legs and knees and feet, a little of his shirt, but hard to turn to see his face, with him so much higher than me. I can see his wrists, his hands clasped in his lap.

"Hey, Connie, you awake?"

"Yeah."

"I meant to ask you, what did Harlan want last night? He was pretty well plastered, you know. What was he talking to you about for so long?"

"I don't know. Lately, it seems, I have these conversations with people without knowing most of the way through what we're talking about."

"But there must've been a *reason.*"

"Oh, I don't remember. Something about how tours make him depressed and cause all his problems to seem bigger than life."

"I heard he's having trouble at home, you know, with his wife."

"But he's upset . . . about me, I think. Having me along is . . . an . . . an added complication, I guess. I guess . . . I guess . . . because . . . because of some pretend union . . . or phony contract . . . something about money . . . paying me cash. . . ."

I'm slipping in this unyielding bus seat, sinking, trying to hold myself up with my palms pushing down into the seat beside each leg, but still keep slipping, sinking, until I'm leaning against him again. My pulse thumps in my middle ear where my balance is . . . or *was* . . . Now, in transit, that's where I'm out-of-whack, out-of-phase, whirling off-balance. . . . I feel him staring at me.

"What? Wait, Connie, don't go back to sleep yet. Go on with what you were saying."

"About what?"

"The union . . . paying you in cash. . . ."

"Oh, that. God it sounds silly . . . doesn't it? Playing house . . . then playing doctor . . . then playing union. . . . How fast we grow up. I say, if a union is gonna make you sign a contract that gives away your original work, why sign, why work with a contract, it's better without one, isn't it?"

"You're working for cash, Connie? Why?"

"Maybe it's cheaper, I don't know. Money never meant a hell of a lot to me, but it does to them, I guess. And to you? If getting paid means you're professional, I'm *not*. Who cares? They got the publicity they wanted from me, I'm good for that, so now they also get a free bit-part player who they *wished* they could've fired before anyone found out the whole story wasn't even true. One story wasn't true, but there's another whole story to tell. But let's just finish the show and forget it."

The bus purrs under me, all around me. Conversations fade and what remains loud is that pulse still in my ear, not necessarily mine anymore. . . . I never care that nothing makes sense when my breathing is this heavy and deep, and I know I'm not moving, my eyes closed permanently for several hundred miles—so I'm no longer even seeing the transient light flashing on the other side of my eyelids as trees or buildings flip past the window. Words make no sense, but everything makes perfect sense in my heavy chest and jellied head. Like right now, feeling a heavy shoulder beside my own . . . like warm water surrounding me, no jolt or bump we hit can hurt me. . . . Not a rigid wooden rowboat in choppy seas, but a soft inflatable raft holding me. And I'm not the only one in it. We can be rescued together, Harlan. Abandoned adrift at sea. But not alone. And not seasick. Because the ocean is air. That's where I am. A speck in the middle of the air, exactly in the middle . . . which direction would I fall . . . or is it really *falling* . . . ? Skydivers aren't falling . . . until they drop each other's hands and pull the cord. But there'll be no thin flapping parachute so far above me, dangling me from taut nylon ropes . . . instead feathers by the thousands, and I watch the ground approach, nestled in fleecy down, silky, firm, and not alone. . . . He shifts again and I moan and feathers blow everywhere, explode away from me like a dandelion head, cloud out around me, falling free, just before I hit the ground—

Thunk.

My head in the empty seat beside me. My forehead and nose on the rough carpet upholstery. I can't move. Something heavy in my spine, a fist, a knot, a clotted fracture. My eyes must've flicked open for a second because I saw, up close, the brushed blue-green fabric, but I haven't moved—*can't* move—but still, now, somehow, through my closed eyelids, I think I can see two feet: from the ground, the victim with a broken back watches the rubbernecker who's staring down . . . I can only imagine what Harlan sees looking down at me from way up there. Is my body crooked and horribly contorted, my eyes staring as though I'm dead in the parking lot? I wonder if he knows . . . how soon until he hears . . . that the girl in the cocktail dress is a sleeping-pill addict who couldn't even feel the agony of her back breaking just now. . . . But I do know . . . there's not really any sidewalk sand grinding into abrasions on my face . . . just a vibrating bus and carpet-burns that will become sleep-blushed pressure-spots when I sit up. . . . But if I *could* move . . . if I could reach to touch that ankle I saw there—on the bump of it or just behind the bump, in the tender spot—Harlan may bend to kneel beside me, put his face next to mine, his hand on my numb broken back which is swelling, swelling. . . .

A fade-in of bus conversation. Cranking gears shift like a key change. I stare at the seat back in front of me. Air leaks in around the rattling window, like a cold stare chills slowly. I draw my legs up, knees to my chest.

So I *can* move.

Reach around and take a book out from between my spine and the back of the seat. Randy is gone. I hear him laughing far away, and dice rattling in a cup.

The bus begins a circle, like rotating on its axis, and I'm awake, I know it, because as the bus circles I spin twice as fast. I'd better look out the window at least until we straighten. Must be a freeway-change loop.

We're going across the Columbia River from Astoria, Oregon to Washington. The bridge arches high above the water, then drops halfway across and sits right down on the surface. Something clunks in the bowels of the bus, and a buzzer blinks on the front panel. "Shit," says the driver. People lean sideways to poke their heads into the aisle. I say, "What is it?" I'm not sure to whom, but nobody answers anyway. Maybe I didn't say it. Nobody kneeled down when I touched that ankle either. Or did I ever get to touch it? I disremember waking up. The bus coasts off the bridge and grinds into the gravel on the side of the road.

"What's happening?" I ask, kneeling backwards in my seat. In the back of the bus, everyone bends far too intently over a backgammon board. Doesn't Randy look up slightly? He puts one finger into his mouth then closes his lips down on his finger, points both eyes narrowly on the game.

"Hey Randy . . . ?" Is my voice working? "Where are we . . . ?" He moves a game piece with a wet-tipped finger. "What's going on?" He touches himself behind his ear. Nobody else is even moving. The driver crunches outside on the highway shoulder.

A metal hinge groans. I turn and sit again, facing the glass, cool on my forehead. "Did we break down?" I ask. My words fog the window. Proof I said something.

Through the film on the window, or on my eyes, I see Harlan out there walking around the bus. Where did he come from? Was he maybe the bus driver all along? His gait seems vaguely rigid. I force myself up and out of my warm seat.

Outside, on my own two feet, I seem to be functioning okay.

"Why are you looking so glum?" Harlan asks me. He's on his way back to the car, parked behind the bus, Windrem waiting in the passenger seat. He walks too carefully.

"Because of this."

"This is nothing. Just a mechanical problem."

I don't give a damn about this shitty bus! I know you warned me, maybe I said too much this morning but couldn't stop myself. Well, I don't care, it doesn't change anything . . . maybe this is better, let them ignore me, Really, when the drug wears off, I'll probably love it. I'm a photographer, aren't I? I work best by myself. Now I've got the old hidden camera trick without the clunky disguise. And you and I . . . you and I . . . you can't shut me out because we both know.

"I know." My voice, when I finally find it, is early-morning low. I can't stop staring at him—still noticing that stiffness, even when he talks, almost unnatural, gawky, like the bus wheezing to a halt. "What happened to you?" I hear it like I'm asking from far away, as though he's the one who limped off the road and I pulled up afterwards. He *is* actually broken—one hip is lower than the other, one leg seems rusty, and he's bent to one side.

"My hip went out of joint last night. I don't know how. I didn't sleep too well."

"You're crooked!"

"Yeah, I am." He twists his shoulders one direction and pushes backwards on his hip, wrapping his arms around himself. "It doesn't want to go back."

I nearly smile—the drug doesn't vanish simply by waking—

because I'm sure if I touched him, if I touch that hip with just one finger, or with the uncapped end of my telephoto lens, I would probably cure it.

The actors begin to wander off the bus, shaking and stretching, looking around, sniffing, exploring. They apparently don't see me . . . aren't looking this way. I glance at them, then back at the hip. "Why don't we—" My voice stops as he falls back into the front seat of the car. And Windrem says, "Come on, let's get out of here."

"See you in Canada," Harlan says.

They pull out around the bus and me standing here. Someone yells, "Hey, come back here!" Someone else: "I guess we cramp their style." And I also wonder why he needs to go on ahead, leave us behind, leave me stranded here. . . .

Take my pill jar from my warm pocket. . . . He had to go. Windrem says go and he goes. He doesn't have a choice. So let them look at me and wonder—*who is she . . . what's going on . . . what does she know . . . ?* He left me alone here and the distance between us gets longer every second, but . . . he'll be waiting in Canada. In the meantime. . . . Too much difficulty to get my camera out. Too complicated to try to read. Too much trouble to cry—too much work—until the morning pill wears off . . . but it won't have a chance to wear off now . . . already another pill is acrid in my throat, without using water to get it down. I don't mind—if it's bitter, it means it's really there and will work and I can forget everything else and sit back on the bus and doze and wake and doze again, catching pieces of someone's wedding story. . . . It's already been told over and over the entire tour . . . once while I was part of the smiling audience . . . recited yet again now for someone who missed the beginning, the part about the stubby thick-leaded pencils pushed at them through a window at the county courthouse. Not sure if that was before or after the crying reverend, or if the car broke down going into or out of Vegas, and *she's* not sure, after all, if it was actually official, but she says she doesn't care, in five more years it will be common-law. Love the way she says that—she doesn't care. Likewise I can go back behind my camera. I don't care, as long as Harlan's waiting for me in Canada. I keep thinking about his hip, the way he limps with it.

I loll sideways in the seat and end up face-first, once again, laughing or sobbing into the rough material. How many thousands of hours have I spent alone in my studio, in my darkroom, under a safelight, and did I ever care? I could say it the way the little blond freckled dancer did: *I don't care.* My voice squeaking, laughing, I don't care I don't care I don't care. . . . But if you're going to leave me here, Harlan, I'll need another few shots, to look at and remember the last time I saw you, your face through the window as the car gathered speed, nearly crushed my toes under the tires . . . and I haven't had my camera out in days . . . wait a second, let me go get it, stay where you are . . . *please* . . . stay up there on the ladder. . . . I've often seen that ladder on stage, gingerly placed among the set and props, and a man on top checking the lights. I didn't think it was you, Harlan, way up there, while I've been lingering below, waiting for you to climb down. But have *you* been up there waiting for me, holding a hand down to me as I sling my camera over my shoulder and place my foot slowly on the first rung . . . ? I've had it all backwards, haven't I? Waiting for you to come to me, waiting for the photo to find the photographer. But if I follow you, you'll be there, in Canada or wherever. The ladder can't fall until we're up there together, in the lights, swaying gently before the long slow graceful dive to the ground. You'll catch me or I'll catch you. No one's back will be broken. No one will be crooked or bent or paralyzed. And the camera, with the shutter running by motor, making pictures of us as it falls freely. Pictures of us only we will recognize. Pictures of us we'll never have to see . . . photographs to feel in the pleasant ache of our heaving rib cages, in the boom of our heartbeats . . . not in a darkroom but in the darkness we'll share behind our eyelids. When I get to Canada. When I get to Canada. Or wherever you are.

I sleep in embryonic heat until somewhere around two or three o'clock when the clouds crack along the coast and the sun makes a painful attempt to break the chill. I realize the bus won't be moving for quite some time.

People move up and down the aisle—too cold to sit still. I pull my feet into my seat and look at my former colleagues over my knees. They seem to want to remain candid and therefore never look directly into the photographer's eyes. But each time one turns, and a face goes past in front of mine, it's like they're swinging an arm around, fast, on purpose, and smacking me in the jaw. When you get hit, you know you're really there. Put my forehead down on my knees. I'm completely surrounded—everywhere I look a part of myself blocks the direct light. If the bus restroom were converted into a developing closet or printing lab, would I be a recluse and go crawl into it?

There's only so much to do now that I'm truly—if not fully—awake: get out and look at the hole in the bus where the radiator used to be; watch the road from Astoria to see if the prop truck is coming back with the mechanic; kick a few stones; look at the ocean or river or whatever they call this thing which is sluggish and timid and just pats the rocks on the shore; get back on the bus where it's hard to breathe. Gasp and gulp at the air, like chasing something, falling down in the dirt and sucking up dust, then running again, breathing from the bottom of my lungs, but getting nothing, and getting nowhere. My muscles and blood and airless lungs are still here on the hostile bus, but my heart and head and the eyes inside my eyes finally catch up, five hours up the freeway where Harlan should be keeping one eye on the mirror, waiting for the welcome image of the bumbling bus he left behind.

I play the scene over and over, joining them inside their car—except I leave out Windrem's beady head, so I can say anything I want. I'll be in the back seat, leaning forward behind Harlan's neck. No, I won't whine . . . won't even have to use a voice or words, but can ask: Why did you leave me behind? I can picture the Harlan I'm chasing now, the same Harlan I remember from another day when he was sick and his face pallid and his eyes sunken into his skull, cold-foggy as an unwelcome morning, and he put his hands around the back of his neck, and seemed old with turned-down mouth and sallow complexion. And it was not awfully pretty . . . to anyone but me. Why did you leave me here? Why did you leave? There has to be an answer. Has to.

But there is no sound of his voice in this picture, only the eyes flashing up in the mirror, silent, still blue compared to the dreary sky outside the windshield, but awful grey compared to the color when he has answered other questions, other times.

It was hardly him in the bulky coat, hiding his neck, crunching around on the patches of snow, rocking on a wooden leg like a sailor put in dry dock. His eyes were opaque, like someone else's, not looking at anything, seeing only enough to pull the car out from behind the bus without plowing me under. When I find a photograph in my mind, an image of the way his face opens up while waiting for a question, and the way that question settles into his eyes—like paper hitting water, caressed there a moment, then soaked and turned over and drawn inside so slowly no one knows the last moment it was afloat and the first moment it was beneath the surface—even then he is incomplete and won't answer, won't beckon, won't acknowledge that I asked.

When the costume/prop truck comes back from Astoria, drops off a mechanic, then prepares to leave again, take off for Canada, I climb into the cab and say, "Let's get outta here."

I wish it were a one-way street, no-stopping-anytime, no

merging traffic, so I'd know the bus would never catch up and breathe on me with its headlight eyes. But would that also mean I'd never catch up to Harlan?

By nightfall I doze with my eyes like slits, blocking out the unbroken thick black on either side of the narrow road. No domestic lights are twinkling. No street lights. No other headlights. Where is everyone? And as the truck flies off the lip of each road lump, I nearly expect to see Harlan in the splash of lights, having ditched the car somewhere, standing on the sandy shoulder, hitchhiking, running away, or running *back.* We'll stop, freezing him in the headlights, and I'll jump out—join his melodramatic scene, share the steady spotlight in the center of a black dream. But what do I do next? Question him silently or touch his crooked hip? Maybe both at once . . . reach out and at the same time ask "What now . . . ?" The camera on him from every angle, we begin to move, together we whirl, parallel circles that never cross, one around the other. Good, a blurred background. Indicates action. Now what will I ask him? But before any words come out, there, over my shoulder, my house is on fire. It's not even recognizable. I reach for fresh film—color—because the flames are pretty, red and yellow and blue and orange all mingled up inside. Dark sky, dark ground. I am fumbling in an empty camera bag. Did I leave it inside, in the fire? Sun through my upturned lens sparked my film to flames? Is that how it started? "*Run!*" I don't hear you. Maybe afterwards I'll remember that you yelled, after the sun comes back up. But the fire is louder than you are. My camera is in there. I dodge flames and get past the door. You don't try to stop me. I thrash from side to side, tangled in my sweater, dousing the blaze. There's no smoke from this fire, but everything's as dark as ever. My camera is black, lens-up on a burning bed, fire in a ring—red, yellow, like sunlight, moonlight, stage lights. I have to reach through to touch it, hot, blistering, but whole. I clutch it to me, pressing it to my chest, my stomach, a hot lump against my heart. Treasured photos inside. Photos I save but will never see?

There's nobody up and dressed and waiting for us in the lobby when I slip through the two glass doors at half-past eleven. I have to spell my name for a man at the desk, wishing I could tip my head back, look straight up, through the ceiling. Harlan is somewhere up there, doing what . . . waiting to hear if the bus arrived? The counter man keeps getting the letters screwed-up. Do they spell differently in Canada? Everything's too exact and loud, the way television sounds late at night. And I'm floating across the lobby to the house phone. One ring . . . two. . . . Close my eyes and arch my stiff back. . . . And the thick voice that answers has obviously been asleep.

"Harlan . . . I'm . . . we're finally here."

He says something that sounds remotely like "What?" but more closely like "So what?"

I don't remember closing my eyes nor how much I slept nor if I slept at all, which I never do much after the pills wear off, but I don't remember *not* sleeping either, and finally open my eyes amid a tangle of sheets, neither pillow under my head—one is like an extra mattress beneath my stomach, one on the floor. One thing I do remember as I lay here last night—their noise in the hall when the bus arrived. The ungraceful footsteps. Loud voices. Some angry. Some laughter. Someone was supposed to share my room but didn't. I don't care. I put two yellow pills down and walk out to the bus with my toes dragging.

On the ferryboat to Vancouver Island, waiting to get seasick in the wind and salt spray, I'm standing at the rail near Windrem when he tells some actors—laughing!—how Harlan was hurting yesterday from lack of food, lack of sleep, too much coffee, cancelling the performance in Vancouver, and a lame wheel—

that's what he calls the aching hip. I still must be crazy-sleepy when I finally find Harlan eating in the cafeteria with other laughing actors around him, no doubt filling him in on what he missed yesterday in Astoria. They all look so happy to at last be together. I'm nearly sorry to break into it. I sit behind Harlan until he notices me and turns around.

"I didn't know you were sick yesterday and I forgot about you being hurt. Otherwise I never would've called."

"Perfectly all right. You can call me anytime. I don't mind."

As good an answer as any I could've imagined.

IX

The Audience Isn't Ashamed to Sit and Stare

• • •

We're milling about in the wormy lobby of a downtown hotel in San Francisco. It might've been a nice place once. The gray walls are actually wallpaper that used to have textured, pseudo velvet red scrolls, but now crusty with age, most of the texture has been brushed or scratched off. I scrape off a little more, left untouched in a corner near the public telephone box. It's brown powder in my hands.

How many days has it been . . . ? All the way down from Vancouver Island, waiting for a sign that he even remembers my name. . . . No words addressed to me. I've only heard his voice in dark run-through rehearsals giving terse instructions, have hardly seen him at all, never alone, never relaxed, never without the remote, abstract opaque haze around him.

I've mostly kept my face to the walls. I sign myself into single rooms. Save them the trouble. But I don't know what it's like—avoiding me, I mean. Everywhere I go, *I'm* there too . . . I'm hard for me to avoid.

I return downstairs after piling my bags and camera onto the no-color bedspread in my fourth-floor room. I don't need a camera to go back to being a recluse photographer. I didn't take a pill this morning. My hands are a little shaky, another reason to leave the camera behind. So, grimly awake now, it doesn't matter so much, being an outcast. I get a seat to myself on the bus and a table to myself in crowded coffee shops. Besides, if I'm a photographer, here I am with my subjects perfectly unaware of my presence. This is much better. Perfect, in fact.

"Excuse me." It's Randy, behind me on the shadowy stairs. I flatten my back to the wall of the stairwell to let him pass me. "Connie, I can't explain anything to you with the rest of the cast around. We all know someone in our classes or workshops who desperately needs a part—like yours—to get started. . . . Management as it is would like to own our talent. But when someone who doesn't even care just *gives* it to them for free . . . that hurts *us*."

From here I can see Harlan—in the lobby, giving someone a big hello, opening his coat before wrapping his arms around the person. Then he steps back to speak and I see it's a woman. Looks like an actress but isn't one of these.

I have to look away, wish I could run back up to my room—perhaps to get my camera—but Randy's still standing there, blocking the narrow stairway, looking over my head at Harlan and the girl. The half of his face near the wall is in almost absolute dark. The other half is grey, but dark is caught around his eye, under his cheek, and in the corners of his mouth. He squeezes past me without even brushing against my bulky sweater and joins a group near the front door, glancing back once, not at me, but at Harlan.

Harlan speaks to the girl in his old familiar way with his hands on her shoulders, his face alert and eyes sharp, momentarily his former self . . . without the limp.

I take the last step onto the carpet floor and begin to follow the others following the girl and Harlan out the lobby door and into the street. In the cadence of conversation, I hear someone's voice behind me, "Who *is* she?"

"Jenny Something. I think he worked with her once back east."

"So is this meeting a coincidence or what?"

"Why not ask him?"

"Yeah, sure!"

From behind, Harlan's limp is abstract—his gait obviously wrong somehow, but unless a person already knew, no one could tell where he hurts, what makes him limp. He is lame all over.

It's been like this since the few words he said to me on the Vancouver Island ferry . . . they've surrounded him, guarded him, protected him. That day . . . how many days ago . . . for a moment I faced him in the wind and salt spray. But he looked over my head, far into the colorless sky, saying, "I'm going to shake it off, get the job done . . . then there're those two free days in San Francisco . . ." before he turned without glancing at me and walked away.

Now when he looks around himself on the trolley, past the girl, he and I plug each other with sulky glances.

Are we supposed to be angry at each other? Did something happen while I sat dozing, lobotomized, on the bus, day after day? Did I say something I shouldn't? I haven't even spoken for days, except to order my meals—toast and black coffee. I don't bother to say please anymore. My throat's getting rusty, but, after all, it's just a non-speaking role. Except in that rehearsal a few days ago, a cue-to-cue in Seattle—when he shouted from a dark place out in the house, "Connie, you look like a hag, play your character," and I actually replied, "So dock my paycheck." I wish I could've seen it—not been there and watched it.

What did I want from him when I caught up? I don't know . . . but not this.

I roll off the trolley and wind up seated next to him at a large round table. Jenny on his other side, players and crew fill the remaining chairs. And Harlan, a cripple, smoky-eyed and somewhat quiet, keeps everyone's glasses filled. He pours and I drink, and he fills and I drink again, and his voice dims like incidental music. I don't think he's talking to me. Or is he still glaring at me? No, he's not looking at me now. Maybe I really am invisible. Part of me is still in present tense, remembering how to hold a fork and chew with my mouth closed. The rest wants to wait in the future and watch this happening in the past.

So all along I continued taking yellow pills, continued being rocked by warm lapping waves of sleep, passing then returning, taking everyone else out of the picture, but keeping him there, cutting slices of bus conversations for me to fool with and put together my own way, the difference between sleep and consciousness becoming more and more fuzzy. Did I only imagine propping my elbows on the window ledge and not feeling ill as the horizon slithered sickeningly past the lens?

On my right, Harlan is smilingly wondering why all the wine stains on the tablecloth are near *his* place. He moves around from the waist up—reaching for the wine, the food, turning toward Jenny, turning away—as though there was no sharpness in that hip joint when he bent to sit, as though it's not, even now, stiffening, waiting to trip him when he gets up to walk again.

The trouble is—I realize as we hit the misty air outside—I'm not drunk. If I am, it's not nearly enough, not sloppy-happy like the rest of them. Dancers begin serenading the streets, baying the moon, wooing something—probably each other. Our parade finds another place where we're given a back room of our own, steaks and all the beer we can drink, and I finally find myself with my own dark corner and the familiar shameless vantage point—watching, the way an audience isn't ashamed to sit and stare. Harlan and Jenny, side-by-side, in that unnatural position always used for on-stage interaction, cheating front to keep their faces in the light. The audience gets to see it all by sitting out there alone in the dark, quietly, not participating, easy to ignore. The audience should be a photographer. Or might as well not be there at all.

All this activity buzzes around Harlan. Now and then his hand disappears under the table and a grimace flickers across his face. None of his happy entourage notices, even though he is the center of attention. I wonder what it feels like . . . I mean how his hip feels to him. I pound one of my own hips with a fist, several times, but my hand hurts before I accomplish anything. Does a dislocated hip feel anything like my broken back? Wait . . . was my broken spine real? I remember it so clearly. Slide my fist around behind myself, between the chair and my spine, lean back into it. Yes, like this. A book broke my back while I was asleep, after I fell from something miles high, isn't that what happened? I was flying, I hit without emotion, but I was deadweight even before I landed, and I felt my spine sever, so I *knew* I couldn't move my limbs, couldn't turn my head, open my mouth or squeak out a call for help. I looked down one long arm lying dead beside me, and there beyond my fingertips were his two soft shoes. . . . But I felt my whole life flow down that arm—all my breath and all my blood—and I did lift it, so many pounds, but I lifted it and reached for his ankle. He took a step backwards . . . my arm fell dead again. Isn't that what happened?

The dinners are served and I don't need anything passed to me. I cut my steak into microscopic pieces so I'll hardly need to move my jaw to chew. I'm not hungry. The fork makes too much noise against the dish. Lean back in my seat, still holding the fork, feel the points of it with my other hand, down under the tablecloth.

Harlan also leans back, tilts back, and the ceiling is stretched in front of his eyes, an empty screen, the same screen I stare at on the ceiling of every motel room. Across the table from him, actors urge more beer into each other. On one side someone sets up an imaginary stage—a beer glass as himself and the salt as someone else and a wadded-up napkin as a prop. On his third side—the bent hip side—Jenny can't sit still. First she leans across the table, putting a silly emphasis on what she's saying. Then she is laughing at someone across the room, then answering someone else on her other side. And when she turns to Harlan, she uses her hands, clutching his arm once, and patting his knee. And she lays her head on his shoulder, then quickly removes it. She is lonesome, she says, and wants to go home, away from this cold foggy town where no one knows her.

He turns, finally, with something to say, and begins an almost one-way conversation with her. As he leans sideways I see his acute profile pointing to the center of their conversation, somewhere between them. He holds his end up better, points farther, shoots stronger, so probably the little she does say just drops on the table in front of her. Suddenly he is in focus and no longer frail. I can't hear. But it's easy enough to see that his words soar over her head. His eyes are just as vigorous on what he says, on why he says it, as they are on her, in between words. I did once, not long ago, see his face become soft with drink, tender lines near his eyes and the corners of his mouth. Not now, though. This is almost even better. His eyes have no soft light, are brittle but not breakable . . . different from everyone else in the room. So how can she continue to effervesce like a bubble-machine—he can even make *her* listen hard because his voice, his urgency is all hardness.

I feel like I'm squirming, unable to sit still or find a comfortable position, but my shoulders have been pressed against the back of this chair, it seems, for hours. Maybe it *has* been hours, maybe it's late tonight or maybe it's already tomorrow. But we're going home tomorrow. Are we on our way home yet? We've been on our way home since we left . . . heard Harlan say that to someone who asked *Where're we going?* one morning as we boarded the bus outside a motel. But it certainly doesn't feel like we're on our way home right now. I've plenty of room, even with close to thirty other people in the room, so it's not claustrophobia, but keep wishing I could find a more comfortable position. They're chasing wine with beer, ignoring me, a show unfolding, a blurred plot, something for me to innocently watch. It should be so easy, since no one speaks to me nor I to them and they see only themselves or each other, like a room full of mirrors, none of which holds *my* reflection. Nothing blocks my view, nothing to peek around, my eyes a one-way street, no one at my back, no one to tap me on the shoulder, no one to divert my attention, and naturally no one's attention *I'm* diverting. I've done it before, countless times when I was behind my camera. How is tonight different? His eyes are looking over the empty frothy beer glasses . . . looking at nothing . . . not at me. . . . But Harlan, you *could*, if you wanted, change everything, glance at me for a second, remind me that without a doubt, yes, I am here, tell me that *you* know I'm here. Tell me you know about the photos and what's in them . . . that you know I was there. Tell me what to do with them. His eyes used to be blue—even one night earlier this week, on a writhing bed in a bewildering distorted motel room, with the TV shrieking, its lights flashing, when I lay down alone fully clothed but woke in disarray, legs tied by my underwear, the cord to my discarded sweater still wrapped around my waist . . . never saw anyone with me, yet knew his eyes were blue. But this night is so black-and-white. Does Harlan see anything when, again, his eyes cut the smoke, looking around the room without touching anything, without focusing, without caring?

Standing, I suddenly notice the side-show that has been acted out between tables as people stumble and sway back and forth, back and forth, it should be funny, a great ebbing and flowing, like waves roaring onto the beach, foaming there and giggling on the sand, then drawing away so meekly. Soon there are less of them in the room than are outside, still crashing back and forth on the street somewhere. At the long banquet table. Harlan has one untouched beer which casts amber sparkles through the hundreds of empty mugs. He is alone with Jenny—she's taken his arm, holds his eyes, devours his words, except one last sentence which he finishes straight forward toward me, but I don't hear it. Shocked by his direct look. But his eyes are glazed. Still not seeing me. Then he says, "You have a question on your face."

Jenny leans a little more toward Harlan, pretending to be reaching for a clean napkin on his other side, using the hand that isn't already hooked around his arm. But after she wipes her fingers, she puts that hand on his arm too. He picks up his beer, looking at it. Not drinking. A table between us. More than an arm's length.

"Can you get back to the hotel okay?" It's hard to ask. I had to.

"Yes," he says. "Thank you." Still looking into the beer.

Jenny smiles at him, patting his arm, then looks down, still smiling—smiling at his hand.

I have to go. *Now!* Dodge through the chairs, knock over a few more—so what?—feel for the doorknob, why can't I see? Outside that door there's another dark smoky room, much larger, full of tables and happy people stuffing their faces, damp steam rising from bowls of clams and mussels. I slip a little on a dropped piece of lettuce, grab the back of someone's chair for support. Where's the door? The man in the chair turns and stares at me. I haven't even said excuse-me yet. I've spotted the exit sign. I think the door to the back room is opening, but I get myself outside before I can see if it's Harlan coming out . . . with Jenny . . . or maybe even alone. I don't want to know. I don't know which trolley to take to which bus to get back to the dirty section of town our hotel is in, so I run and walk, run and walk . . . run along the damp shiny-dark sidewalks as though being followed, but the only one that could be chasing me is someone named Constantina, trailing me, trying to catch me, used to be so far away, how has she gotten so much closer?

The hotel is pretty quiet, even the fourth floor where the drunken company has its rooms. I am next to the elevator, so I hear the comings and goings. I leave my door open.

A man, a stranger, comes to wait in the hall for the elevator. He turns toward the open door, stares at me stretched across one bed, and I stare back, a long time, far too long, until the elevator comes. I get up and shut the door and hear the automatic lock click. Still on my feet, leaning, I turn, roll against the wall through the bathroom doorway. The mirror is tarnished at the corners, a little warped, hard to tell if it's clean or not. I watch my hands turn the water off and on. Maybe Harlan noticed my shaky hands today as I reached for something at lunch. With no yellow pill, my thin blood pounded in my veins, and yes, I wobbled but never spilled. In the darker place, that last place, his hand sat on the table, probably for hours, not stirring . . . his left hand, the one on Jenny's side, each knuckle slightly red or pink, not at all knobby. Did she pick it up and lick between the fingers? Or did she pick it up at all? I'm calling his hand "*it*" like a piece of cake or an apple.

Every time the elevator rattles past the bathroom wall, my head jerks up, but once again I am only facing the tarnished mirror. I look at the brown discoloration of the glass, not the reflection. I could take out my camera, use a medium long lens, rest it on the window sill and see the sidewalk. Unless I pan properly, people will flit past too quickly. What good is a camera in a hotel room? The photographer is supposed to be pressing in and out of crowds—at concerts and speeches and games—watching, always watching, and catching everything, without anyone noticing. *That's* how I caught Windrem backstage opening night . . .

but caught Harlan too—seeing what he shouldn't know or knowing what he shouldn't see . . . knowing nothing . . . refusing to know . . . probably not even knowing *he* was exposed too, by mistake . . . paralyzing the photographer's right to prove she was there. *Please* . . . how can I know what to do with those photos?

Finally, voices on the stairs, two at once, then none at all. I jerk the door open and there they are in the dim corridor lamplight—she's ahead on the stairs and Harlan behind, climbing with a limp. There's not a whisper of drug left, however, to suggest I can comfort him by touching him there. I only look at the crooked place where he's joined together, legs and body not knowing where to meet.

"What room am I in?" Harlan asks. I wait. No one else answers.

"The one next to Windrem." My voice.

"What number?"

"Four-O-Eight."

"Thanks. I'm beat. 'Night, girls."

She fades from my view, a blurred-edged scene, and the camera pans on him, watches him turn—almost normally but too slowly—and walk with a silent creak, a little bent to one side, transformed into an old man in three weeks. His hand creeps under his jacket and presses low on his back. Down the hall eight doors. Alone. He takes his aching out of reach.

I don't want to be doing this! Even *in* this dream I hear myself asking: why tonight? *Why now?* I'm too weak or hungry or drunk to fight it. I don't remember any self defense. Too tired to wake, but is this really sleeping? But I ask all my questions and make all my excuses only at the beginning, before anything happens. Am I paralyzed again? Am I asleep or dreaming that I'm asleep or dreaming that I'm awake or not asleep at all . . . or . . . asleep and dreaming that I'm dreaming of being asleep . . . ? I can't move and I know, like impending doom, what's coming—someone in my dark room is going to tip-toe to the beside and scare me. My ears strain to hear the creak of a floorboard or the whisper of his shoes on the frayed carpet. My eyes struggle to see a shadow, a place in the darkness that's more dark than the rest. But my eyes aren't even open. *Don't scare me* . . . that's all I ask . . . tell me when you get to the side of the bed. Tell me when you're going to touch me. Suddenly the waiting is over, no one startled me, nothing made my heart flop like a hooked fish . . . no questions, everything is perfectly natural and relaxed. It's slow motion, no sound, soft colors, low lights—greys and blues—hard to see but I already know what's going on, like a movie I saw only yesterday, or last week, but don't remember actually seeing it, it's just so oddly familiar, nothing surprises me, feeling myself smile as he tickles the insides of my ears with his mouth, sucks gently on each of my closed eyes, bites my lower lip, pulls it out then lets it snap back. I can feel everything he does somewhere in my stomach too, or deeper than my stomach . . . I can feel it, and I can also see it, as though watching from the foot of the bed or sitting on the window sill . . . his tongue, my neck, his hands, my skin . . . the only thing that astonishes me, when I stop to think about it, is that I haven't actually seen his face, can't be sure it's him at all. Can't even be sure it's *me*. No time to wonder about it because suddenly *she* has recovered from paralysis. She can stretch and roll and arch her back and *move* . . . and he is long and smooth and erupts as soon as she touches him, as soon as she strokes him once on the silky underside. She holds him in her hand like a torch, a sparkler fizzing at the end. It throws light onto her face. Makes her look shiny . . . flat and frozen . . . and happy.

Morning comes so early, although I waited most of the night for it. I think I thrashed about—in and out of sleep—until I wake bruised, more tired for having tried to sleep than I ever was before lying down. In dark silence, I whirled and swelled until morning finds me sore. I wake myself moaning.

The elevator seems tired, and makes me sick anyway, so I push myself down the stairs, sit in a linoleum cafeteria. How can anything else surprise me? Harlan brings his coffee and rests his hip on the chair across from me. Every bit of the hard-light intensity I saw last night is gone. It's only me reflected back in his fragile eyes . . . with swollen eyelids and soft blue skin underneath.

He says, "Look how big that donut is."

"Huh?"

"That's what's so neat about being small. You have lots of food. You wanna know what it's like for the rest of us? Buy a hamburger and cut off an inch all the way around the edge. That's what a hamburger looks like to me."

"Oh."

It's quiet, too quiet, and this silence is thin, allowing anything to get through. We look at each other.

He says, "Are donuts carcinogenic?"

"I hope so."

He lifts his coffee mug, puts his mouth on the rim but lowers the mug again before drinking anything. "Tell me," he says. "I may be able to fix it."

"Fix it . . . ?"

"You were up most of the night, weren't you?"

"That hardly seems to matter."

"Something matters."

"I guess so."

We both drop our heads to our coffee, then rise, eyes first. And we each seem to notice at the same time, as we glance away from each other for a moment, that the rest of the company is sitting down and eating, getting up and walking away, paired up, leaning on each other, couples who would never speak to each other off a stage, except on tour.

Harlan says, "Have you had a tour-romance?" His eyes crinkle carefully.

I let the steam of my coffee rise straight into my face, the hot dampness overcoming some of the chill I feel. And I lift my head, slowly, swing toward him, not sure what I'll do next. "Have you?"

He manages to smile again, making the corners of his mouth white. It's a turned-down sort of smile, and I want to cry.

"Have you ever fried an egg?" he asks.

"No. Maybe. Yes, probably."

"Then you know how you can let it get too hard on one side, then you turn it and over-do it on the other side. The cell breaks down, changes composition, corrodes, changes color and gets really ugly."

I nod.

"That's like thinking too much, especially when you haven't slept, you have no resistance. Everything changes color."

I feel my mouth parting, my head moving back, myself falling backwards until I hit against the back of my seat. Want to be angry. But want to be soothed.

Home is only a day away from San Francisco. Didn't he say that *home* was the destination since the first mile of tour? Well, I'm home now, until rehearsals start again for the next tour. Five days with nothing to do but think. Yesterday, five-hundred miles ago, Harlan walked with me from the cafeteria to the parking lot where the bus was already warming up. When I turned away from him to get on the bus, he said, "Wait," then led me over to Windrem's car and asked me to get the state map out for him. I didn't even pause to ask why . . . opened the door and stretched across the seat on my stomach, kneeling on the doorjamb, digging through their ratty pile of unfolded maps.

"I can't find it."

"Okay. I'll get it. Come on out."

I backed out and he leaned in, sitting on his good hip.

"I really wasn't sending you for the map," he said. "I wanted to show you something. Did you notice anything?"

That he was out-of-phase.

That I was just as out-of-phase because it didn't really faze me.

I shrugged.

"Didn't you notice how the inside of the car *smells?* I've already emptied the ash tray five times. I've had to live with this for three weeks."

I ran my finger through the dirt on the hood of the car and shrugged again.

"What does the bus smell like?" he asked.

"People."

But all I could smell right then was the exhaust as the bus idled. The company was getting aboard, the driver snapping down the luggage compartments.

"That's better than this smoke," he smiled, ". . . sometimes." Then he laughed a little to go along with the smile, but I didn't stay to hear any more.

I looked for him at the truck stop where we had lunch, but I guess they stopped somewhere else, and the bus was back at our own theater by early evening. No sign of the car.

Sitting all day, how could I be so tired? Dragged myself from the bus to my car, three trips to get my luggage. But far past midnight I was still awake, went to the bathroom where I'd dumped my clothes and fished around in the pocket of the jeans I'd worn home for my bottle of pills.

•

In my black-windowed kitchen, not even sure what time it is, morning or night, I prop a single black-and-white photograph in front of my mirror-finish coffee pot. Should be easier to think clearly while not being jiggled and bounced by a bus. I like the silence here. There's no one across the table from me, telling me how big my donut is or how to fry an egg, no one facing the blank white back-side of this picture—the backstage circuit board photograph. Windrem and Harlan. But it's Windrem's hand, Windrem's cigarette, Windrem's glaring eyes. Isn't Harlan's face simply in the background? Couldn't I have shown someone the picture and *explained* that? Would the show and everything else have ever gotten this far if I had? Why didn't I do it? I know Harlan's face tilts up, has always tilted up as long as Windrem has held the light jack—neither of them has ever moved, no matter how much happens between the times I look at it. Some elements are unmistakable, fixed: the characters, the circuit board, the cigarette, Harlan's face toward the rafters, his mouth slightly open, lips parted, a microscopic bit of light shining on his wet tongue . . . and the shadow across his eyes, cast by a rope or curtain or Windrem's arm. . . . His *face* is tilted up but his eyes *could* be looking *any*where. He could've lowered his lids and looked down his cheek, off to his left. . . . Maybe he saw me. . . . Maybe he saw what Windrem was doing. Harlan, maybe you realized you were in the wrong place at the wrong time, that you would just *look* guilty if anyone saw you. But if you *didn't* realize it, maybe it would help if I told you . . . that you share the red spotlight only because you, like me, were there without being there. I should've told you sooner.

I'm suddenly sweating as I pick up the phone. The dial tone penetrates my ear, jars my head.

"Hello."

"Hi."

"Who is this." A demand.

"It's Connie."

"What d'you want?" Another demand.

"I have something I have to tell you—"

"Not now. We have rehearsals starting again next week. Take a vacation like everyone else."

"It's pretty important." I have my chin on my fist on the tabletop facing the photograph.

"It can wait."

The pause is only a second, but he might be hanging up—

"Wait! Why didn't you tell me about their us-against-them mentality, that it would be *impossible* for me to be included as a member? If I'd *known*. . . . How many other things have you not told me?"

"Connie, I don't have time for this— I'm having some rough times right now. . . . What makes you think I should tell you everything?"

"But you—" I start, but hang up in the middle. I click it with my finger, just let the receiver fall on the table. And I sink down to the tabletop too, cheek on my bicep, looking down my arm, so far from me, waiting uselessly. My own arm, the skin so transparent and bluish and thin, stretched too tightly around the bones. *I'm* not like that. Only sickly people, starving people.

Sometimes, when you looked at me, I let myself think it mattered that I was there. How long ago? Not recently. Before tour? Maybe you only really noticed me when they told you something was wrong with me. And maybe it is. And maybe I'll never get it right.

He probably didn't even notice I hung up the phone.

The bottle of yellow pills is sitting beside the coffee pot, in front of the wet glass I used last time I took one. If I could move, I'd take off the lid and roll them onto the table. Then what? Pound them to dust with the salt shaker? Throw the handful across the room? There's not even a handful left. I wasn't going to take another one today. . . .

I'm tired . . . tired . . . and the outside of my face holds me together like a sack. Without lifting my head, I see down my arm to the photo I'm holding, way out there. . . . I thought you were different. You *did* know what Windrem was doing, didn't you?

You may not have told him which jack to pull; you may not've told him where to leave his cigarette . . . but . . . you *knew*. So I'm going to show the picture . . . at least finish what I started to say, what you didn't want to hear . . . after all, the photographer who no one thinks is there *is* at least *some*where. . . . I don't care how innocent you actually may or may not be, Harlan, why do I have to continually remind you again and again and again. This photograph proves it. . . . *I was there.*

X

The Photo Booth in the Adult Store

• • •

"Not Glen Peters," that jerk, I tell a receptionist with eyes like pointed pencils, sketching her own version of me straight from some television show she saw last night—another doper with a little trivial information to trade for a dollar. I promised myself I wouldn't take any more pills.

And with all her scrutiny, she still doesn't hear everything I say, because she calls someone then points me to a desk, and it's *his.*

"I *said*. . . never mind." I try to walk steadily, and not too slowly, in case someone's watching, but of course no one's looking at me, not even Glen Peters himself until I arrive at his desk.

"Whatcha got?"

"This." I put the photo squarely onto the desk. No flippant toss—not sure I could keep it from landing on the floor.

"What is it?"

"What's really important is that I can show you where this shot appeared on the negative strips—it's marked number *one* on the *first* roll I took that night."

"What're you talking about?" Probably now remembers I'm a strange girl.

Just listen. This particular shot was *first.* After this, I took pre-curtain dressing room shots. *Then* the fire.

"This is the same night?"

"Now you're catching on."

He picks it up to look, makes notes on a pad, then asks, "Who is this?"

"In front—that's Windrem. Hal Windrem, the producer, but he's not top money anymore."

"What's he doing?"

"The lights were messed up that night. Someone fell into the pit."

"Oh, I remember," he says, "right before the fire. Who's this other guy?"

"She was stupid to try to move in the dark like that—"

"Who's standing in the background?"

"—so near the pit."

"The picture's kind of grainy, I can't tell who—"

"I wasn't working under optimum conditions. It's not *posed,* y'know." My voice comes back to life.

"Okay, then tell me—what're they doing?"

"He switched two jacks . . . Windrem—"

"Oh! Is this the guy in the fire . . . ? Harlan, the director?" He flips little pages on his note pad. "Do you know Ron Galvin?"

"Why?"

"Don't have a heart attack."

"I'm okay. . . . Um . . . that's all I had to tell you, I guess."

He's holding his pencil in both hands, as though he's about to break it. "Well, this Galvin fellow was in here, oh, a few weeks ago, I guess—maybe more than that—asking about these two guys."

"He didn't mention me did he?"

"What is he, a detective?"

I try to laugh. I'm not sure what it sounds like. "What happened to you—too many years on the police beat without a big story? Galvin's the music director!"

"So why was the music director asking about these two?"

I shrug. "Why doncha ask him."

He puts his pencil down, still whole, and sits on the edge of his desk. "You know, Connie, I don't believe you're being this difficult just because you want your photograph to speak for itself."

"Well it *should.*"

"I think there's more."

"Think what you like—you'll be making a big mistake and find yourself back in obituaries in a week."

"You're really scaring me."

"Shut up."

"Okay . . . it didn't take long for this interview to cover your entire vocabulary. How much d'you want for the picture?"

"Constance Zamora, full name, on the credit." He keeps looking. "Yes, I know, I'm a strange girl. It's stamped on the back if you forget."

•

Some secretary left a message on my machine reminding me about rehearsals starting Monday. I heard her say it while I sat here and let the machine do its job. Why pick up the phone? That was Friday. No other calls. Thursday, Friday, Saturday, Sunday—the photo didn't appear in the paper at all. Did some editor ax it? If so, it's over. Just like Harlan wants. So, okay, I'll go to rehearsal tomorrow and play my uncontracted bit part. That's what they're not paying me for, isn't it? I guess I am running a little low on actual cash so I go down to the darkroom just long enough to get Harlan's check off the drying line. I'll try to get that check from Windrem for my cello on Monday too, if I remember.

Monday morning I'm at the newspaper vending machine at five A.M., buy one, flip through, find my photo, put one more quarter in the machine and take the whole stack. I don't know why—I have no one to mail it to and don't keep a scrapbook.

Instead of going in the side door straight to the backstage areas and dressing rooms, I park on the street in front and bang on the heavy doors to the lobby until some technician finally comes and lets me in. "Why doncha go around back like everyone else?"

Why answer? Why bother? One newspaper under my arm, camera on my hip, I go down the center aisle, hardly making a sound on the thick carpet. But when I get to the front I hear Harlan's voice—no words, just the familiar hum of him talking—coming down the stairs from the office. I toss the newspaper into the pit, then follow it, boosting myself over the wall, cradling the camera, jumping down on Galvin's podium. Harlan calls, "Connie!" But I gather up the paper in both arms and dodge through the music stands and light wires to the back door of the pit, through the narrow hall, then run up the stairs two at a time and find myself at the dressing rooms coming from a different direction—people laughing, lockers banging—so I turn into the prop-storage room, push hard on the door to get in, then the door sticks on the floor and I can't close it.

The storage room hasn't changed. The air is dusty gray, like thin white paint over black walls. The same stuff lying around, not even moved to new positions—the cap with deer horns, the lifeless potted palm, the shell of a knight with his legs bent under him. There's some things I didn't notice before. A moldy bale of hay, a red wagon, a window frame with curtains. The props we've been using are all new. After we close, they'll be put in boxes and dragged here. And the sets will be loaded onto carts, wheeled down the hall and unloaded here. Nothing is ever re-used but nothing is ever thrown away.

Sitting on the bale of hay, I spread the newspaper on the floor in front of my feet, then bend over, camera hanging down, swinging between my face and the page. . . . The photograph is dead center, an italic header in bold quotes above it: *"The Lights Were Messed Up That Night . . . He Switched Two Jacks."* Ink soaks into newsprint, so certain details are lost—not a shadow of the cigarette remains in the picture. But the words are clear enough:

> . . . According to unnamed sources in New York, several years ago Harlan misrepresented a financial disaster in an off-Broadway production to scare investors, which allowed Courtney Harlan, his wife, to buy them out under an assumed name. In his recent ill-fated production at the Guild Theater, the financial trouble was obviously more real as technical mishaps and a backstage fire interrupted the opening performance. But once again a generous donor has rescued the show. The name given by Hal Windrem, producer of the Guild production, of the benefactor is Stella Green. Sources in New York claimed Courtney Harlan used the name Stella Green when buying out the allegedly troubled show there. Reached at her home in La Jolla, Courtney Harlan did not deny the donation to the Guild production following the disaster-riddled opening-night performance. . . .

Then there is the photo caption, with the credit *first,* bigger than usual . . . in fact as big as *his* name over the story. *Photo by Constance Zamora,* bold italics . . . then the caption:

> The fire department spokesman said their investigation of the fire at the Guild in February determined it to be accidental. However, local sources, including a member of the production, feel there is reason to believe the events which halted the opening-night performance weren't entirely an accident.

Voices in the hall. I don't look up and they pass without noticing me. A few more lockers bang shut next door, and more voices fade down the hall heading to other direction. Kind of quiet. I do hear the piano in the pit. I think next door is empty now—I'll have time to stuff my sweater, camera and the newspaper into my locker and get on stage while the rehearsal is still disorganized. It always starts at least five minutes late.

But I stop in the doorway of the storage room. Harlan is down the hall, coming toward me, sees me, doesn't skip a step. I back up into the storage room again and he replaces me in the doorway, back-lit, dark-faced, undefined expression.

"What're you doing in here?" he says.

"Nothing much." Why should I be hiding. I *was* there. I *did* see it. "You look like you did in a dream I had last night." My voice churns out the words without a pause. "I came to the theater, a Monday morning, and met you coming in also, and you spoke to me so I knew it was really you. But another you walked past, coming out of the theater, and I wasn't even amazed, only said, 'There's two of you.' You said, 'This is my Monday self. That's my Friday self leaving.' That's what finally astounded me—your Friday self just leaving on Monday morning!"

He smiles. I can see it in the dark. And he steps out of the doorway, toward me.

"I suppose you saw the newspaper—"

"Connie, I'm sorry about the other day, how I spoke to you." His eyes and mouth talk together in a blur. "You couldn't have called at a worse time. It's probably going to be this way for a while, if you can bear with me."

His skin is yellowish, his mouth tired, his eyelids still blotchy blue. I drop my gaze to his pale neck, gaunt collarbones, shirt-front, belt buckle. "I'm sorry I called."

"No. *I'm* sorry I spoke to you that way."

"It's just that I've . . ."

He puts one hand on my shoulder. I didn't know we were only that far apart. Looking up, his arm between us, to his clear eyes. . . . Then, smoothly, like falling, he sinks to sit on a wooden trunk. He holds the edges of it on either of his hips, which are level and balanced now. "Connie, why are you doing this?"

"This—?"

"Why are you doing this show?"

"Oh." Why is it so hard to think? I'm not still taking pills, am I? "The show? I don't know. I don't remember. My father wanted me to be a cellist . . . but I also needed . . . something different. I thought I was becoming too much of a recluse again, alone in the dark with bad vacation snapshots and backyard barbecues going past me like a conveyer belt." Braced on my legs, slightly apart, arms folded across my chest, camera on my navel, newspaper still under my arm—something unfamiliar gushing out of me? "Sculpture and oil painting weren't taken over by the general public as a toy, so why photography? It's almost been ruined. Everyone and his Aunt Jane thinks they're a photographer. And all those snapshots—the zoo or Disneyland or some picnic—the people who take them, well, the whole reason they have a camera . . . it's as though taking the picture will make the time they're having better. They think if they've got a snapshot, then the time they're having is more special. . . . And then they want big poster-sized blow-ups to plaster on their walls . . . I'm surprised they don't go ahead and put vaseline on the lens."

His lips twitch, actually tighten, cheekbones rise a little. The light mirrored in his eyes—the weak bulb in the ceiling behind me—flickers slightly, a faltering candle which grows strong again, a flame to be fanned or blown out or just left alone because it's pretty without my help.

"Have I answered your question? I saw the notice. I auditioned."

He continues smiling. "I knew a director who saw everything as a scene being acted out, with scripts and characters. He even tried to make his wife start over when they were having a fight—to change the blocking or make it more dramatic. It really upset him if she used a cliche. *Who wrote this drivel*, he would shout. Their fights never ended up being about the original subject."

"Really? Is that true? I don't believe it."

"Well . . . I might've exaggerated a little. But pretend it's true."

"Why?"

"Connie, I think it would be a very simple matter to show you what's wrong with the way you see or look at things. With or without a camera, I don't think there's any difference for you." He glances down at his knees. "I'd like to talk to you." Then he looks up again. "But not here." He stands. "Come on."

"What about the rehearsal?"

"There won't be one today. I don't know when or if there'll be any more at all. The cast decided not to do anything more until all their questions are answered. Windrem isn't here today. Everything's on hold."

I'm following him out the door, down the hall. "I'm really not surprised!" My voice does surprise me. Louder than usual in the empty hall.

"I didn't think you would be, but you have to realize, they're all practically amateur. In name they're professionals, and I've tried to treat them that way, but none of them are very experienced. I've had to coddle this company like none other I've ever worked with." He looks at me quickly over his shoulder. "And everyone's still blowing things up out of proportion, aren't they?"

After I move my car off the street, into the parking lot, so no careless truck or taxi driver, or even a bike rider, can get too close and make any more dents, I get into Harlan's car which is waiting, idling, at the parking lot exit. Leaning back, the morning sky floods past a window in the roof. Tinted dark blue. A red lens filter will make the sky dark but keep the clouds white. My camera on my lap.

Everything's so quiet as the car rushes underneath me.

Twice I open my mouth—then don't have anything to say. It's not that I'm thinking twice or reconsidering anything. Is there *any*thing more to say? Where are we going? And why? Beautiful weather for April but we could use some rain. Read any good books or magazines . . . or newspapers lately?

Mouth open again, and closed without a word.

"What is it, Connie?"

"Oh, I just had a question, but I forgot what it was."

"I have some answers—yes or no or maybe—which do you like?"

"None."

"They might fit the question."

"Not before I ask."

I stare into the sky. It *was* the only thing I could do. Not for legality or ethics or to make the cast walk out on him *too*. What difference does it really make—one red light, one small fire, one broken leg. But if no one saw the picture, I would have stayed invisible. I *had* to release it. I had to.

"I used to play a game," he says, "where one person gives an answer and the other makes up a perfect question for that answer."

"Okay. . . ."

"Try one. The first answer is . . . ," he pauses. Lucky the road is so straight here because he faces me, thinking with an odd smile or something like a smile tugging at his mouth. "A pleasurable pastime."

"Uh . . . what is . . . photography . . . ?"

"That's not a pastime, it's an obsession. Boy, Connie, how can anyone be *wrong* asking the question? Come on, try again." His mouth thinks again in its funny tight way. "Marriage."

"Why that?"

"It's an answer."

"But one I can't question. I don't know anything about it."

"Well, you almost have a question there: What is just *one* of the *many* things you don't know anything about?"

"Oh. Okay."

"Get the idea? One more try." This time he doesn't even face me. He watches the outside rush toward us and around us, a blurred world in every window and mirror. "Fidelity."

His voice focuses.

"What did you say?"

"That's a good question for it."

One hand half curled on his leg, he drives the car with the other, just two fingers hooked on the wheel at the bottom. Then he flips on cruise-control. The doors all lock together when he pushes his button. The power pushes me back deep into the soft seat, cushions every jolt.

He flicks up the locks when we stop, and I step out onto a sidewalk. We're in front of a barbershop. He comes around the car, takes my camera from my neck and puts it on the car seat, locks it there, then touches my arm and I follow beside him two doors down. Here he takes my arm and gets me inside before I can read the glittery neon sign, all lit up in the daytime, but I think I know what it said.

"What me to show you around?"

"You come here *often*?"

"Connie, look around . . . stop looking at *me*."

Unexpected, tears streak sideways on my temple as I spin-turn and nearly walk into an island three-shelf counter. A row of flashlights standing on end totter as I knock my knees into the glass shelf. I catch one. Not a flashlight at all, but the same size, fits two batteries end-to-end, a blunt point on the top, flat cap on the other end. I cradle it in one hand, keep looking down at it because he said not to look at him.

"It's a vibrator," he says. "Just a plain one."

"I know that." Smooth tan plastic. I run one finger from tip to base. "It's awfully phallic, isn't it?"

"Connie, that's the *point.*" He takes it away and smacks it back down on the glass. "I bought one for my wife . . . just before tour."

I look up at him. "To *use?*"

"Of course."

"What did she say?"

"She was pissed. Surprised me."

My cheeks tingle. Most of the time in bookstores I find the photography section and kneel on the carpet in front of a bookcase, browse through a book, read opening chapters, careful not to break the spine or soil pages, touch gently the glossy dust jackets. I think most bookstores must be dark green, or brown inside, and have oak doors with brass handles, and peaked roofs and a chimney. I know most really have glass fronts and share apartment walls with western clothes and shoes-and-boots, but still when I settle onto the floor, the walls become books and blend into dark green or brown, the realness, the thickness that a wall of books is, like glossy wood-framed photographs in geometric intervals on the wall. The floor here is rolled-out hard plastic and the walls a shocked violet, and I don't dare kneel for fear the floor's been spilled on and not mopped up. And if I did sink to my knees, behind the glass counter under the cash register, one box says, *Ribbed For Maximum Pleasure,* another: *New Lifelike Rubber.*

"So many things which aren't books, for a bookstore. Why do you come here?"

"Connie, it's an *adult* bookstore."

"Still, it's a *book*store. . . ." Selling printed material which someone thought of and wrote . . . and photographs on covers of magazines, and these other things. Someone else peeks out from behind me, grinning, not shocked—*she* knows about these things, not flashlights at all, no need for light when following *their* factory instructions, tab A into slot B, no need to see anything. Yet without sight there is no reading, and without reading, no books . . . we'd stumble in here blind, merely an adult store.

Some of the other toys are big as dolls, soft pink plastic like dolls, many can wet like dolls if you fill them first. Arranged in sizes like an artillery exhibit, rockets to the moon, the way lenses lie on velvet in a glass showcase. I reach to touch one, to hold it in my fist, but turn quickly and take a book from a rack, cheap dull paperback cover, recycled paper pages already folded like a bookmark to the middle where I open it, one speaking to another: *"I can't love you," she purred. "It's not you're love I want so badly," he answered thickly. . . .*

"A misspelled word," I say.

"What?"

"They misspelled a word in this book." I hold it up to show him, but he takes the whole book, closes it and puts it back on the rack. He seems to lift his gaze, hold it over the tops of the counters and racks. "You would notice a wrong word," he says.

"Well, I just opened it in the middle. I didn't know the plot or what they were *do*ing."

Something flat in a cellophane package claims to be lifelike. "Do you think it really is?" I ask him.

"As much as it has to be to someone who thinks he needs it."

I touch the tip of a club-like phallus on a shelf at face level.

"Come on," he says, a hand on the base of my neck. "Come back here."

Hand still on my neck, from behind me he firmly steers me down an aisle, quickly past slick magazine covers where girls are foaming at the mouth. We pass through a bead curtain hanging from a doorway.

"Here," he says, next to a black cloth curtain—the door to a small booth.

"I'm gonna have my picture taken? Or is it a darkroom?" I smile. He stares at me.

The bead curtain rattles open. A man says, "Hey buddy—"

"She's old enough," says Harlan.

The guy's hand is out, he wags his fingers.

"Connie—your ID."

I pass over my license. The guy says nothing more, passes it back, swishes through the beads to the front of the store.

"Come on," Harlan says.

"A *peep show?*"

We look at each other. He doesn't tell me to stop looking. "That's a typically narrow-minded label for it."

"I don't want to watch it."

"Why—have you seen one before?"

"No."

"Then how do you *know*?"

"I *also* know I don't want my arms cut off, but I've never had it done before. This is where deranged voyeurs go to—"

"Look—humor me, okay?" he says. "I've had a rough week. Just sit here during the film. Close your eyes if you want to."

"Why?" He's already ushering me—half pushing me—into the booth. "Where're you going to be?"

"Right here." He's kneeling beside the only stool in the booth, holding a quarter in the entrance of the money slot. "Sit down, Connie."

"What are you going to be *do*ing?"

He laughs—a lot harsher than his usual laugh—and the quarter drops. Silence for a moment, a machine hums, a picture flickers on a tiny screen.

"How do they get close enough to photograph *that?*"

"That's not the point. You're not the photographer here."

I watch the first few minutes, someone else's bad dream, then turn to watch the movie flash lights on his eyes. He's looking back at me. "I've already seen this one," he says.

"Do you *really* come here often?"

"Only when I need to see the world through a vaseline-covered lens.

"*Here?*"

"Why are you getting hysterical?"

"I'm not!"

"You don't understand, do you?" he says. "I thought this would be perfect for you—the way you like to look at everything as though it's a picture of what it is, then you want to blow it up even further."

"I didn't *ask* to come here."

"Hey!" A voice from the front of the store. "Quiet down back there!"

"Open your eyes, Connie." Harlan's voice is a hoarse murmur rather than a whisper. "It's so simple here, so uncomplicated, it is what it *is*, dammit, there's nothing more to be *made* of it. Can't you just enjoy it?"

"No! It wasn't *my* idea—don't try to force me to share your perverted hobby!" I'm standing, holding his arm with both hands, twisting the skin in opposite directions . . . he's still between me and the door of the booth, still kneeling, the stool bolted to the floor between us—I can't get him in the nuts, so I bring my knee up to smash him in the face, but he grabs my knee with his free hand, pushes me back, off my feet for a second, throws me against the back wall of the both.

"Hey—I said knock it off in there!"

I'm on my butt, my knees drawn up to my chest, and now *he's* standing. I only see his feet and ankles. His voice is almost gentle, "Connie do me—and yourself—a favor and remember what happened here. I wanted to give you a perfect example of how you make a wall poster out of everything . . . you get yourself all worked up over nothing, or over something with a simple explanation, or something that's none of your business. Believe me, though, I didn't know it would work this well." He sits on the stool, scraping his feet on the plastic floor of the booth, sending chills up my spine. "This is really a harmless place," he says, "probably sometimes downright lonely. . . . But I've never been here before."

I try to look at him, but it's too dark. The movie has already ended.

He pulls into the parking lot and stops beside my car. Afternoon and sunny, but not hot. I notice my sweater still in his back seat where I threw it this morning, but I'm already out of his car, leaning against my own car, against the dent . . . a flaccid moment . . . try to remember to blink now and then, and keep breathing. I don't know what else to do. His hair is so straight—the wind decides where it will lie. He reaches out and brushes some wispy, fuzzy strands of my hair from where it was blocking my eyes. Should I keep watching him the way he looks now, in the hazy breeze and windy sunlight, or slowly raise the camera in my hand—an intellectual lens ringed by aperture numbers and speeds. Suddenly he pushes his fingers deeper into my hair, tangled for a moment in the frizz, then slides his hand down to my neck, his thumb on my throat, moving up and down.

The inside thud of a slamming door, then another, and someone in the theater fumbles with a locked side exit door. Harlan drops his hand from my throat. "I knew it," he says.

"Knew what?"

"Let's *go*."

But before we move, a service door beside the trash dumpster opens, all the way—the knob cracks into the wall. The sun is glaring on the side of the theater, and Windrem is still beady, more than ever, his eyes and shiny round nose and little pursed mouth. I didn't even notice the newspaper he's got until he throws it at Harlan when he gets near. The pages flutter briefly, but Harlan catches it against his chest with both hands, part of it over his face, just for a second.

"I hope you're both satisfied," Windrem says. "This finished everything here . . . including you, thank god, but you had to drive all those kids out of work too."

"Wait, it was *you* who—" I'm stopped by Harlan's palm, firm on my mouth, a backhanded swing that knocks my head against my car and holds me there.

"I never considered any type of gossipy publicity important," Harlan says. "The cast made their own decision."

"You know," Windrem says, "I'm not at all surprised to find the two of you together. I should've known all along you'd use her. Well, you got trapped in your own little plot this time."

"No," I say against Harlan's hand, but only manage to hum and get his palm wet. He tightens his pressure on my mouth.

"This time the loss is all *yours,*" Windrem says. "I'm paying those kids what they deserve—out of your wife's money. Wha'did'ya think—that I wouldn't find out it was *her* again? I knew it was her in New York, after it was too late, but never heard the name she used. Wish I had since she was stupid enough to use the same name twice, or was it *your* lame idea? It backfired on you this time. Those kids have principles and they walked out on you."

"You know as well as I do why they quit," Harlan says.

"Those *lies?*" Pointing at the newspaper, now held in Harlan's other hand. "Invented by your personal whore. Your wife paying her *too?*"

"Her professional life is *her* affair and has nothing to do with our relationship in or out of the company. The same goes for Courtney."

Windrem sticks his beady face right into Harlan's. "You blew it this time. That much almost makes the rest worthwhile, but it's not stopping my lawsuit. You're not gonna drag *me* down with you."

Dodging Windrem's breath, Harlan loses his grip on me, and I try to duck away, beyond him, to get away from him so I can help him. Windrem is still talking—"You think it's over? No way, nobody's heard *my* side of it yet, but they will."

My mouth is free. "Even the tabloids won't care . . . you're not big enough, good-looking enough, or rich enough." Harlan reaches for me, backhanded again, grabs me fish-mouthed, his fingers in my cheeks, reeling me in. Windrem is shouting, "Shut that sleeze up!"

"Leave her out of it." Harlan pulls me closer, practically behind him, practically twisting his arm to keep his grip on my mouth. Windrem's eyes are still bulging. He says, "Like you left your whore in New York out of it?"

Can't move—I try but can't.

"Yeah, she told me what *you* offered her." Harlan's voice.

Windrem lunges forward, and Harlan, moving sideways, gets me all the way behind himself, pins me against the car with his back, so he can let go of my face. The newspaper flutters against our legs. I think Windrem is trying to fight, but I can't see anything. I'm trying to push Harlan off me, but suddenly he steps forward by himself. I hadn't realized I was having trouble breathing. Now Harlan is holding Windrem's face, but not the same way—using his whole hand, spread out, like trying to gather Windrem's skin into a fist, making his eyes bulge even more, dull little pebbles glaring the only way a pebble can glare.

"Don't try it again," Harlan says, and throws Windrem free, opens my car door, sort of pushes me inside, but puts his hand on the top of my head so he doesn't clunk my skull on the top of the car. I'm on the passenger side, quickly roll the window down. Windrem is still out there, looking over the roof of the car.

"You're finished," Windrem says. "As good as dead."

So was another man out here once—dead—and they took

pictures of him too, old fashioned instant photos. The next day I found the negative backs they rip off and throw away.

"It's different than you think," I say out my window. "I know what you did."

"Hush, Connie," says Harlan, getting into the driver's seat.

"I was there and I saw you . . ."

"Connie . . ." Harlan is trying to grab my arm, but I lean farther out the window and his fingers only brush against me.

"I was there! How the hell can you stand there and deny it?"

"Hush up, Connie." Harlan jerks me inside. "Give me the keys." I hand them to him, suddenly surprised—he's driving *my* car. "You've got to stop letting your mouth be such a know-it-all." He drives without jerking, knows just where the clutch catches, knows just how much gas, how much acceleration between gears.

"You drive it better than I do."

"You destroyed it, remember?"

He chooses a booth rather than a table in the open, but much different than the photo booth in the adult store. Old-America sepia photos are on the table beneath a thick glossy layer of varnish, and on the wooden wall behind my head hang rusty artifacts. One looks like a giant nutcracker, or big pincher-pliers, a yard long, maybe to pick fruit high in trees.

"Do you know what that is?" Harlan asks.

"Big pliers?"

"That's a tool they use to castrate a calf."

I turn and stare at it again. A giant nut-cracker. "Really?"

The girl stands beside him and he orders beer and cheese fondue. I keep my face toward the table, rest my eyes on the soft ripe photos under the table gloss. Two women in a Model-T and a man near the door, off on a vacation to Atlantic City.

"What're we doing here?" I ask when she's gone.

"I'm not going home yet." He studies his palms. "Your steering wheel comes off on my hands."

"I usually wear gloves. You've a beautiful car."

"Yours was closer at the time."

"I knew you had to get away from him, but I— Well, he wouldn't have hurt me if I'd stayed."

"I couldn't leave you alone there with him."

"He wouldn't touch me."

"Probably not." He smiles. "But with you thinking you had to set him straight, and him with a different story—also believing he knows everything—no telling what you'd say to each other."

"What's the difference? To you, I mean."

His eyes don't shine, but are soft in the dim gold light. I hate that thing hanging over my shoulder.

"There're several things you would need to hear from me before you go telling anybody—not that I want you to. . . . The trouble is, when people want to know something about me, they never ask *me*. Don't you think I would be the best, most logical source?"

"You mean the newspaper?"

"Forget the newspaper for a minute." The waitress comes back with napkins and ice water. "I have to admit, the reporter *did* try to ask me, but I didn't want to talk to him. He called at a bad time. Courtney was—well, that doesn't matter now.

I drink half a glass of water.

"No one likes rumors going around about themselves," he says. "*You* know that."

"You think *I* spread rumors about you?"

"Maybe, without knowing you were."

"Other people kept telling me about you."

"Did you believe them?"

"I didn't listen."

"*Some*one did."

The waitress brings his beer and a glass. She starts to pour it for him, but he says, "I'll do it, thanks." After she leaves, he picks up both the bottle and the glass, tilts the glass and he pours the beer into it. It's dark brown beer.

"I know a theater is a gossip mill," he says. "This one perhaps more so because everyone was so young. It seems someone—probably more than one person—was bound and determined to find something to talk about."

"I know who you mean."

"I don't think you do." As he swallows, his lashes drop in a familiar way. "I guess sometimes people might do *any*thing to get information they feel is being withheld from them. Know what I mean?"

"I guess not." I almost reach for his beer, but pull my hand back before I move.

"How about a gay man giving heterosexuality a try because he thought *you* knew something he should know. Didn't you figure that out?"

"I—" Can hardly picture his crooked front teeth, low-necked leotard, perfect nose. . . . "It doesn't matter. Both of us had the wrong reasons."

"I can only imagine how the stories started and developed . . . I'm not saying it was rumor-spreading that killed the show. And the death of this show certainly isn't the crux of my problems, either. But it's something I want to tie up, just for my own satisfaction, before I chalk this up as just another disaster."

"*Are* you a disaster area?"

He laughs softly. "What've you been reading, back issues of *The Village Voice?*"

"Just something I heard."

"I've made a lot of mistakes, Connie." The waitress is standing by the table, smiling, a fondue pot and a platter of bread cut into cubes on her cart. "Thanks," he says. "I've been looking forward to this all day."

"You have?" The waitress is gone again.

"Yup—when I woke up, I thought, a good day for cheese fondue. I just didn't know who would be sharing it with me. Help yourself."

I watch him swirl a bread cube in the cheese, then put it in his mouth, catching a few drops of cheese in his hand rather than let it drip on the glossy tabletop, on someone's yellowed vacation photo.

"I've never tried to hide it," he says, swallows, takes a sip of beer. "If anyone asked, most of my, well, disasters—for lack of a better word—*were* my fault. Also bad luck, I think, but I was pretty impulsive. No, I think *reckless* is a better word. Reckless out of confidence. Didn't pay enough attention to technical areas of the show. And, yes, I had some bombs that quickly went up in flames—figuratively speaking . . . one in particular during dress rehearsal when the sets literally fell apart on stage." He smiles, swirling another bread cube in the cheese. "I guess stuff like that only makes what happened here seem worse." This time he lets the bread drip off over the pot before transferring it to his mouth. "I think that's the real danger in rumors and stories: they let the past get mixed up in the present—just because people are talking about the past during the present—when actually the two times may have nothing at all to do with each other." He drinks a few more swallows of beer. "That's an awkward way of defining *reputation*, but that's what it all boils down to, I guess. Right?" He looks at me for a second before putting another bread cube on one of the long forks. But this one he hands to me, then loads up his own fork and puts the bread into the cheese. "Excuse me for thinking out loud," he says. "But at least a few things are clearer to me now. There was a rumor on tour—maybe you heard it . . . ?"

"No one was speaking to me." I finally dip the bread on my fork into the fondue pot.

"Well, anyway, it upset Courtney, but it didn't *cause* the trouble we're having. It didn't help either."

"Trouble?" I look up from watching my fork stir through the thick cheese. Let go of the fork and leave it there.

"Something's splitting us up. I'm not sure if either of us knows the real reasons. We go around in circles. Not fighting. But not communicating either. It's hard to describe. I don't know what she wants. She's upset about something. Publicity about me never seemed to bother her before this." He's turned sideways in the booth toward me, his hands not resting but holding onto the glossy edge of the table, his back erect, his head up, his mouth still slightly open. But his eyes are gentle.

"The photos—?"

He shuts his eyes while inhaling. "I'm not sure what's really going on in her head. I made a simple suggestion that if she wanted her own publicity, she could try *really* being a producer, finance her own projects, take some chances, make some decisions." He turns back to the fondue, lifts his bread out, then drops it again. "Maybe that's what she's doing." He finishes all the beer in his glass. "She says I'm not real anymore."

I reach for my fork. I can't move it. The cheese has hardened in the pot. "I don't understand." Barely more than a whisper.

"I know." He seems to wait. Then goes on. "She thinks I don't either. Maybe she's right, though. Reputation, photographs, more rumors.... I think I understand." He pours the last of the beer from the bottle into his glass. "I think you have the same problem in a way. You call yourself a photographer. But what's a *photographer?* There's no such thing... there's only people who take photographs."

I sink backwards until my shoulders hit the padded back of the booth. My head just below the rusty pliers, sitting on my hands. "Was it a rumor about a girl?" Still feels like I'm falling backwards.

He holds his beer glass again, but doesn't lift it, then lets go. "Connie, when are you gonna trade your camera for a mirror and see how your face is falling apart."

The back of my head clunks against the wall. The artifacts and tools shudder.

XI

The Fog Remains Fog Even Through Binoculars

• • •

He drives, I lean back, eyes shut. My car isn't as comfortable as his. The air from the open window dries my wet eyes and cheeks. It's chilly. Only three or four o'clock, I guess. My face is sticky. At the theater we once again park beside the other car. I get out and stand on an oil spot while he goes to his car and unlocks the door. He looks at me, then motions me to get in. So he drives again, and, once again, I lean back, eyes open this time, already dry.

"Where're we going?" My throat is dry too. Or it's my voice that's dry.

"To my house."

I press my foot to the floor of the car, searching for a brake there—a passenger brake for emergencies. "*Why?*"

"Why not?"

"Isn't your wife there?"

"So? Don't you want to share some of our home life?" He's actually smiling.

"She'll think it's *me*."

"What'll she think is you?" He turns on the radio. A news station. Switches to rock 'n' roll. Puts the volume up, tries another station, pushes in a tape—jazz—puts the volume still higher. He looks at me and grins. "I could put on a tape of the show if you want." Practically has to shout.

At three sides of a kitchen table, Courtney Harlan and I watch Harlan's fingers as attentively as he does, while he rolls the fragile white paper, licks it with the pointed tip of his tongue, twists the ends.

They're at the two ends of the table, and I'm on one side. I can't see both of them at once. But I don't think either of them sees the other without also seeing me. I keep my head turned toward Harlan. I should've stayed in my car or standing on the oil spot in the parking lot, or remained in *his* car when he parked in his carport, or stayed in the garden on the meandering cement path—shouldn't've been following him through his front door while he said, "Courtney, you remember Connie."

"Of course," she said. Of course. And she smiled.

Harlan holds the smoke down wide-eyed, staring straight forward at her. She holds it in with eyes pressed shut. Then my turn.

"Suck hard," he says. "And hold it."

Immediately I need a drink of water.

"You took too much. Watch me."

His lips press on it, the way he looks when determined. Is *sad* a better word? While Courtney drags, I say, "I wish you could know what I was doing, giving that photo to the newspaper."

His eyes flicker . . . glaze over. "I don't wanna hear that stuff."

"I know. . . ." I take the cigarette from Courtney's limp fingers.

"Just a little . . . good . . . hold it, real low."

The smoke comes out of me when I say, "I didn't sell it, there was no money involved."

"No matter."

"Because sometimes it seems money is important to me, but it isn't. I didn't care about the money. That goes for the contract too."

"Use it or pass it."

It burns. Coughing doesn't help. The cigarette seems to circle the table and come back to me so quickly. I suck on it twice, so maybe it won't come back so fast this time. "You remember . . . that store—?"

"You mean on tour?" he says, nearly too rapidly to understand, quick glance at drowsy Courtney.

"No. *Oh.* Yes. That one." I can go along with it. I have to, don't I? We *were* touring, I guess. He gave me an adult-store tour. "I didn't get to look at much of anything. You wanted to take me there but didn't want me to look."

"See, not look. I wanted you to see, not watch."

"Watch what?"

"I don't know. I don't remember."

"Witch watch," says Courtney.

"You're forcing," Harlan tells her.

She stares at the table top without blinking. If she were a photograph right now she'd be flat black-and-white with no contrast. She used to be in color, causing a sun flare on the lens, the last time I saw her. "It isn't me," I tell her.

"I couldn't believe it was me my first time either," she says.

"Huh?"

"I know what you mean." She hasn't looked up.

"It's sad," I say.

"Yes, it's sad," Harlan answers. "What's sad?"

"Sad stories are sad. You've told me lots of sad stories."

"I have? I don't remember any. I didn't tell stories just for their sadness."

"But it makes me sad to see people get excited and then let down." I take the little cigarette. I want to cough. I want him to help me cough, massage my shoulders and the back of my neck, pat my back and clear my head. I'd like to feel if his brown hair is as fine as it looks.

"Did I ever tell you about that?" he says.

"About what?"

"The kind of sadness which makes you sad."

"Huh?"

"What did I ever say to make you sad?"

"Oh." Again, my turn—I've lost count—hold the smoke down, belch it out. "You told about when you were a little boy all excited about singing a solo on television with a school choir, but when you saw it later, it was flat, more shouted than sung. . . . I could picture it perfectly."

"I told that story?"

"It's funny I remember it 'cause I can't remember something else."

"What."

"Why I said it. Why I remembered. Why I'm sad, I think. I can't remember why I'm sad. You told it on tour, at a run-through. To the whole cast."

"Tell me a sad story," he says. "It's only fair."

"Well . . . I can't think."

"Here." He hands me the cigarette. It feels as if the smoke fills my back and shoulders like balloons.

"I remember being sad when I was little too. Five I think. What's the difference. We were going to have a barbecue, my father and I, and he was happy. I liked it when he was happy 'cause usually he was nothing at all—I mean no particular mood. He'd look at me if I asked a dumb question. I mean look at me for an answer. But we were having a barbecue and I was sitting at the picnic table outside, the barbecue hot beside me, and he came from the kitchen with a tray of hot dogs and mustard and ketchup and pickles and other crap probably, how should I remember, but he was proud of that tray. He smiled over it at me and was proud that we would have a barbecue together. Then he stepped on a little train I'd left on the patio and fell. The last thing I remember about this is the spattered trail of mustard across the pavement."

I touch his fingertips as I take the cigarette. He's soft there, the pads of his fingers, like a cat with no claws. "I used to have a cat I liked to sleep with."

"Is this another story?" he says.

"Could be. Not really. She got old and was squashed in the driveway. She couldn't hear my father's car."

"I know a sad story," Courtney says. "When you brought home that painting, the one in the living room. You liked it. I didn't. But I let you hang it there."

"Why did you think of that," he asks. He looks at her.

She looks back at him. Both of them are profiled to me.

"I want to take it down," she says.

"Go ahead." He closes his eyes to pull smoke from the shrinking limp cigarette. His neck is hard as he sucks.

"Just a minute," Courtney says when he holds it out for her.

"Too fast?"

"It's pretty fast."

"Feel anything, Con—?"

"Everything. Too much of everything."

"It's not *that* fast."

It circles, twice more, in silence, and Courtney presses her forehead with her thumbs. Harlan leans back, pushes back, unbuttons his shirt. I watch like touching: the skin on his chest, brown arms and light hair, a muscle which makes a smooth ridge along the sides of his legs. Maybe I could reach around and touch the backs of his knees.

"Hey—when did you change into shorts?"

"Right when we got here."

Oh yeah, when he left me and Courtney uncomfortably alone

in the kitchen, nervously smiling, I put my camera on the table. Then she said "excuse me" and followed him into another room.

"I didn't remember."

"Sorry," he says. "What don't you remember?"

"Well, what're we talking about?"

"Something."

"That's for sure."

"I don't remember it either."

"I feel like for a long time, someone's been rubbing me, on my spine in between my shoulder blades, rubbing with their knuckles, for a long time, and now I need . . . what am I saying, anyway? Have you been rubbing me with your knuckles?"

"Not for a long time."

We laugh. Courtney doesn't . . . it doesn't matter. I think it's the funniest thing I ever heard.

"It's hard to remember. Do you remember . . . *any*thing?"

"Probably," he says.

Courtney skips every other hit. There's a blur in between when I swing from him to her. Like I'm not turning my head fast enough or smoothly enough. Maybe to them I look like a flicker-frame special effect, where I leave a shadow of myself frozen in several angles as I turn, creating a double-double exposure, four of me or more and a blur in between. I wish I could see it instead of feel it. It's dizzy . . . *I'm* dizzy.

"I know how to fix it," I offer.

"What," he says. "Fix what?"

"The painting. My father was a painter. He'd never paint anything like that. Never painted anything that good. But I'd add something alive."

"Nothing's alive in a painting."

"I'd add a gull. Two of them. No . . . just one. Crossing the horizon. It'll take a long time to cross. Forever."

"Real gulls get across. Use it or pass it."

"They take a long time."

"It might seem like it to you . . . it seems like he's just killing time . . . but *he* knows he's working—straining to stay aloft. And succeeding."

Courtney says, "Nothing can make it a better painting."

"Okay," Harlan says. "Whatever you say."

"I'm sorry I called," I say.

"What?"

"But you should've told me what to do with that picture. Because I just *gave* it away." I close my eyes. Urgent words are escaping before I can say them. "No, it's not the money! You believe me, don't you? They were worth something I can't explain. What did I want?"

Courtney is face-forward down on the table, her forehead on her knuckles. A tear drips out of her lashes to the table top.

He offers me the joint on a pin, but I shake no, hand on throat. He looks at it, twirling the pin, both eyes focused there, says, "What were you looking for? What did you find?"

"Huh? You mean backstage?"

"What good does talking about it do?"

"What are we talking about?"

"I don't know," he says. "Do you think I owe you an apology?"

"For what?"

"I don't know. Three months of work for nothing."

"Why can't you understand—I don't give a shit about the money, *any* of it."

"You were cheated."

"And *you* allowed me to be cheated, because I wasn't anyone important to you."

"If that was an issue," he says, "no one would ever be cheated." He smokes, then takes the piece of cigarette off the pin and crumbles it between his thumb and fingers. "So are you saying we're even now?"

"It doesn't seem very even, does it?"

"Unless you still haven't gotten what you wanted for the picture."

"Huh?"

"Didn't you just say you wanted to be important? Is that why you did it?"

"No. Did what? Maybe. I don't know . . . I guess so . . . No, I don't think so."

He laughs. "We'll have to set that to music." I watch him leave, a long dizzy look. He goes past Courtney. I don't care what she thinks. I don't think she's thinking anymore. I follow him before he calls, follow the backs of his knees, red from sticking to the vinyl kitchen chair.

More jazz. The volume too high. A screaming trumpet sounds like a frightened animal. A thumping bass—my own heartbeat—echoing through the house, will knock pictures off walls, china off shelves, break windows and mirrors. A frantic saxophone, going crazy, doesn't know whether to go up or down. My knees wobble and give in, I sink to kneel on the floor, on the thick carpet, hands over my ears, watching him . . . he's no longer touching the stereo dials, but the music suddenly steps into the background where it probably belongs. He joins me, kneeling, both of us, sitting back on our heels, face-to-face, but his knees are on either side of mine. He leans forward, holds my head by an ear on each side. "Incredible," he says "*You.* Because of you. Everything that happened became worse than it actually was just because *you* thought so."

"Huh?"

"Down in the pit that first day, looking up at us. . . ." He leans farther, one hand on my breastbone, fingertips on my throat, pushing me back as he leans forward until the dull ache between my shoulders is touching the rug. I'm folded back, bent at the knees, feet under my butt, completely supple. And with both hands he clears my face of hair, pulls it tight. My lids flutter shut with his mouth against one eye, saying, "... like a captured squirrel. You seemed so ... harmless."

I arch, struggle against him and he rises so my legs can pop out from underneath me and I can lie flat, but he settles down again, on top of me. "Too bad I never put a mirror in the ceiling."

With his forehead down hard against mine, the only ceiling I see is his eyes, wide open, we're lens-to-lens, I'm talking right into his mouth—"Why didn't you stop him?"

Suddenly he curls, folds around me, draws his knees up to my ribs, pulls his head down, his face grinding against my protruding collarbones, shaking, laughing, maybe crying, can the two be the same thing at the same time? His fingers blunt, digging into both my shoulders. "Connie.... Maybe I deserved all this—"

"No!"

If he was crying, now he's laughing. Also, if he was laughing, he might've cried some too. "And you knew," he says. "Didn't you ever wonder *why* he would do what he did? Why did you only wonder all the wrong things?" He sits up and pins me, kneeling over me, knees hugging my hips, settles his weight and sits *on* me. "It got a little out of hand ..." he laughs. "Maybe it's funny to say that, but ... I thought I could keep everything under control," no longer laughing, not even smiling, "and I could've, except for the publicity."

"But the publicity helped find the new backer, remember?"

"My *wife*, remember? She can find me without publicity. If she wanted to find me right *now* she could. Shit, Connie, *why?*"

"I asked you first!"

"Why!"

"Why *what?*" I gasp. "I don't know!" His hands are on my throat, but not tight. He's heavy—my stomach's going to give in and he'll sink down until he's sitting right on the floor, just a flap of skin between him and the rug. "Get off me—please?"

"I felt like I was being watched by a goddamn detective, why didn't you quit when I gave you the chance?"

"I couldn't!"

"*Why*, dammit!"

Did he hit me? I don't know where. I ache all over. Someone is whimpering "I'm sorry, I'm sorry." Maybe lyrics to the ballad booming through the speakers. Maybe my back is broken. How many times can it break and then mend itself? Maybe this time I'll never move again. Never recover. Not even when he lays on me again, knocks his head against mine, breathing hoarsely, vibrating against me, softly but heavy, a smooth rhythm like a heartbeat, up and down. He moves over me again and rubs against the length of me, brushing like wind-teased branches against a window without breaking it. Maybe the glass is already broken. Go ahead, I must've already done my struggling and broken every bone, ripped every muscle, it's no use now, can't fight if I can't move, go ahead, go ahead. . . . His fingers move, slowly probing, up my sides to under my arms which makes me jerk when he presses there. A hard tickle. My arms flop—the last jump of a dying fish, already unconscious, already out of the water and drying out on the sand—two useless limbs in a limp pile on the rug over my head, they don't move any more. Can't. And his hands . . . huge hands, soft on my skin, tightly bound underneath and inside my shirt, touching all over, neck to waist, side to side, and I can't do anything to stop him. The music is like wind, someone's voice in the speakers is a hurricane, and my shirt is swept over my head, remains tangled in my arms. The only rule I can remember: keep breathing. There's no confusion meter to check before increasing or lessening the air-speed, before opening or closing apertures. Seldom have the conditions been perfect enough, seldom do I trust manmade machinery enough to switch to automatic. Now, I have no choice. All I can see is the top of his head, his nut-brown hair falling straight in a fringe against my ribs—it tickles, as does his breath on my skin, bared in glaring lamplight, unfiltered and direct, caught in a strobe shine, warm as the sun. . . . Electronically-lit skin makes for terrible photographic skin tone, but I never worried about my own—how could I photograph myself without the camera being in the way? Why would I want to?

Where *is* the light source? Is it natural or what? All I know is it's not fluorescent . . . and there's an open window somewhere. Where am I, anyway?

Last time I was here I would've been trampled if I lay on the rug like this . . . so many people, ice plinking in glasses, low rumble of voices reminded me of the ocean, rough and random, peaked periodically, breaking sometimes, once or twice even burst open like fish jumping out. There is an ocean down the hill from us. As I think of it, my body jerks once—a quick mistranslated instruction to get up, go to the window and see the waves. Harlan holds me still, rubs his mouth and nose up the midline of my body, bumps my chin with the top of his head, then moves back down toward my hips, holds my sides with his hands, holds me like a pillar.

Over his head, back on the wall, the painting Courtney doesn't like, perhaps because it likes to hang crooked. When it's crooked the boat is level and in no danger of sinking. More likely—although she didn't say so—she may hate it because of the man, the one in the boat, *he* likes his painting because thick mist makes the fishing better and no wind makes the rowing effortless . . . although right now pure wind blows soundlessly through the alert stereo speakers. Is it the same man—holding me under my hips, lifting me up, breathing with a voice in his throat, pressing me against himself—as the one out there in the fog, which remains fog even through binoculars, casting about, casting, casting, and reeling in Windrem every time. Windrem, who I can suddenly picture quite clearly, sharp edges and detail, reading a magazine on Randy's tight bed, or peeing into Randy's violet toilet. I giggle and see his eyes, Harlan's, come out of the mist—blue eyes directed toward me.

"What's so funny?"

"I should be defending myself."

"Against what?" He puts his mouth to my belly, pulling at me with his teeth and pushes his tongue into my navel which swells as though he's blowing it up, bigger than my head. I can't do anything to stop it. But I wouldn't have to stop it if it wasn't me . . . if I could *see* this, just watch it, under Windrem's red spotlight—it's Harlan and Constantina, unaware of the audience. The photographer steps back then zooms in. Even with eyes shut the scene will remain the same. . . .

She bumps her fingers down his sides, over each rib, to his waist, then tries to twist sideways, to turn her body into a C and reach farther, to his leg.

"What the hell're you doing?"

"I want to touch behind your knee." She doesn't whisper. She doesn't giggle. But she smiles, I think.

He does something like a push-up, holding his body off the ground while she turns sideways, so when he lowers himself again, they make an X, joined at the stomach. He's heavy, but it doesn't hurt. He props his head up with a hand on his ear, his mouth against his shoulder, looking over at her while she finds his knee, the back of it, slides her hand onto it. He's cool there—without even looking at it, without needing to see it, it feels happy to her.

"I don't know about the rest of you," she says, "but the back of your knee is happy."

He laughs but doesn't fool her. He doesn't sound very glad, but hooks his arm around her and pulls her back to him; her shoulders burn against the rug, but she's reaching for him, laughing silently or crying, who can tell anymore. He doesn't kiss her tears—he licks them, so then she *does* laugh, I think.

Skin against skin, his and hers, no friction between them, the jeans, the shorts, the shirts are a nest around them. He pinches a nipple. Her head thrashes back and forth, crashes into his, they both grunt. He pulls and nips with his teeth, pushes one knee tight between her legs. Her arms circle his neck, pat his hair, then drop again. She never touched his face. Constantina traces the length of his sex with a forefinger as though remembering something. He is long and smooth and pretty. His hand, on a roller coaster ride, slides down the inside of one thigh, jumps across her crotch without touching, then tickles up the inside of the other thigh. Her bare body flops fish-like, bruises itself against his teeth; her hips pound on the rug, cushioned, the sound muffled. Back and forth, from knee to knee, just his fingertips make the trip, down one thigh, up the other, and she brazenly lifts her hips off the floor, tries to catch his hand as he passes over the middle—because the air is cold on her there now, that's all she knows. She chokes on a sob and he chuckles, a low moaning laugh, and presses himself into her hand so she closes her fingers like an anemone, and, like an anemone, also swallows *his* fingers.

It's not true—who said so, anyway?—that her insides would melt. That her vision would be misty. That everything would be warm. She is alert, inside and out, eyes dry, cold and goose-bumped wherever he's not touching. And the movement of his fingers: not anything like the previously presumed—or dreamed—hot electric power. It's just a licking tickle, and Constantina is focused there, arches and tries to stay with him as he pulls his hand away. She is holding onto him still, grips harder as he backs away, and he jerks like something bit him, a guttural voice, nearly collapses. He's grabbing her legs, fingers leaving bruise-marks on her thighs, spreading her like a wishbone. . . . His fingers licked and tickled but his mouth has teeth. Who's laughing? He growls like a puppy and shakes his head. His hands under her butt now, cupping softly, lifting her up, then his fingers dig in again, leave prints on her ass. His razor-face is expressionless, then he ducks his head again, pauses briefly, uses his knees to push her legs farther apart. Breathing like she's crying, extremities buzzing, face numb, fingers stiff and cold. . . . All her blood is gushing to meet him *there* where he pushes at her . . . opens her with his hands, forces himself into her. . . . And she smiles . . . feels herself not smiling with mouth or eyes, but only there where he's pushing—she's grinning where she aches because he bruises her, and he rubs away the bruise and bruises again so she aches again and aches for him to soothe the bruise away before he bruises her again. She feels him breathing there, feels his heart there, feels his voice growling there where they touch. His hands flat on the rug are on either side of her ears, propping his body up, his head hangs. They touch no where else except where her muscles are standing at attention, and he beats them down to mush, to jelly, but they stagger and writhe and strengthen again, and hold onto him and hug him, wrap slick around him, suck and stick to him. The theater could come down around them and they'd never know. The flimsy sets could fall apart over their heads . . . or there might be a fire! And ashes would rain in their hair. His eyes cry . . . or maybe it's sweat falling on her. An orange flame licks its way up the right leg curtain. But the photographer is still watching.

I won't ask myself a single question. On my stomach, cheek to the rug, naked, not touching him . . . he rolled the other way. I might've even been dreaming, it seems as though I was . . . would it make any difference if I were? Don't answer that. Dreaming was once clinically described to me as the storage of memory—as the cells are shuffled, programmed, transferred to microfilm, as new memory is filed in among the old, a jostled cell accidentally spills a scene. But that doesn't explain why Constantina stars in the dreams and Constance watches without ever wanting a guest appearance. I'm incredibly lucid, aren't I? Asleep or not asleep—I can't even tell the different anymore. Except I *thought* I would dream about him, about what just happened—did it really happen? I *never* dream about my mother, except in nightmares of my father's painting, which I threw in the garbage—the only one I ever put out for the trash men. It's the day my mother is going away. In movies the lovely young mother dies and Daddy tells Baby-toddler that Mommy is going on a long trip, going away. My mother, neither lovely nor young, but older than my father, just left, without dying, walked out the door and three-year-old Constance—so named, already, in her own mind—watched, hands on hips, and didn't care. Didn't, as movies would have her, declare to Daddy that she's waiting up till mother returns. Little Constance just watched, not even yearning for a photo to keep of Mother's last glance. Flat-eyed child and flat-chested mother with but one communal feeling—I don't care about you. We understood pure unaggressive indifference. A rare treat. I don't really remember it, but that's how I decided it should've been. So now I remember it that way, so it *was* that way. Except when I picture her, she looks strangely like my father's painting—crippled, misshapen, patches of bizarre color. But now, again, it's her departure day, and I must go along, she says, though I'm fully grown. She holds my hand and I pull away. We're getting into a horse-drawn carriage with lacy window curtains, and I say, "I don't wanna die with you." She says, "We ain't gonna die, we're going to St. Louis," and smiles a red smile below Windrem's pug nose and tiny eyes. We sit in the carriage a long time, but it never moves.

Someone is snoring and it isn't me. I curl around my nakedness, burrow my nose into the rug. The light's still on, and a light in the kitchen—is Courtney Harlan still asleep at the table? How could I forget about her? Why'd I have to remember her? Is the rumor true now? I swear—it wasn't *me!*

I roll to the wall, to the socket, and unplug the living room lamp. Harlan is asleep on his back, shoulder up against the opposite wall. I stand like a shadow against this wall, press cheek and palms flat to the plaster and creep to the kitchen doorway where a sliding door comes out of the wall. Roll it shut, then drop to my knees and crawl to Harlan, asleep with both hands cupped over his genitals below his flat belly, protecting himself. From what? Kneel beside him and edge closer. My head nods a couple of times. I catch my chin falling toward my breastbone. My eyes won't stay open so I hold the lids with my fingers. Who'd have thought my eyelids could be stronger than my hands? I'm stoned . . . my god, I'm so thick-headed I can hardly remember anything. Why is Windrem taking me to St. Louis? Why not New York where he came from, if he's got to take me somewhere. And where did my mother go? Did I miss her? Is she already gone? But why is that dream more vivid than what actually just happened . . . ? Precisely why photographers shouldn't work drunk or stoned—it's too hard to remember what they just witnessed, in the darkroom they'll be facing something they never saw before. Harlan, wake up and talk to me—what happened? If I could remember it, I'd always have it . . . to keep. . . . Why does it seem as if maybe it wasn't real and *nothing* happened just now, a minute ago, an hour ago . . . how long ago did it happen or not happen? I don't want it to be nothing, so help me, I can't work this way, we've got to go back . . . like the time I had a glass of champagne at someone's victory celebration and forgot to take a single photo, we had to go back the next day and pose a few staff members around a punch bowl filled with colored water. Creep closer, swing one knee over him, straddle him without touching. Very white skin in his groin, in the soft joints, and his hands cover the rest, cupped tight but gentle against himself. I take his wrists. Harlan, if I can't remember, if I can't hold the memory, it was all nothing!

He doesn't open his eyes, but groans . . . as *she* pulls his hands away. His head tilts back, chin up, and under her hands he stirs. She runs a feather touch along his groin joint, white and pampered, sticky, the skin where he is youngest, softest, fearful sometimes. Tendons tighten as she teases him there, using his own trick—a slow zig-zag from his pelvic bone, across the vulnerable joint, down between his legs where he is no longer protecting with his hands. He makes a sound with each breath, begins to rock, moves his hips forward and back, up and down, gently.

"I learned self defense once."

He doesn't answer.

"I was supposed to use it, times like this . . . I don't remember who told me so. . . . Aren't you afraid I'll hit you . . . or something?"

He hasn't opened his eyes yet, his body heavy, arms limp. He's completely flaccid, but there may be fireworks as soon as she brings her hands together and holds him. That's what she's remembering, as soon as she touches him there'll be a Roman candle, Mexican firecrackers popping in rapid succession like a machine gun.

He says, "Maybe someone ought to defend himself against you."

Something strikes me on my chest as though I, flying, smashed into a wall. With both my wrists in one big hand, my jaw held like a vise by the other hand, Harlan slams me up against a chain-link fence—that's what it *feels* like, anyway, this ache is a pattern in my back like that, criss-cross. I didn't feel my head thump on the rug when he rose beneath me and pushed me backwards. I'd like to see my wild face—my hair tangled like weeds, my mouth held awkwardly half open by his hand squeezing it, lips drawn back, teeth bared. All the power is his . . . my own bleeds away from me, a harpooned frog, writhing on the prongs, jerking my legs and thrashing underneath him, his knotted hand like a rock pounding me, bouncing my head off the floor. He's reaching for something, scattering paper and envelopes off a coffee table, holding me down with his other hand on my chest. "Help," I croak. He's holding a wooden letter opener. Halfway want to say, go ahead, but my open mouth cries, the sound of a seal on an iceberg . . . my own short wail makes me shiver, and I collapse the same second he throws the letter opener across the room. Instantly, again, everything is soft and quiet, Harlan on top of me, motionless, as though he's fallen here, afraid to move or he'll discover his own broken ribs, or newly dislocated hip . . . or severed spine. I feel his power leave through his breath, slowing, becoming shallow. "No." The sound has edges, beginning and end, corners and sides before it is a word. "No." Said against my neck.

He rises, lifts himself on wobbly arms, and bolts away—snatches his shorts, jumps into them, flings open the kitchen door and vanishes into the glaring light.

After a moment I roll over and begin crawling about, gathering clothing—most I don't remember shedding. I didn't feel sweaty but now that the clothes are on, they're clammy. I feel very far from the ground, standing up, looking back down.

The front door has a deadbolt lock and needs a key to be opened. The only other way out is through the kitchen. Or I could jump off the balcony and hope to land feet first on someone's patio furniture—maybe my legs would break but my back would be saved. But the sliding glass door is also locked. I can't figure out how it works. I brush my hair with my fingers. Now Courtney won't have to wonder if it's me she heard about. But I can still say that it wasn't. Swear it. Take a solemn oath.

She may have been stirred to life by the swift wake of his departure through the kitchen—he split the thick air, blew her out of that chair. She stands at the sink, without motion. The room doesn't stop turning right away after I move my head, which this time is not true dizziness, just a slow spin, my eyes not moving with the rest of my head, a lazy panning photographer who can't understand why her action shots are so blurry. Courtney's chair is still warm. I sit, stretch one arm its length out in front on the tabletop. Lay my head on it and watch her at the kitchen sink window, her back to me. Watch her with one eye because one is squeezed shut on my arm. One dimension. A cut-out paper doll against the night sky over the black ocean. A picture which I could put my hand palm-flat against, spread my fingers, and be touching all of it at once: sky, window, wall, sink, ocean, stars, Courtney Harlan, as motionless as the rest. Is she breathing, is she living? No matter, she's in the scene, as touchable as any of it, no more so, no less, and she turns to ask, "Does he ever talk about me at the theater?"

"What?" No question. My lips didn't move. I drool on my arm.

"I mean, I thought he *wanted* my help. He said you and he came up with the idea to have a new patron who saw the pictures and felt sorry for the company. . . ."

"We did?"

"I knew how much he cared about this project, he really did, why else would he have taken it when Windrem asked—he knew how Windrem felt about him, but he didn't care—I know it's hard for anyone to believe that now. What's going on, Connie—*really*. I've lost him, haven't I? I don't even know if I can believe him anymore. Can I, Connie? It sounds so stupid, like play scripts I've seen him turn down."

"What're you talking about?" I raise my head, stretch my fingertips to the carefully rolled, untouched joint he left on the table. Put it into my shirt pocket.

"I told him I wanted to hear *his* version of the rumors I heard. He said the only thing he could think of which remotely fit the rumors was something that happened *years* ago. But I already *knew* about that—why would I ask him?"

"You mean the girl-rumor?" *It's not me! You couldn't've heard about it this fast!*

She crosses the floor between us, like approaching a fish-eyed camera. Face thrust forward. "You heard about it? I can't believe he would lie. Maybe he's right—somehow the cast heard about what happened in New York and that's what they were talking about."

"Huh?"

"Tell me what you heard, Connie."

"I can't remember. Nothing to worry about."

"Was it a story about the time he suspended a production? He was waiting for a new version of the script to be written, but no one would change it the way he wanted, so he let the whole show die rather than try to stage a flop, even though it was by an established writer. It was *terrible*. I read it. He let everyone lose their money and disappeared to avoid being hounded. He *had* to, and I went with him, that's why I already knew about it. There were rumors about it *then* too—nobody seemed to realize who I was. But why would that be an issue *now?*"

"Oh. *That* girl-story."

"That's *it?* That's the one you heard?"

"No. I mean yes."

She cries prismatic tears, large and lens-clear, and pulls me out of the chair without touching me. I rise as though I'm growing. She has very strong fingers for such a lithe body, when she does touch me—has me by the shoulders, bone-to-bone, the bones in her fingers against the bones under my skin. She digs in. Also her eyes dig in, and she cries against me, against my breastbone, the hard part of my chest, suddenly like paper, wants to cave in, wants to let her cry directly against my heart. Her or anyone else.

XII

Other People's Dirt Plastered on a Mirror

• • •

It's not late but is dark, and the night is like a series of hanging black curtains I'm walking into and through, my eyes a half-step behind the rest of myself. I don't see or hear anyone else around. The ocean fog doesn't come all the way into the manicured garden, but I'm having a hard time staying on the twisty path. This is what the pills are really for! Not because of a car or bus—the road itself makes me dizzy. *Stop, please stop.* That's me, isn't it? Sounds like my own panting voice, somewhere behind me. But I don't care—I've got to find him. I don't know what I'll do if I don't find him . . . I'm going to be alone again—all night, tomorrow, forever a recluse—if I don't find him.

But I don't know where he's gone. At least in Washington I knew he would have to take that single road—he was somewhere on that dark bumpy highway, or he was at the end of it, in the hotel. I knew the name and address of the hotel, I knew the phone number, I knew what room numbers we had reserved and knew which one he'd be in. As though there was only one road in all of Washington—the one highlighted in yellow on the maps. Harlan must've had a map like the truck driver had. I don't remember seeing any maps in his car today. It can't be that late! I can't see my watch. The carport is empty, smells like exhaust—I retch once silently, hand over mouth, but recover. Not a single car. Over each empty parking space there's a light bulb with a chain hanging down. Some of them are on. I go down the middle, hopping over grease spots, turning off lights . . . sometimes I have to jump to reach the chain. I don't remember where his space is, but it doesn't matter, does it. Even though I go back through the grease spots turning on *all* the lights, I'm still undeniably alone in this carport, letting the lights stay on as I leave.

Camera in my lap, on my butt on the curb, staring into the gutter—the yellow street lamp reflecting in a greasy puddle. Or is that the filtered safelight shining into a tray of chemicals? Where's the photographer? Even with a tripod, the shutter-release set on timed-automatic, as soon as the photographer jumps in front of the lens, into the scene, she'll no longer be the photographer. The photographer who's not there. Okay, I quit. Don't bother scheduling your special run-through for publicity stills, I don't want to be the only one in the audience, sitting out in the dark house where the actors can see only my flash. I'll go back to the pit, I'll pull the curtains open and shut, I'll sweep up the sequins dropped off the chorus girls' dresses, I'll be the understudy. Because if the female lead doesn't show up—because she doesn't have a contract?—how can her counterpart practice their scene? He'll be sitting in a room memorizing his lines without knowing what she'll say in between.

How can I catch you, Harlan? I have to! I've never been dizzy this long . . . scared I'll never find you . . . need someone to grab my shoulders and stop me from spinning, shake me, rattle my eyeballs in their sockets, snap my head back and forth, break my neck if you have to, then I'll crumple against you and let you hold me up for a while.

Lean panting against a pole. Yes, this is what I want, a bus-stop.

I even have enough change for a one-way fare. He gave me a quarter to go get some coffee, but before that I gave him two quarters for winning the pencil bet. I still have three quarters and four dimes . . . no, one of these dimes is a penny . . . we should've marked those quarters with some nail polish from makeup and charted their course. Where do I want to go? Don't all the buses go downtown at night? The doors open in front of me and suck me inside, and I doze, eyes open, ring the bell and get out before the doors snap shut again. A block past the theater. I rang right in front, but he wouldn't let me off there. They've changed all the streetlights from white to yellow. The marquee is lit up, but the box office is dark. A light on upstairs. The parking lot gate is chained and locked, but I can squeeze through. A parking ticket on my windshield. Where's the dent? I feel all the way around the side of the car—disremember where it is—then find it practically where I started. But the doors are locked and I have no keys in my pocket. They're in *his* pocket, in the pants he's not even wearing anymore. Kick a tire and keep moving. A few blocks away I can make a shortcut through the park. No crippled bicycle to slow me down. Don't need a quarter for the phone, don't need to decide who to ask for help. There's no one around to ask. What help could they give? Maybe in the shadows of the trees I might see cigarettes glowing. Or it's reflected light off discarded beer cans. There's no one there.

On the other side of the park, I pass a dark, closed-up barber shop. Hey, isn't it just a few more doors down . . . no, it's not here. I don't know where we were . . . just this afternoon? Is that where he'll go tonight? I might find him in a photo booth, alone, not even watching anything. You dropped the quarter into the slot, Harlan, and neither of us saw the whole movie. Did I give you that quarter? Did you really want to go back to see the end?

Next block over, there's no barber shop, but neon lights which say 25¢ ADULTS ONLY. I don't know if it's the same store. Does it matter? The shelves and counters are in different places, but it's the same—the glare hurts my eyes, it smells thin and acrid, there's a slight buzz in the air from the neon lights. I'll rest a minute, kneeling between magazine racks. "What're *you* doing?" My voice, out loud, in front of one of the slick covers: a chained girl, twisting to get away, but reaching for him with her mouth—the only part of him that's showing. Raise my camera, hands not too steady, can hardly hold her in the lens.

"Want somethin', girlie?"

"He called me girlie," I say through the camera to my friend on the magazine cover.

A man with thinning hair, his scalp red, showing between the sparse strands. He is diamond-shaped. What does he want? Oh, yeah—do *I* want something. "*You* tell him," I whisper to my buddy. She never moves. So bold, with the camera on her.

"No pictures, sweetie."

"I'm leaving. I won't touch nothin'."

"Touch all you like. What're you looking for?"

"He ain't here."

"Which cover was he supposed to be on this month?"

"If he was, I'd've shot him. That's why he left me, isn't it?" I'm backing away, crawling backwards. A few covers down is another chained girl, two iron clawed feet with talons clamped to her chest. Can't give her any answers to her predicament, she's in a bookstore—pretending to be a book? Can't tell whether the posture, the positions, the lurid detail would prefer to be literature, or if the books wish they could be real sex. Can't figure it out. Squat and push the viewfinder back into my eye-socket. I need to cry. About what? Maybe for you, Harlan, because I *would've* shot it—would've had this camera on my face during my most private dream . . . one night in San Francisco, you were long and smooth and explosive . . . would've *had* to take a shot to prove it was real, but it *wasn't.* Not that time. But tonight you *were* real, and I have no picture of it—should I cry for that? For all the photos I would've taken, pictures to keep in a book that wishes it could be real?

The diamond-shaped guy is gone. Raise my head, drop my knees to the floor. "He's gone," I tell the girl. She knows it, she doesn't have to sell her magazine to me . . . the boss is gone, she can relax. "You're trapped. Wish I could help, but I'm so far from you. I should take you with me, but I have no place to keep you. I hope you become a famous actress, and when we meet, we'll pretend we don't know each other from these days." I crawl all the way to the door, then stand in the open doorway, holding both sides of it.

There's no longer no one else around. Couples and singles and gangs and crowds and single-trios and double-couples. The cars in the street only point one way—that's what the sign says—but the people go both ways. Without crashing into each other. Amazing. Across the street, in between the current of cars, I see the same thing—sidewalk and people. Three men pause to window-shop outside a boutique, *Between The Sheets.* The one in the middle deftly removes one of the hands from his backside—his smooth pocketless pants—but he allows the other hand to remain; it pats his rump.

I take a few steps out onto the sidewalk, look both ways, look back at the bookstore, through the window between letters painted on the glass:

U
NAME
IT
I
GOT
IT

Someone passing shoves me a little. A few jerky steps . . . I'm leaning against the window. Turn and go back inside, now looking out through the letters.

U

ƎMAИ

TI

I

TOↃ

TI

Beside me the diamond-shaped man is polishing his glasses, standing behind a counter. "Someone chasing you?" he says.

"Me? No."

"Looking for something in particular?"

"Oh . . . I don't know . . . maybe . . . I'm supposed to *see*, not look. . . . Suppose I name it and you haven't got it?"

The man smiles. If someone slugged him and his lips swelled, it would look the same. "Come over here and name it."

"Um . . ." moving toward the counter. There's a rack of sunglasses. Try a pair—dark mirror lenses.

"You incognito?"

"Huh? No, I'm on vacation." I can see out, but hold the glasses in front, facing myself, and I can't see through. They warp the images reflected back at me—my own face? I'm not looking at that.

"Anything else?" he says. "Need a mirror to see how they look?"

"No." Try another pair—pink glass. Eye level, behind the counter, three shabby signs, ALL CIGS $1.59, HOTEL 4TH STREET, and ONLY $20 IN THE CASHBOX AFTER 10. He's staring at me. I know, I know— I'm a strange girl. The deranged voyeur who patronizes adult stores alone, late at night.

"Hey, your shirt's buttoned up wrong." His lips swell more.

"Did I punch you?" Looking down . . . one shirt tail hanging well below the other. I tuck them both in. My eyes shut . . . standing here, holding onto the counter, I could fall asleep, just for a minute, and maybe, for that minute, be like thousands and thousands and thousands of other normal people, in their beds at home.

"Hey—you gonna pay for the glasses or you want somethin' else?"

Pointing at the signs, "You mean you've got beds somewhere?"

"Oh, I get it, you were waiting for someone, weren't you?"

"Huh? I'd like a bed, please, just for an hour or two."

He clicks a key on the counter.

"And. . . ." I don't suppose he has a tripod here, stashed somewhere. My hand cupped around the camera lens on my hip. A recluse even stranger than the deranged voyeur—drop a quarter in the slot and *I* get a camera on a tripod instead of the movie I didn't watch. See, not watch, he said. Don't look at everything, Connie, as though it's a picture of what it is. With only me in a room, why not leave the camera outside the door, in the hotel safe—does the HOTEL 4TH STREET have a safe? You're a director, Harlan, would *you* ever put vaseline on the lens? It's a cliché, now, Connie. *Constance.* I know, but, if it's the way everyone wants to see things. . . . For me to see what other people see, to fit in and belong, isn't that what you want, what'll make you come back?

"Got any vaseline?"

This time his fat lips crack and show teeth. "No, but this'll do the trick." A tube of K-Y on the counter beside the key. "I'll send him up when he gets here."

"You think he'll know I'm here?"

"If this is where you told him to meet you."

"He brought me here once for . . . something important. To see something important. What was it . . . ?"

"Hey, how strung out are you?"

"I'm okay."

"Who'll he be looking for?"

"Huh?"

"How'll I know it's him, who'll he ask for?"

"You mean me? Constance, of course."

"Okie-dokey."

"Were you ever a newsman?"

"What?"

"Never mind."

"Okay, Constance, I'll send him up when he gets here." He picks up the key and the K-Y and puts them into my hand. "Constance, huh? Pretty classy, you think that up yourself? Upstairs, on your right."

"It's my name. But—wait, *Constantina* is who he'll be looking for . . . probably . . . that's who he'll want. Just tell him she'll be waiting . . . where did you say? Upstairs? Constantina F. Zamora. The F's for Fortunata. I forgot about that."

"Oh. Italian this week. I get it."

"Huh? Got any matches?"

"Sure. Don't burn the place down, darlin'."

"You sure you weren't ever a newsman? Why're you guys so preoccupied with fire?"

It's a box room with peeling paint, a low flat double bed with yellowish white sheets and a faded blanket which might've once been red or brown or even purple. I put the sunglasses and the camera on the nicked-up nightstand.

The joint in my pocket is bent but not broken. Lumpy, damp, mashed a little . . . not anything like it was when Harlan rolled it, thinking we might make it through the first one and into the second, thinking we might stay longer at the kitchen table . . . or thinking nothing . . . trying not to think.

Flat on my back on the bed, I remember to suck hard, hold it down, let the smoke out and watch it rise. On the ceiling there's a smoky, streaked mirror with yellow stains. Harlan said I needed a mirror . . . he wanted one on *his* ceiling. . . . The smoke spreads out when it hits the mirror, joins everything else up there. If I looked, I might almost see myself through a lot of crap. But what would never show in a mirror is my heart blasting away inside my chest, one adrenalin-rush after another shooting into my stomach, earthquakes moving up and down my spine, my mouth dry, my palms wet, cold all over, then hot. . . . What'm I so afraid of? I'm scared to death. What should I do? Is there something I should do? What am I doing here? Where is he? I want him back, I want him back, I want him back. . . . I need him to pry my fists open, make me let go of this filthy bedspread. God, look at this grime under my nails. Will he find me here? Impossible. Only in the movies. Not like the movie he tried to show me . . . which he didn't want to watch himself. See, not watch. Where are you? I could see-not-watch if you were with me. You can't possibly find me here, can't know where I am, *what'll I do?*

Wait a minute, wait a minute, calm down.

I think I watched someone else say that from inside the mirror. The mouth moved. A dirty face. Sullen. Dark. Drastically straight features. Sooty eyes. Just lying there. Constantina F. Zamora. The one he's looking for? Wait for her to say something else. I'm watching and waiting. . . . The photographer waits and watches for the best shot, the right shot, patiently, doesn't rush it, the experienced finger in sync with the experienced eye, knows when to squeeze the button. Experienced arm stretching to the side, reaching for the always patient camera, blind and waiting to fit back against my eye. Two legs in faded jeans, a rumpled shirt coming untucked, buttoned-up askew, hair like a dark crushed tumble-weed, is this some homeless wretch, discarded by family, maybe set free from a state institution when funds ran low, a hurricane victim—

A *survivor.*

Of what? **Of what?**

Was it a whisper or a shout? No matter. No one heard. No one knocks on the walls or pounds on the floor or ceiling to shut me up. Lying here. Staring up through the lens. Staring back down. Not the zoom, not the telephoto, not the wide angle, not the panorama, not the fish-eye. The lens that distorts nothing.

You've never seen *me* through a vaseline-covered lens.

Never wanted you around

I know. You think I didn't know? But *why?* Ask yourself that.

You're probably too much like **her.**

And you always wanted to imagine her like a dry brown leaf that just blew away. You don't need a camera to remember her, to recall what she was doing to herself in bed before she left him. You were there, little Tina—that's what *she* called you.

Shut up.

She was just loving herself because *he* wouldn't. What's wrong with that? Aren't you old enough to understand that yet? And all these years . . . no one's loved you either. . . .

Watching her hand creep down to touch me, to strangle or soothe—to kill me, maim me, protect me, console me. Inside my jeans, my pulse hits her palm, her fingers like curious animals. But her soft hand could turn into a claw without warning. Afraid of her, always have been.

Stop it!

You don't mean that. You watched her, you played on the bed beside her. She didn't stop, and when she cried, you stared, sucking your finger. No camera. You saw.

Stop. Please.

Make me.

I'll take a picture. I have film loaded, I'll have to focus and set the exposure. I'll need **both hands** *on the camera.*

But what'll you have a picture of?

Me? You?

A camera.

And you!

Just a camera. *Two* pictures of a camera. Your camera takes a picture of the camera in the mirror. The camera in the mirror takes a picture of your camera.

Which would be the real picture?

None of your pictures are real. Remember? They *wish* they could be real. *This* is real. Feel it?

Oh god.

Don't stop watching. She's pushing my jeans down the same way she did with him—*she* stripped herself, he didn't have to, there was no rape, I remember that. But I don't remember such dry flesh, this sharp pain . . . she pushes deeper, deeper, scraping her fingernails against me and digging in, ignoring my sobs, my tears behind the camera, my muffled cries, my own pitiful voice, no one hears it. But there's nothing to kick or bite or punch in the face . . . is it all only happening in the mirror? I can see everything that's happening to me. But down here, I'm alone. Alone with my terrified heart, my twitching body, my raw throat, my running nose, the whole horrible mess. . . .

And your camera. You're alone with your camera. No one will find you here. He won't come looking for you. You think he only *pretended* you weren't there, in rehearsals, on tour? He didn't have to pretend. You had your camera—you *weren't* there.

That's what a photographer wants!

So the camera's on your face now. Which of us isn't here? The one on the bed holding a camera and jacking off with one hand, or the one holding a camera and jacking off in the mirror?

Why doesn't everybody leave me alone.

They already have. You took care of that. You can go back to your cave, hermit.

No, I don't want to.

You're a strange girl.

No.

Oh yeah? Look what you're doing. *See*, not look. See, not watch.

How?

I think you know. What did he say? Trade your camera for. . . .

Oh.

When my hand lets go, the camera just falls softly beside my cheek, on its side, and I push it farther away, slowly, to the other pillow beside my head. But up above me, the rumpled jeans pushed halfway down, the V of the open zipper, the thin white thighs, the black hair, the flat caved-in stomach, the finger moving, now so gentle, a bubbling tickle every time it passes over . . . something's rising, waiting to boil over. . . . The heaving chest under the dirty shirt, the dark long neck moving like a beating heart with each breath, the raised chin, the hard eyes, like frozen water, looking down, never blinking . . . pupils opening and closing like an aperture . . . dry . . . now shiny wet . . . what're you looking at?

No answer . . . unless I answer myself.

I'm not looking at a photographer. No photographer is looking at me. No photographer ever called out to wait a second while she squeezed a blob of K-Y onto her finger and smeared it on the dome of the lens, her finger going round and round to spread the thin film evenly. No photographer here at all, anymore. But staring . . . as though we've never seen each other before . . . me in the mirror above me, watching me. . . . Nothing between myself and myself but a column of smoke and other people's dirt plastered on a mirror.

•

Is that my voice again? No . . . a long groan, sharp crack, two quick jolts. Is the bus breaking down all over again? Fling the bedspread over my face, shut my eyes, my breath shoots out of me, leaves me pop-eyed and gasping as the bed frame finishes breaking and the mattress falls to the floor. Everything is still. Everything has stopped. I can't move. My back is broken. This is the last time. I know it. I'll be in this room the rest of my life. No one knows I'm here. . . . Except me. *I* know I'm here . . . slowly starving, bones cutting straight through the tight dried yellow flesh. Lying in my own filth. Seeing only the light change from day to night through this sick-pink bedspread over my eyes. Bugs all over me. Diseases creeping out of the stained mattress and slowly eating me alive. Is this as low as I can go? And no one will come to help. Who would want to help. Would *I* help me if I found myself here? That's crazy—no matter how long I wait and hope, I'll never see myself coming through the door to help me. I'm already here. I haven't abandoned myself. And maybe I still have some luck . . . Fortunata, remember? I can rock myself to sleep or cry myself to sleep or cut my wrists and sleep or freeze in my own sweat or curl up in a ball and smell how badly I stink. . . . My favorite plaid flannel shirt—I wore it on tour, slept in it on the bus after everything broke down and the social standard stopped mattering . . . it stunk then too but no one got close enough to tell. No one can tell now either . . . except me . . . but it smells thousands of times better than the sleazy sheets and bedspread. . . . I'm sleepy . . . and comfortable too . . . that's odd, isn't it? Warm and drowsy . . . my heartbeat a slow soothing rhythm. . . . Like a baby? But whose heartbeat soothes a baby? It *becomes* his own. And is this how a baby feels when his diaper is wet and dirty but also, at the same time, for the same reason, warm and soft?

•

Gray cement. I wake staring at it, spine braced on a wall, head between knees, a pulsing headache, sour stomach.

I haven't been here long. The sun's just now up. It was slightly pre-dawn when I left money on the bumpy mattress, folded in the sunglasses, and climbed down the fire escape. Must've dozed just a few minutes on the sidewalk, trying to settle my stomach. It's no use. I vomit, thinking of Harlan.

That's not what I mean.

I still want to find him. I think I know where he was last night. If I'd had half a brain at the time, I would've realized it. The theater's not far. We might've been a few blocks from each other, and across the park. I could call over there and ask him if he would come get me . . . ask for help . . . but I'll walk to him myself. Breathing at dawn always feels like drinking cold water when incredibly thirsty.

I won't even stop in makeup or a toilet somewhere to push my fingers into my hair and attempt to tame it. Won't bother to wet my hands and rub my face and eyes. I must be smoky and streaked, sweat-trails, tear-trails. Licking my lips, I taste what I think I look like.

Barely can climb these stairs . . . pause to press each palm to my ribs, slide my hands down, pressing hard, wringing out the slow ache . . . like a car crash, barely avoided, which finally catches up to me anyway. Always such a buckled-in, speedometer-watchful driver, day after day, another, another, driving to and from wherever I went . . . I never crashed. My neck was never stiff from collision, from two objects meeting at the same place. If so, I might've crept off like a nocturnal animal to lick my wounds alone. But now, even though I know being alone doesn't always mean being a recluse, I carry every blue bruise, every sore muscle, every rattled thought in one loose bundle back to Harlan.

The door is ajar. I tap it open with one finger. No creak. It opens like a scene. He is packing his stuff.

"Need any help?"

He answers by taking my car keys out of his pocket. When I don't reach for them right away, he tosses them. They bounce, skid on the desk, off the edge to the floor near my feet.

Don't you care where I was all night, Harlan? Don't you wonder . . . *any*thing?

I do start to pick the keys up, but instead I sit, pull a chair close to his desk, move the keys a little with my toes. The chain includes a key to my house, and a key to my darkroom . . . difficult to picture myself there now. Left it a mess last time, when was it? I think I trampled some prints on the floor, wet, unrinsed . . . they'll decay, burn brown and stiff and brittle. Half the times I've seen you, Harlan, I've been unwashed and snarled . . . mostly because of my *own* fingers in my hair grabbing fistfuls. You and I last night . . . don't worry. I'm not shocked or outraged. No feeling of violation. Look at me . . . why won't you look at me? Do you think there's no one here? Who was it who watched you like a captivated audience that flocks to any show as long as you're the star . . . not even knowing why . . . waiting for a chance to play a scene with you . . . then I blew the audition . . . but all along probably loved you like a miracle. Is there anyone here who still feels that way, somehow, for some reason, is there anyone here, Harlan, who still wants a chance . . . someone sitting on this side of your desk. Look at me!

"Did you sleep here last night?"

"Yes." Clears his throat. "It's a long story. I did go back home after you left."

"I went out to look for you." Shut my eyes, recalling his drowsy voice, *What were you looking for, what did you find?* Shake my head and ask, "Where will you go now?"

He's down behind the desk, working on the lowest drawer, the desk top littered, the trash can full, and trash piled around the edges on the floor, wadded-up stuff which bounced off the rim. He says, "I don't know. I'll find something." Slams the drawer. Puts a box on the seat of his chair, pushes the chair up to his desk and sweeps all the stuff from the desk top into the box. I fall from chair to floor, squat, pull the trash can between my knees, pick up the scattered pieces and push them in.

"I could go with you. I can type or run errands—"

"No!"

His voice pushes me backwards. I fall off my heels to my butt, whack my skull on Windrem's desk and stare like he used to, bulging, dry-eyed. Harlan stares back. And says again, "No."

In the parking lot, before he opens his car trunk—the box of stuff balanced between the bumper and his knee while he searches for the right key—I take my wallet out of my jeans and find the check he gave me for pictures of the show. A little dog-eared. And it must've gotten damp in the darkroom. I put it on top of the box of stuff. Habitually glance at the place where the chalk outline has already, long ago, vanished, rubbed into the asphalt, under skid marks and foot steps and dripping oil and leaking radiators.

He looks at the check.

"For the pictures, remember? You never got any."

"I think I got my money's worth of pictures." He turns the key and the trunk springs open. The check blows off the box, but he catches it, then hands it to me.

"I don't want it."

Shrugging, he folds it and puts it in his shirt pocket.

In the trunk of his car, his clothes are all stacked, folded so neatly. Harlan throws the box on top.

"You'll get wrinkles."

"Don't see how I can avoid it."

"No, I mean your clothes."

He laughs, then says, "Connie. . . ." Chuckles softly. "I mean, Constance. Are you still Constance?" His hair has gotten longer. He pushes it out of his eyes and says, "I'm going to live in a bachelor's mess with stiff laundry and carcinogenic canned food and never read labels. I'll probably live forever, embalm myself on a diet of preservatives, how's that? And if you go back to hide in your darkroom, you can do the same with your photo chemicals. Go back to blowing things up, without getting yourself caught in the explosion." He laughs again, then, unsmiling, says, "That's a great smile, Connie, I hope you realize it. A smile that forgot this day, this minute . . . and everything else. We could live together forever in that smile, so use it more often, okay?"

When did I catch up? Somewhere he slowed down and I shortened the distance between us. . . . He limped and headed for the side of the road with a blow-out or clanking gears, opened his hood to let the steam pressure out, then turned grey-faced to the road, wiping his brow with the back of his hand. But at least the one chasing him didn't just pass and stare . . . even though all I can do is wait to make sure his engine starts, maybe offer him a quarter for a phone call if it doesn't. I know I'll be all right by myself when he drives away today.

COLOPHON

This book was set in Spectrum and Helvetica types using Adobe Wood Type dingbats. It has been printed on 50 # Windsor Offset paper by Friesen Printers and Smythe sewn for readability and durability.